The Soul Whisperer

A Tale of Hidden Truths
and Unspoken Possibilities

The Soul Whisperer

A Tale of Hidden Truths
and Unspoken Possibilities

J. M. Harrison

Winchester, UK
Washington, USA

First published by Roundfire Books, 2016
Roundfire Books is an imprint of John Hunt Publishing Ltd., Laurel House, Station Approach,
Alresford, Hants, SO24 9JH, UK
office1@jhpbooks.net
www.johnhuntpublishing.com
www.roundfire-books.com

For distributor details and how to order please visit the 'Ordering' section on our website.

Text copyright: J. M. Harrison 2015

ISBN: 978 1 78535 246 1
Library of Congress Control Number: 2015946136

A CIP catalogue record for this book is available from the British Library.

Design: Stuart Davies

Printed and bound by CPI Group (UK) Ltd, Croydon, CR0 4YY, UK

We operate a distinctive and ethical publishing philosophy in all
areas of our business, from our global network of authors to
production and worldwide distribution.

CONTENTS

'The soul answered and said, I saw you. You did not see me nor recognise me. I served you as a garment and you did not know me.'
The Gospel of Miriam Magdalana

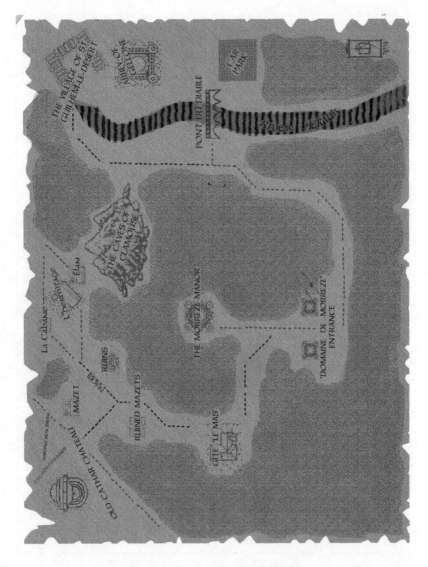

Map artwork by John R.L. McNabb.

One

Rain

In the cobbled square of the normally serene and welcoming village of Saint-Guilhem-le-Désert, darkness had arrived. In the fading light of the Languedoc day two hundred and sixty-five people – men, women and children – silently huddled together. They were surrounded by a horde of mounted, heavily armed mercenaries, whose leader now commanded them to speak, 'Ignorant fools... do you really think you can stop us? This... is your final warning. I will not ask again. For the last time... tell me where it is!' His rage and frustration were as clear as the reddening of his face and the sweat pouring from his steed's breast, as he drew his large sword high above his head for all to see. But still no one spoke.

Turning his attention to his men, he bellowed out what was to be the final, ominous command, 'Get these heretics into the Abbey. As they will not speak when I demand, then I charge you to make sure they will never speak again!' It was like a battle cry that unleashed hell. The villagers were kicked and beaten as they were herded into the abbey. With the doors sealed behind them, the debauched, horrific slaughter began.

Men, women and children were ferociously attacked; arms, legs and heads were hacked off with such force that fountains of blood spurted high into the air, causing warm showers of red viscous rain to fall, splattering across the cold grey stone floor. Their body parts piling up in the aisle, their blood now flooding the abbey, spilling out under the doors into the market square, until it looked as if the building itself was haemorrhaging. Shrill, stomach churning screams pleading for compassion fell upon deaf ears, as the bloody faced army of Christ descended into hell. Pity, shame and mercy were abandoned as babies and children small enough to fit in the font were drowned, in full view of their mothers, before, in turn, each of the women's throats were slashed open in the name of the Father Almighty. The poisonous stench of evil was suffocating, causing one frail old woman to cough and choke so violently that she suffered a fatal seizure. And still, through all this, no one gave up the secret.

'No!' Sara sat bolt upright in her bed. Heart racing, sweating profusely and tears streaming down her flushed crimson cheeks, she struggled to clear her head of the terrifying vision she had just witnessed. Memories of the awful nightmare lingered in her mind, and then the pain hit. Like a lance to the stomach, a wave of hot, searing cramps pierced her womb as the agonising memory of last year's trauma reared its ugly head. Sara relived the heartbreaking moment when the precious lives she was carrying inside her were unforgivingly torn away, as she became consumed by the excruciatingly painful realisation that her precious, unborn twins were well and truly gone.

Standing there, unshaven and barefoot in torn jeans and old sweatshirt, a tall, dark haired figure looked down at the world around him. In the murky street below, he caught sight of a boisterous group of teenagers smoking, giggling and texting, an old man half bent over with arthritis struggling to see where he was going, and a hooded youth running at full pelt along the pavement, holding what looked like a large jar of change in one hand. *What a crazy mixed up world*, thought the man as he shook his head and turned away from the window. It began to drizzle for the umpteenth time this week. Depressing. 'Bloody rain!' he exclaimed aloud, in typical English fashion. The last ten months of Alex Brunton's life had left him feeling very frustrated.

From being a successful musician, making jingles for TV and radio stations, he now found himself reluctantly selling his Victorian apartment as the economic slump drained him of all work and what little savings he had. The latest financial crisis had just about squeezed the very life out of him; he was barely hanging on when suddenly a highly aggressive cancer reduced his beloved mother to a shell, before stealing her away in the night like a thief... no warning, and precious little opportunity for goodbyes.

And then there was the seizure. With the worries of losing his income, his home and his mother, Alex had collapsed on the bathroom floor. The resulting out-of-body experience shocked him to the core. He didn't fully understand it, as in some inexplicable way it had changed how he looked at life, radically altering his thoughts and beliefs. Consequently, it was a subject he preferred to avoid, rarely talking about it even with his nearest and dearest.

Alex's saving grace was Sara, his blonde, blue-eyed wife of two years. She too had suffered when, having strived so hard for her dream job, it failed miserably to live up to expectations. Today was her last day at the office. She was quitting her civil servant post following too many disappointments and ethical inconsistencies, having undergone a general loss of faith in her fellow beings. But for Sara the real blow had been the miscarriage of their twins at twelve weeks, and they never talked about that either.

And yet here they both were, still together, now realising it was time for a change, time for a new beginning. Using what equity they could muster from the sale of their home, Alex had finally convinced a rather reluctant Sara to travel the 'Way of St. James', the pilgrimage route to Santiago de Compostela in north-western Spain, where it was said that the remains of the apostle Saint James were buried. Not that they were religious, but since his seizure Alex felt pulled by the undeniable simplicity of a pilgrimage. And since the miscarriage, he thought the change of scenery would do them both good... and perhaps offer a little adventure along the way.

Alex's mobile phone vibrated in his pocket. Tightening his neat ponytail, a habit he employed when deep in thought, upset or anxious, he moved away from the window, passed the map of their 'Spanish adventure' lying on the coffee table and slumped himself down on the sofa, before finally retrieving the phone to answer it. The warm, comforting voice of his grandmother, Lucette greeted his ear, 'Hello *mon chéri*, just seeing how you're both doing...'

'Oh, we're okay thanks Lucy,' replied Alex, sounding unconvincing, and tired.

'Well listen, I've got an idea, I've been thinking about it, and I'm going to treat the two of you to a break in France. You both need it. I've made contact with old family friends near Clermont, and they have a lovely little *gite*... you know... cottage, which you can stay in for a month. I've looked into flights and car hire, all you need to do is to say "yes"...' she paused for breath, awaiting his response. 'Oh go on... it'll do you both so much good.'

'But Lucy it's too much, we couldn't...'

'No dear, I can afford it, and I'd much rather see to it that you have whatever you need now, than not be able to help you when I'm gone. Just say yes and I'll take care of everything.'

'Oh, it's such a generous gesture Lucy, but I've planned this trip across northern Spain. It took Sara a little convincing, but I think this pilgrimage might be just what we need, you know... a breath of fresh air, take our minds off stuff, meet new people and see new places.'

As soon as he had uttered the words he knew Lucette wasn't buying it. Just as Sara hadn't bought it when he sprung the idea of the Compostela pilgrimage on her two weeks back. She'd left the apartment, needing to clear her head, having told him in no uncertain terms she thought the idea a selfish form of escapism for him at best, and torture for her, being left to walk in the bloody heat with only her thoughts of 'the loss' to keep her company.

After a short pause, Lucette responded calmly but firmly, 'Eh oh Alex, don't tell me you really think Sara's happy to traipse around the baking Spanish countryside, day in, day out. A relaxing holiday is what she needs and deserves... what you both deserve. You two have been through so much.' She paused a moment, moved by the thought of the loss of Alex's mother – her daughter, dear sweet Marguerite, 'Now come on be a good lad and let me indulge your happiness... just for a little while, ah?'

Now come on... be a good lad, the words rang in his ears, triggering memories of his mother's voice when she wanted his agreement on something. The room temperature appeared to drop, something Alex was more aware of since his seizure, and he saw his mother standing before him, a vision of comfort, and support, filling him with an overwhelming sense of love. Her arms outstretched and her smile lighting up her whole soft beautiful face, her warm brown eyes engaging him once more as she nodded her head... Then she faded away. But in that brief moment he understood Lucette's invitation made absolute sense. Besides, who in their right mind would turn down such a kind offer? Alex accepted there and then.

Putting the phone on the coffee table he gathered up the map and other 'pilgrimage artefacts', scrunched them up and tossed them into the paper recycling bin, letting go of the idea of the Spanish trip completely. His mood was finally lifting, he even managed a little smile to himself, and in that moment even the constant rhythmic assault of the rain mattered very little. He got up and, almost in defiance, left his coat on the banister as he made his way out and headed for the local store.

Alex bought all Sara's favourites, part of his plan for a delicious meal to celebrate her last day at work. With the sale of the apartment almost complete, they would have a lump sum soon enough to allow a little splurge right now, so he put the Cava back and picked up the Champagne. Coming out of the store, he narrowly avoided bumping into a couple of Muslim women completely masked by their burkas, their anonymous eyes barely peeking through the fine dark linen mesh, as they struggled to control an uncooperative umbrella. Now running down the street in the torrential rain, with two plastic bags full of shopping, he really wished he'd grabbed his coat after all.

Sara slid her key into the lock, having to jiggle it slightly because it was such a poor copy. Once inside, she noticed the dimmed lights and the scent of flowers in the air. She almost smiled when her eyes caught sight of a huge 'Congratulations' banner hanging along the mantel in the living room.

Alex saw her half-hearted response in the mirror above the mantel, and, admiring his partner not only for her athletic appearance but strong mind too, jumped out.

'Surprise!' said Alex, tap dancing and waving both hands like Al Jolson performing 'Toot Toot Tootsie!' Sara tried to keep a straight face. They hugged and he planted a loving kiss on her full pink lips, leaving her unable to hold back a smile any longer. She shook her head and giggled (a rare sound over the past few months). Handing Sara a glass of bubbly, Alex looked her in the eye and offered a toast, 'Here's to new beginnings.'

'To new beginnings,' she echoed in relief, desperately hoping the clear 'ping' of their glasses was heralding in better times ahead.

Over the celebratory dinner, Alex explained Lucette's French remedy. Like Alex, Sara thought it was a wonderful opportunity to get some autumn sunshine, revitalise, and maybe uncover some of Alex's ancestry too. Why not, and anyway, they both knew how determined Lucette was once she'd made up her mind. And it was a far better idea than a long distance hike across Spain. They chatted happily about the future and their hopes and dreams. It was a touching and romantic way to bring the London chapter of their life to an end.

As they were enjoying dessert, Sara slowly put her spoon down and looking intently at the man she loved with all her heart asked, 'What will we do when the holiday ends?'

Not wanting the happy spell broken, and seeing her genuine concern, Alex took her hand and answered, 'Well let's just wait and see, let's live in the moment and not in fear of what may or may not happen next.'

'But it's not that easy, is it?' queried Sara, as a little disbelief crossed her striking face.

At which point Alex took hold of both her hands and very slowly and steadily explained, 'When we experience fear in ourselves we will attract people and situations in our lives that reflect that fear in order to make us conscious of it. When we are aware, and allow ourselves to experience those fears, we begin to clear our system, so that fears gradually have less impact on us because we're empowered with the love from within.'

'Where did you read that?' Sara was now less unsure, but rather surprised and a little bemused.

Alex's eyes had glazed over a little, and he let her hand go. 'I'm not sure.' He paused a little while as if pondering the meaning of life, then just as suddenly his eyes refocused and he continued, 'maybe it's the Champagne!' They both laughed. Their laughter was combined with such a deep sense of relief that it was the real therapy they had been craving for months. Later that night Alex and Sara made love for what seemed like the first time in an age, it was sweet and tender and filled Sara with new hope...

The next day, following breakfast, Lucette rang saying she would email the details of the trip. Alex put the call on loudspeaker and thanked her once more, as did Sara. It was a welcome blessing, to feel so spoilt and cared for. 'Oh, by the way, if you get the chance, please go and visit Jean-Michel, he's an old childhood friend, and, er... maybe you could send him my love.'

Alex and Sara agreed without hesitation. But unbeknown to

them Jean-Michel was the real reason Lucette had booked the holiday cottage. When she was a young girl living in southern France, Jean-Michel had helped her, well more than that... he had healed her. Lucette also never mentioned that Jean-Michel was her childhood sweetheart, and her first love. Deep down Lucette really hoped he would now be able to help Alex and Sara in the same way. 'And maybe, if I get the chance, I'll come out and visit you too!' Lucette added, as Alex and Sara gave each other a knowing glance.

A week later, the estate agent called, informing them that completion of the apartment was due in a matter of days. They would be coming away from the sale with a reasonable enough sum which would allow them to live for the next few months, maybe a little longer, but once they had spent that, there would be nothing left. Nonetheless the French trip was approaching and Alex and Sara's woes and frustrations began to give way to a feeling of excitement. Lucette's email was full of details, maps and explanations, they were sure to never get lost and it seemed they would have plenty to do too!

The synchronicity of the sale meant that they would be out of the apartment the very same week they were due to leave for the self-catering holiday in France. There were three nights between the completion of the sale and the departure of their flight, and Lucette offered to put them up for as long as needed before taking them to the airport. She really had thought of everything, but that was how she was, and how she loved to be. She had an uncanny ability to know what was going to happen, it was almost as if she could foretell the future.

Leaving the smog and mental chaos of the city on the National Express coach bound for Bournemouth (neither Alex nor Sara owned a car) seemed to take hours, weaving in and out of rain and traffic jams. By early evening they were nearly at their stop, a place called Ringwood. Lucette found it easier to pick them up there, as she could take the quiet country lanes and not have to go into the hustle and bustle of Bournemouth. The coach was slowing down, approaching their stop. Alex put his hand up to the coach window to peer out, and in the arising darkness and drizzling rain, he caught sight of her.

Lucette was there as promised. They clambered down the steps of the coach, took their suitcases from the large boot in the side of the coach, and walked across to the waiting Lucette, who having recognised them, leapt out of the car like a vivacious teenager. You would never have guessed she was now well into her sixties.

Following hugs and kisses, Lucette opened the boot of her little black Volkswagen Golf, and Alex put the cases inside.

'About fifteen minutes and we'll be there,' said Lucette joyfully. The car was warm and peaceful, just what the doctor ordered. Lucette could sense they were tired, so she didn't bombard them with too many questions during the journey down the winding country roads. Crossing the speed humps, they entered part of the New Forest, at one point slowing down to a stop to allow a small band of wild ponies to cross the road. Twenty minutes later they finally arrived at 'The Lodge', Lucette's idyllic little rented cottage. It was a round thatched property, once the gatehouse of the large stately manor, which lay hidden somewhere farther down the old carriage driveway. This lovely 'hobbit-like' dwelling looked like it had just jumped off the pages of a fairy tale, and although not grand by any means, it beckoned you to stay. Sara and Alex felt right at home.

Over the next couple of days, Lucette prepared everything for them, just like staying in the most wonderful country hotel. She pre-planned all the meals, whilst at the same time giving them the space to do whatever they wanted. And it was while she was engrossed in her patisseries that she got an unexpected phone call. Hearing the phone ring in the living room, she wiped her floury hands on her apron and went to pick it up.

It was Marianne, calling from France. Lucette's initial thought, that the holiday was about to be cancelled was soon overshadowed by the palpable strain in her old friend's voice as she said, 'Lucette, I've heard a rumour that Jean-Michel's memory is failing him more and more each day, what if he starts to forget important things… like the shell?'

'Marianne, what I told you that night when I'd had one too many all those years ago is between us and no one else, it's *our* little secret. And it's important you keep it that way.' Lucette's voice was calm and informative, but a little menacing. Aware of her harsh tone she softened it a little and added, 'Please don't ever break that trust, Marianne, it's all in hand, now I must go,' and put the phone back on its receiver, returned to the kitchen and continued to bake as though nothing, nothing at all, was wrong…

Alex and Sara walked a lot in the privacy of the two hundred acre Estate, spotting deer, birds of prey, and even a handful of rogue guinea fowl that had escaped and taken up residence with the local pheasant population. One morning as they explored the beautiful woodlands, they became separated as Alex went wandering off, immersed in his 'mission' to uncover wild mushrooms. Sara, no longer able to see Alex, continued down a track leading her deeper into the woods. 'Craaaaaack!' – she was startled by the loud noise of a falling branch. Looking about she could see nothing. The noise of her boots on the broken twigs and leaves that covered the woodland seemed to get louder and louder.

'Alex… Alex, Alex!' she called out with increasing urgency. She looked around and called again, but still no response. Sara was becoming fearful, and, thinking she was lost, stood at a cross-roads in the forest track. She felt her head spin as she realised she had no idea where to go. Feeling her breath, tense and heavy in her chest, she teetered on the edge of another panic attack.

Then suddenly, just ten feet away from her on one of the grassy pathways appeared a most incredible sight. A white stag with megalithic antlers stood proud, soulfully gazing directly into her captivating blue eyes. Sara froze on the spot. She was speechless, but no longer panicking. As she continued to admire the stunning animal, a palpable calm seemed to fill the air, as if holding time still. There was no noise, no movement, and no thought. In that magical window, Sara was sure, had she opened her mouth to speak, the magnificent creature would have understood her every word.

'Sara!' called Alex as he finally spotted her from another track. Sara turned to see Alex, waved, and then quickly turned back towards the stag only to find that the handsome beast had vanished.

'Are you alright?' asked Alex approaching her.

'Yeah, I've just seen the most amazing thing.'

'What…what was it?' enquired Alex coming closer.

'A white stag,' came her somewhat hesitant reply.

'Really? Whoa! That's insane! Did you know that in the past white stags were considered to be messengers from the "other world" and their appearance was said to herald a profound change in the lives of those who encountered them?'

'Yeah, it kind of feels like something's just happened to me,' responded a dreamy looking Sara.

Alex put his arm around her and led her down the pathway. 'In the Arthurian legend, the white stag is the creature that can never be caught. King Arthur's repeatedly unsuccessful pursuit of the white stag represents mankind's quest for spiritual knowledge,' Alex recalled from his computer-like memory, another 'skill' he had acquired since his seizure.

They walked on for a while in silence, till they broke out in unified laughter at the site of a herd of rabbits leaping several feet in the air as they darted madly in and out of the undergrowth.

Within half an hour they had made their way back to Lucette's cottage, and that night they slept like babies.

The following morning the long-anticipated call finally came. The money from the sale of the apartment was now 'in' their joint account. Alex and Sara felt an unexpected sense of relief in no longer owning or owing anything of great value. It was the opposite of what they'd imagined. They had both been brought up being told that ownership of bricks and mortar was the way forward in life, and yet experiencing the financial crash had definitely taught them otherwise. The sale of the apartment provided a mortgage-free life, which was accompanied by a newly discovered sense of liberation. Even the 'not knowing' of what was going to happen next provided the couple with an exciting outlook on life, a feeling they had almost forgotten.

On the last evening before the flight, Lucette prepared a lovely meal, after which they gathered around the little green enamelled Godin log burner in the tiny circular lounge. 'I'm so glad you both said yes, I think you'll have a wonderful time. Jean-Michel is such a kind and beautiful person. You remember Alex, the story of the little blind girl I used to tell you... it all happened there you know... Anyway you will be sure to say hello and send my love won't you? I've given you a clear explanation and map of how to find his little house... it's not far from where you'll be staying... not far at all,' said Lucette looking at the young couple as if to make sure they were paying full attention. Sara and Alex gently nodded. Alex hadn't a clue about the 'blind girl story'; perhaps Lucy was confused, so he smiled all the same. Unnoticed, above their heads, the dreamcatcher turned gently from side to side.

The next morning they awoke to the all-too-familiar sound of the English rain, which only served to increase their anticipation of being touched by the warm glow of French sunshine they so desperately craved. With the car packed, Lucette drove them to

Bournemouth Airport, where she refused to pay the entry fee which she labelled as 'immoral', dropping them a short distance from the departures entrance. This was followed by firm hugs and heartfelt kisses all round. 'Enjoy yourselves, I think you're going to have the time of your lives,' said Lucette with a knowing smile. Alex and Sara watched and waved as the little Volkswagen sped off into the distance.

With their bags in tow, the young couple entered the departures building through the sliding doors, hand in hand and beaming. In this moment Alex thought life was very good, yet Sara seemed a little distracted. 'Are you alright?' he asked, hoping he was just being over-cautious.

'Yeah, just a little nervous... but in a good way,' said Sara, turning her head and smiling back at him.

They joined the queue for the flight to Carcassonne, passing through the electronic detector without any nasty surprises. And, despite even more rain, which looked and felt like it would never stop, the plane arrived on time. Following a coffee, and a good chunk of Sara's time surveying the interesting hodgepodge of characters and personalities gathering in the departure lounge, their flight was announced, and they joined the queue for boarding.

Unfortunately, Alex's hand luggage was deemed too large and he was asked to repack it or remove items so that it would meet the regulations. Not one to be easily embarrassed, Alex put his suitcase on the floor and sat on it. 'There you go,' he said to the girl, as the now squashed bag slid easily into the metal frame. A middle-aged couple behind them raised their eyebrows and glanced at each other, as if to share their disapproval of his actions. Alex smiled, and he and Sara walked through the passport control area.

Shuffling along like sheep heading for market, no one spoke. Getting wet standing on the metal steps whilst boarding the plane seemed a small price to pay, and was almost pleasurable in a strange way, because they knew they were escaping to the sun. They were welcomed on board the Boeing 737, found their seats and readied themselves for the safety announcements.

'There must be a hundred and fifty people on board,' Alex said to Sara.

'One hundred and forty-nine actually... but a very good guess,' interrupted a friendly air hostess, forgetting to include herself in the count. The safety announcements came to a swift climax, the flaps on the wings whirred as they were tested, the engines began to rumble and the plane slowly taxied down the runway. Then with a force that noticeably rocked the passenger's bodies forwards and backwards, the pilot accelerated and they were airborne. Up, up and away! Little did Alex and Sara know that what was waiting for them would change their lives forever...

Two

A Welcome Break

A pproaching the airport at Carcassonne, strong gusts of wind blew across the runway, tilting the aircraft wings just enough to convince most passengers to brace themselves for a nail-biting landing. But touchdown safely they did, albeit with a bit of a bump and a bang, as the tyres of the Ryanair flight steadied themselves and the reverse thrust of the engines took control. Alex could feel the collective sense of relief as the recording of a bugle played announcing another successful, on time arrival.

Collecting their bags from the overhead lockers, and following a bout of 'holiday rugby' (as Alex liked to call it), he and Sara scrambled their way along the centre of the plane towards the exit. They thanked the cheerful cabin crew and clonked their way down the metallic steps, immediately being struck by two things. Firstly, the wind really was very gusty and, secondly, it was lovely and warm. In fact, it was just right, thought Sara, because it would have been too hot for them without the giant refreshing fan of wind.

They strolled across the tarmac towards the terminal building, to join a short queue. *Ahhh...this isn't so bad*, thought Alex standing quietly, basking in the healing rays of the Languedoc sunshine. Once inside the terminal, they showed their passports to the French customs officers. A solidly built, middle-aged, dark haired man with a well groomed, formidable moustache glared suspiciously at Alex. The officer was silently mocking what he considered to be a rather pathetic attempt at facial hair, as he surveyed the wispy goatee and rather 'girlie' ponytail.

Not sinister enough to warrant further inspection, he put it down to an Englishman's poor attempt at displaying virility and, with a brisk 'Okay', sent Alex on his way. Alex now stood patiently waiting for Sara to come through. Would she get the same disdainful look and curt acknowledgment? At 5ft 7 Sara was far from statuesque, but something about her confident stride, her strong, toned physique, and those fascinating blue eyes got a gaping smile and a gentle waving on from the moustached officer, as if he had known her all his life. *Typical*, thought Alex, as Sara winked at him and they headed off to collect their luggage from the carousel.

Sweet, dear Lucette really had thought of everything. The hire-car station was only a few metres from the flight arrivals area, and even though there was another queue, it wasn't too long before they were served by a plump pregnant French lady who spoke English, but not as well as she thought she did. Anyway, it didn't matter as Sara was fluent as was Alex, albeit in a grammatically non-exact but chatty kind of way.

'Zeees ar yorr keees,' said the mum to be.

'*Merci*, Alexandre,' replied Alex, having noted her staff badge. He signed the necessary papers, and was handed the keys.

'Nowwer, all you arf to do iz check zee vehicool for damages. It izz on zer rait zerr,' she pointed to the parking zone on the far side of the chain-link fence.

They quickly found the car, gave it the once over, cross-checking the list of damages, marks and scratches, and set off across the ridiculously bumpy car park, until they reached the main road and stopped at the roundabout. 'Remember to keep to the right love,' suggested Sara in a helpful manner, but Alex found the advice rather obvious.

'Mmm humh,' came his mumbled response. He really didn't like being told what to do by anyone. They got underway and celebrated the wonders of the sat nav as it led them out of the industrial area near the airport in the direction of the A61 Toulouse to Narbonne *autoroute*. They collected their tickets at the toll-barrier and were on the way.

'It really looks and feels like another country, another place,' said Sara, Alex nodded; he knew exactly what she meant. After a few minutes they were able to see the medieval city of Carcassonne on their left. 'Wow, look at that... it's like a real-life Disneyland for adults,' remarked Sara.

'Yeah, it always reminds me of mythical stories and medieval knights in armour,' added Alex nonchalantly.

Sara twitched her shoulders. She was eager and excited – since arriving she really did feel like it was a proper holiday. With her anxiety about the original idea of a pilgrimage in Spain now long forgotten, her feminine sense of curiosity simmered as she turned to Alex, 'Shall we stop and have a look around?'

'I'd rather get to the cottage if you don't mind, love. We can always come back and visit sometime during the holiday,' replied Alex, who was still getting accustomed to driving on the right.

'I'd like that,' said a satisfied Sara adjusting herself back on the headrest.

They sailed past the old city in their little rental, and continued east towards the Mediterranean and Narbonne. Having already programmed the sat nav from the details contained in Lucette's email, Alex hoped to get to the cottage before nightfall. But in the meantime he was mesmerised by the views. The countryside seemed to emanate a secret, inexplicable magic. The collection of vines, honey-coloured stone and soothing sunbeams evoked a sense of being completely nourished – mind, body and soul. Feelings of relaxation, freedom and an irrational yet undeniable sense of home engulfed them both. The colours so vibrant, so alive and so different, that even the golden brilliance of the sun and the shocking blueness of the sky were refreshingly alien. 'Look at those vines Alex, what do you think they grow here?' enquired Sara as they flew past a blue sign for Narbonne.

'If I remember correctly, we are going through the *Corbières* vineyards. Lucy told me there were a series of disasters around the Narbonne area during the Middle Ages. As I recall there were floods, the port silted up and the plague hit.'

'Blimey, sounds rather biblical,' said Sara, half joking.

Leaving the A61 they joined the A9 to Béziers, which Alex remembered had something to do with a slaughter and the Catholic Church, although the details escaped him. They continued on to the A75, leaving the *autoroute* at Clermont L'Hérault.

The sun's warming embrace could still be felt, and visibility was still good. Sara's mind wandered as she became lost in the beauty of the multi-coloured skyline, now seemingly alive with all the hues of the rainbow scattered across the sunset. With daylight finally fading they arrived in the town of Clermont L'Hérault, found a little store still open opposite the church, and stocked up with the basics they needed for the next couple of days. Alex made sure they had enough bread and wine, while Sara was more concerned about getting her hands on some fresh milk. Out of the town, in the direction of St-Jean-de-Fos, they faithfully followed the directions of the sat nav for a further fifteen minutes or so. 'You have arrived at your destination,' it eventually announced.

Entering La Domaine De Morreze they passed through an impressive pair of tall, ornate, metal gates guarding a wide gravelled, tree-lined driveway. After one kilometre, they caught sight of the sign for Le Mas – 'Gite de La Domaine De Morreze – 3 epis'. They continued for another few hundred metres. There, sat in the tranquility of the valley was their 'sanctuary', a modest white building, tucked neatly into the stony hillside. Alex parked the car in the designated space, pulled the handbrake, turned off the engine and opened his door, stretching his legs, 'Listen,' he said.

Sara waited a few moments 'I can't hear a thing,' she replied.

'Exactly,' Alex beamed, looking her in the eyes as they kissed.

The unlocked door of the cottage pushed open easily, and inside awaiting its new occupants was a delicious hamper of goodies, including bread, wine, ham and eggs. The brief handwritten note which accompanied it read *Welcome friends. Bienvenue to Le Mas. This is a little gift for you. See you tomorrow morning – sleep well. Marianne.*

It was getting dark, so they took a brief tour around the quaint building, then prepared a simple meal and sat together for a short while at the large wooden picnic bench, on the amber stone terrace. Perched on the high plateau of Le Mas, they felt like Greek Gods in the cloud-palace above Olympus, as they looked down and surveyed the yellowy golden lights emanating from the houses in the valley below. The stars shone brightly, and the crystalline night sky seemed to engulf the whole world.

'I love it here, don't you?' asked Alex, finally breaking the hush that had descended upon Sara's normally hectic mind.

'Mmm, just feels like home,' she purred. The colours were so intense, so soothing she could almost smell them, burning amber, apple greens, rose reds, and lavender like heavy perfume in the air that shimmered.

From this spot they had a bird's-eye view over the entire valley, surrounded by a few scattered pine trees purposefully planted so as to provide a little privacy and shelter from the heat of the sun. Deciding to wash up the next morning, they put the plates, cutlery and glasses on the kitchen worktop, got into bed and cuddled up. Tired after their day of travels, they fell asleep in each other's arms. And just like angels coming to sing them to sleep, they both were serenaded by two young voices in unison, 'We love you.' Had there been someone watching over Sara and Alex at that moment they would have seen them smile in harmony, as somewhere within them the loss they both were carrying lessened just that little bit more.

The next morning, Alex was awoken around 8am by a

metallic banging sound. The noise came and went, and, although not that annoying, it was now beginning to niggle him. Like anything which distracts or disturbs one's chain of thought, the once mildly irritating noise was now becoming the only sound Alex could hear. The sound occurred for about ten seconds, followed by a pause of some thirty seconds or so. Alex tried to imagine who was working so tirelessly, and on what? He turned to his sleeping wife, 'I'll go and get breakfast ready,' he whispered in her ear.

'Mmmm...' replied Sara in slumber-struck appreciation.

Carefully climbing sideways down the rather steep and frail looking *meunier* staircase, Alex drew back the white curtains in the kitchen/diner and looked out at the breath-taking panorama of the ruggedly beautiful, multi-coloured hinterland. He opened the white front door of Le Mas and inhaled, holding it a few seconds before breathing out. A life-affirming warm perfume of pine and thyme filled his lungs. It felt so good. As he repeated the process, he relaxed, beginning to move his body intuitively.

On the in-breath, he brought his hands up from his sides as though clasped in prayer, moved them through the centre of his body, beyond his chin, nose and forehead, then moved his hands and arms above his head, separating them once they reached the highest point of his outstretched limbs. This separation of the hands was in perfect time with the out-breath, which coincided with his hands being turned away from each other, and his arms being brought back down to the sides of his body as he completely expelled the air from his lungs. He wasn't sure what he was doing, but it felt good, so he repeated the exercise a few times. Hearing a loud noise, he came out of the hypnotic breathing as a red sports car passed by on the road below. Alex thought this was just as well, because he was beginning to get lightheaded.

Alex returned inside, went to the kitchen sink and washed up. Then he sorted through what they had bought and also what was in the hamper. In a few short minutes, he was organised. 'Breakfast's ready when you are!' he called, opening the side door to the terrace.

Sara stirred and made her way downstairs. Breakfast at the picnic bench on the old, honey-coloured stone terrace was a simple affair; fresh arabica coffee, and buttered croissants with homemade jam. In the new light of day, the grounds around Le Mas came to life; a vibrant collection of plants and flowers surrounded the terrace, filling the dry morning air with a heavenly, calming scent of well-being. For a short while, soaking up the warm sunshine, looking across the scenic countryside, without a worry in the world, they felt at peace.

'Dac dac dac.' There was a knock at the door. Alex slipped back through the side door of the terrace, into the kitchen/diner and made his way to the front door, closely followed by a half-dressed and a rather shy but inquisitive Sara. Alex opened the door to find a smart, yet casually dressed woman in her sixties, who smiled and nodded, 'Hello and welcome. I am Marianne De Morreze, my husband Jacques and I are the owners of the Domaine and we are very happy to welcome you. Do you have everything you need?'

'Yes thanks,' they replied, almost in unison, with Sara peeking from behind Alex's frame.

'There are information packs in the folders which tell you everything you need to know.'

'Thank you. Can we walk around the Estate?' asked Alex.

'Yes but not this way.' She pointed to the impressively large house in the distance. 'But you are free to explore anywhere else.' She waved her hand in the general direction of the hills surrounding Le Mas.

'Okay, that's great, thanks.' Alex loved exploring and discovering, for it was something which had captured his imagination since childhood. Even now, in his early thirties, he remained intrigued by the idea of seeking. Perhaps it was his creative streak, or at least that's what he'd always put it down to.

'It was so nice to hear from your grandmother, as I haven't heard from her for years, not since...' She paused mid-sentence, unsure whether to continue.

'Not since what?' repeated Alex.

'Oh, it's not important.' She breathed a sigh of relief. 'Anyway as long as you have all you need, and if you find you don't then, just come down to the main house and ask for help. Your wish is our command.' She smiled, turned and began to make her way back.

'We really appreciate everything... Thank you!' Alex called after her, remembering the gift hamper.

'Lovely croissants,' shouted out Sara, as Madame De Morreze turned her head to smile at them and give a little wave, happy in the knowledge that the couple had arrived safely and were settling in nicely at Le Mas.

While eating the last of the croissants, Alex and Sara scoured the folders and leaflets of what to do and see in the local area, which they had found in the drawer of the buffet in the kitchen diner. Sara also produced a file of papers from Lucette, which included a handwritten map, and instructions on how best to get to various destinations. They browsed the information guides and papers, then got washed and changed, with the intention of taking a walk on the hills behind their cottage, away from the main house, in the direction Madame De Morreze suggested.

But just as they stepped out Sara grabbed Alex's arm and with a little glint in her eyes, having remembered Lucette's wish that they pass on her message to Jean-Michel suggested, 'Let's go and see Jean-Michel instead, after all Lucette has gone to so much trouble for us, it's the least we can do.'

Alex could not stop the frustration appearing on his face, he really would have preferred to go on a little hiking adventure and to leave the 'pleasantries' for another day. Seeing this, Sara squeezed his arm a little harder – she had quite a grip – and jokingly raised her eyebrows a little. Alex caved. How could he refuse this woman, who finally seemed to be getting back to her old self? Besides, how long could saying 'hello' take, surely they would be on their way again before too long. He agreed.

Up the hill they climbed with the Tramontane winds offering gentle bursts of refreshment, and the humming and fluttering of various insect and bird wings dancing in their ears. In the distance they spotted a red sports car with nobody in it. They continued, carefully following Lucette's map, for about a mile. In the distance, they were able to make out a small collection of remote stone buildings. Alex, keen to get there, hurried along, leaving Sara a few paces behind. He was always fascinated by buildings, particularly those with a sense of history, they provoked his imagination. 'This is it,' he said aloud approaching the main house which nestled comfortably into the mountainside, as if it had been there since time began.

The garden, given over mostly to olive trees, was set out in steps, like layers of a wedding cake, climbing up the steep hillside, contained by carefully restored dry stone walling, which also surrounded the central building. For a brief moment Alex thought he could see them move, like a waterfall, cascading from one terrace to the next and, at their base, gathering in a pool from which, for just a split second, a golden glow appeared. But then he blinked and all was as normal.

Alex reached the front door and noticed the hand carved sign 'L'Hermitage'. As he peered through the thick single pane glass windows, looking for signs of life, he suddenly he felt a prod in his back and a deep voice barked at him.'Hey, what do you want here?'

Alex turned around, coming face to face with a grey-haired man, and his carved walking stick. The man wore an old straw hat, had a bronzed healthy face, and noticeably dirty hands, which Alex presumed had got that way from taking care of his olive trees. 'We're just exploring, we are on holiday and staying at the cottage at the Domaine de Morreze.'

'Are you now?' asked the grey-haired man suspiciously.

At which point Sara walked up to both of them. Nodding a bashful hello to the man she smiled, confirming, 'Yes, we're on holiday and...'

But before she could finish her sentence, a little dog ran past and leapt up reaching the waist of the grey haired man. 'Pamplemousse, behave yourself!' said the man to the small lively mongrel who was creating pandemonium, begging desperately to be stroked. 'Oh he's beautiful,' said Sara as she stroked the lively dog, which gradually began to calm down.

'My name is Alex and this is my wife Sara.' Alex finally took the initiative and held out his hand, but his words and friendly gesture were met with a stony silence, and a stillness that felt a little uncomfortable.

'And my name is Jean-Michel, this...' he announced raising his stick to sweep through the air, '...is my home.'

A little bemused, Alex wondered if this really was the same man Lucette had mentioned, as he certainly didn't seem to fit her 'friendly' and 'lovable' description. But this was the right place according to Lucette's instructions, and although the man looked far younger than Lucette had described, Alex wasn't planning to hang around, so he took a punt, 'Well Jean-Michel, we may have a message for you...'

'A message for me, really? And who gives you this message?' The old man scrutinised his 'intruder' closely, resting his weight on his stick as if the answer may take some time to pull out of the ether.

'My grandmother, Lucette, in England.' Jean-Michel's mouth hung open like a child's, waiting to receive a teaspoon of medicine. An extended pause took place as Alex patiently waited for a response. But nothing came from the mouth of the man, whose demeanour now seemed suddenly far less aggressive, so Alex continued, 'She says hello, and sends her love.'

And just at that moment Sara could've sworn she saw a tear in Jean-Michel's eyes, but the old man stood firm, giving nothing away, so she seized her moment and with her head cocked slightly to one side and with the warmest of smiles she said, 'It's a real pleasure to meet you.'

Once again it seemed as though her feminine charms had worked, as Jean-Michel replied, now rather softly, 'The pleasure's all mine.' Then, as though they had been chatting for hours, he continued, 'Listen, I am a little busy with my olives at the moment, but why don't you come back tomorrow evening at six o'clock for aperitifs?'

Just then Pamplemousse barked a single 'ruff', which, to the amusement of Alex and Sara, Jean-Michel translated as the dog believing it to be a good idea too. And so they all happily agreed to meet again the following day, the initial apprehension on both sides now firmly a thing of the past.

Meanwhile, an attractive, curvaceous woman with wavy black hair arranged neatly about her face and tumbling down her back, sat listening to the three muffled voices coming through the monitor. The occasional words of what was being said could just about be heard. The mini surveillance microphone that had been placed in one of the flower baskets hanging on the terrace at L'Hermitage was just about doing its job. 'Hey... might have something interesting here. Difficult to make some of it out though!' she called out to her husband.

Upon hearing the news, a slender, grey-bearded weasel-faced man with spectacles approached her and sneered, 'For Christ's sake you stupid bitch, what were you playing at, you should have planted it in a better position. How many times do I have to tell you how to do something properly?' He paused, on the verge of exploding. 'And besides, the old man still hasn't led us to it, so what makes you think these two will?'

Alina Wicky removed her earphones and, looking up at the

man she once loved but had now resigned herself to simply living out this life in his presence, retorted calmly, 'Well look, there's obviously a connection and I have a hunch they're not just here for a holiday.'

Fritz Wicky menacingly leaned down, coming face to face with his wife, no longer captivated by her old school Hollywood looks; he found her very existence a tiresome drain on his being. However, they needed each other right now, if for no other reason than to survive the demands of their notorious employer. After all, the money was very good. Slowly and deliberately he had the final word, 'Well we can't stay here trying to figure out what the hell they're saying if we can't hear it properly, come on, we're off.'

At L'Hermitage, Sara and Alex said goodbye and began their descent. They heard the metallic banging sound again very clearly, and realised that it had been coming from Jean-Michel's farm all the while. They wondered what he was making, and decided they would make a point of asking him the following day.

Arriving back at Le Mas, they decided to explore some more after lunch. The local village of Saint-Guilhem-le-Désert was only a few kilometres away, and according to the leaflets at the cottage, was one of the most beautiful villages in France, so they sat down to a light lunch of pork rillettes, crispy pickled gherkins and divine French bread, accompanied by a glass of Vin de Pays d'Oc, the local speciality from Madame De Morreze's hamper. Again, it hit the spot.

On the ridge a black Dodge Tomahawk motorbike weaved its way deftly down through the calm of the Hérault valley heading towards St. Guilhem. The rider, indistinctive in unmarked clothes and a tinted helmet, brought the bike to a standstill at an imposing electric gate, and entered numbers on a keypad. As he did so, the security gates opened silently, and the rider pulled the impressive motorbike into a large gravelled area, half full of parked cars.

The rider removed his helmet, revealing the scarred face of Zarco De Vlinder. His features were strong, defined, and framed by his platinum blond hairline, the rest of which was pulled back in a small, neat ponytail. His piercing blue eyes were menacing. De Vlinder was not tall, but clearly fit and strong. Now in his mid-forties, the South African mercenary had been a member of Vlakplaas, a secret police hit squad from the outskirts of Pretoria, and he had participated in many raids aimed at wiping out the MK, the military wing of Nelson Mandela's African National Congress (ANC).

De Vlinder rolled up his sleeves to reveal the old Vlakplaas motto 'Who shoots first wins' tattooed on the inside of his right forearm. He was an unusual man, not because he made a living from killing, but because he really enjoyed his work. Recently he had received great financial rewards, thanks to his appointment as European head of the military wing of the privately funded DVK, and was feared and respected by all who knew him. Now he purposefully strode across the gravel to a heavy, steel door. As his hand reached out, it opened and he entered. 'Sir,' chirped the voice of an alert armed guard.

'Ja, carry on.' De Vlinder replied.

Inside the building, an extension to the old castle, De Vlinder made his way to his private chambers and entered. The door swung silently back behind him. With a 'clunk', he rested his Glock handgun on the thick smoked glass table. He took off his leather jacket, throwing it over an old but expensive looking leather chair, and, opening a desk drawer, reached for a much needed cigarette. But even before he got a chance to light it there was a knock at the door. He threw down the cigarette, calling, 'Come on, come in!' The door opened. 'I can spare you five minutes no more. Now Mr and Mrs Wicky, for God's sake tell me you have it right?'

'Closer by the day De Vlinder' replied Fritz nervously and unconvincingly. 'Well, not many fokken days left, are there. Jisis! Do I need to remind you both that we're running out of time on this, and if we do... I will personally ensure you'll be shitting teeth in the gutter!' He reached for his pistol, blew on it, then polished it by slowly rubbing it up and down his shirt sleeve.

'The old man isn't alone,' announced Alina.

De Vlinder noticed her ample bosom heaving a little quicker. Once that would have excited him, now he just dismissed it as a sign of nerves... he had grown tired of her, and just wanted them to get the job done. 'And?' enquired De Vlinder, again engrossed in his preoccupation with the shining of his weapon.

'It appears there are two others,' came her cautious reply, but De Vlinder seemed unconcerned. 'And they're going back to the old man at six... there could be something in it.' continued Alina, now clearly perturbed that De Vlinder was paying her no attention at all.

Finally raising his head slowly to look at them, De Vlinder asked, 'Right, these other two, do you know where they live?'

The couple nodded in unison. '*Ja*, good,' said De Vlinder pointing to the two leather seats opposite his desk, inviting them to sit down, which they did quickly and quietly, with Alina allowing herself a little smile, 'then we need to control this situation. Listen, this is what you're to do...'

Three

Seeing is Believing

A while after lunch, Sara and Alex made their way effortlessly down to the main road. It wasn't too hot thanks to the refreshing mountain winds, and there were stunning views of the gorges and of the river Hérault, after which the *département* (the equivalent of an English county) was named. On the way Alex entertained Sara by mimicking animals, birds and famous actors. He was a gifted impersonator, something that Sara had always found fascinating, funny and attractive. 'Oh go on do Robert de Niro... pleeeease...' she said, jokingly fluttering her eyelids and begging him in a way that he could never refuse. He looked at her sternly.

'There are three ways of doing things around here: the right way, the wrong way and the way that I do it,' said Alex exactly replicating the words spoken by De Niro in the film *Casino*.

Sara laughed, 'It gets me every time... every time.'

'You talkin' to me? You talkin' to me?' said Alex. They laughed hugged and kissed as they continued on their walk.

It took about fifteen minutes walking in the heat of the narrow deserted country roads before they found themselves at the edge of the village. Then, for some inexplicable reason, instead of continuing to follow the signs straight ahead into the village, Alex turned sharp right onto the tall archaic bridge which stood high above the steep-sided, timeless gorge. 'Alex!' Sara called after him in bemusement. She looked on as Alex suddenly fell to his knees.

'Oh my God... what have they done?!' he exclaimed. Arriving by his side, Sara knelt down and could see he was clearly in some distress. He was not himself; his eyes looked as if they were glazed with a strange translucent white marble, and were fixed

29

on something directly in front of him, although there was nothing to be seen. Tears began to trickle down his face.

Whatever Sara did or said made no difference to him, for he had gone somewhere else... Then as quick as a flash he snapped out of his trance, and in silence slowly rose to his feet. Grasping his forearms and staring him straight in the face Sara was more than a little concerned, 'Alex... what the hell is going on?'

'I don't know. I wish I did...' he responded slowly, in an unusually tense, wavering voice. He couldn't remember a thing.

Sara gave him some water from the small plastic cooler bottle which she kept in the belt around her waist. It made him feel a little better. They went over to a stone seating area and sat down for a while before deciding to carry on towards the village. Sara held his hand, keeping one eye on him all the way. They followed the winding road alongside the entrance to some caves, before finally passing the village entry sign.

Walking down the cobbled streets, they came to a stop in the village square. It was full of cafes and shops, a very pretty rural tourist trap which had somehow retained its character of days gone by, all rather quaint and peaceful. Sara thought it a good idea to stop once more, so they sat having cold drinks at a bistro type table. There were other people already enjoying a glass or two. Sara was particularly taken by a very curvaceous brunette sitting opposite a very tall, rather gaunt looking man, rather an odd pairing...

Sara was keen to restore a sense of normality, but Alex still appeared a bit shaken. 'What was all that about?' she said trying to understand the bizarre carry on.

'I still haven't a clue,' replied a confused Alex.

Sara suggested having a look around the village, but Alex said he'd be happier to stay put, which seemed a sensible idea. 'I won't be long... back in a bit.' She got up and kissed him on the crown of his head, careful not to dislodge his sunglasses.

Alex looked up at her and, managing a smile, responded,

'Take as long as you want, I'm happy to sit here in the sun, love.' With that, he lifted the sunglasses still perched on top of his head, pulled them down over his eyes and sat back. So off Sara went. Having completed the round of the small handful of specialist boutiques, and seeing that Alex was still happily relaxing in the afternoon sun, she entered the large ancient doors of the Abbaye de Gellone which, according to the information posted on the walls, was founded in 804 AD.

Sara had always enjoyed the peace and calm of old empty churches, so she thought it would be a good place for clearing her mind after the bizarre episode with Alex on the bridge. But as soon as she entered the abbey, she felt uneasy, instinctively sensing something wasn't right. She couldn't put her finger on it, but the achy feeling in her gut was overwhelming.

The high ceilings seemed so distant, giving the dark, poorly lit abbey a dour sense of separation and hopelessness. She certainly didn't feel in God's presence, whatever that was. She shivered. It was cold, and being the sole visitor in this strange place, Sara felt decidedly lonely. Previously, every time she sat in a church by herself, she'd felt refreshed and connected. But not here, not in the Abbaye de Gellone, this was different; this place was more a purveyor of darkness than a provider of light. Without thinking, she was drawn towards the ancient baptismal font in the left hand corner of the bleak, melancholy building.

She reached out and touched the immense, timeworn stone container. As soon as she did, she felt sick to the pit of her stomach. Shutting her eyes, a flood of gruesome pictures flowed through her mind; vivid scenes of young children being force-fully lifted up by their legs and feet, and battered against the unforgiving solid walls of the abbey. She looked on in horror as younger ones and babies were drowned in the font, one after another. Opening her eyes, she gazed down at the baptismal water, which now appeared to turn to blood. In her mind all she could see was a red swirling tide. In panic, she removed her hands from the rim, and with that, the horrific visions came to an abrupt end. Taken aback, Sara recognised these were the very same gruesome scenes which had plagued her dreams.

A cold draught swept across her face as the flame of a large half-used votive candle blew out, as if extinguished by some ghostlike invisible force. Becoming increasingly frightened and bewildered, she turned, hurriedly making her way to the exit. As she reached forward to twist the heavy iron ring pull of the towering door, it opened towards her, and an elderly French couple appeared. Sara brushed past them, clearly distressed. 'I expect she's confessed her sins and asked for forgiveness' whispered the presumptuous woman as she made the sign of the cross on her body. The man signed himself too, raised his chin and nodded in confident agreement before they both shuffled off into the relative darkness of the abbey.

Escaping the abbey, Sara was relieved to be warmly greeted by comforting rays of sunlight caressing her face. She stood near the entrance for a while collecting herself, breathing slowly to help her calm down and regather her thoughts. She was relieved to find Alex still relaxing in his seat beneath the tree, listening to the soothing trickle of the village fountain. 'Alex, you okay now?' she enquired, fearing a repeat of the bridge affair. Alex nodded and smiled. Sara didn't want to mention her creepy experience in the abbey, because she realised it was neither the time nor the place, and thought it would only burden Alex further. 'Let's have another drink,' she suggested.

'No, can we please leave now?' he asked, getting up and reaching out for her hand, to give it a little reassuring squeeze. Sara, not wishing to complicate matters, capitulated. After all the drama of the last hour, it seemed the most sensible thing. So off they set, walking hand in hand in a wordless silence, heading out of the village, at faster than average walking pace. As they neared the bridge on the outskirts of the village, Sara became anxious that Alex may have another funny turn, but to her relief, he didn't, and they carried on, safely passing it by.

Eventually they found themselves at the enormous ornate entrance gates to the Domaine de Morreze, They entered, following the track back up to their cottage. It was late afternoon, still warm with a slight breeze. Getting inside, Sara asked, 'What about a glass of vino?'

'Yeah, why not?' Alex agreed.

'Do you remember what happened on the bridge yet Alex?' asked Sara as she gently attempted to get some clarity.

'Nope, not a sausage' he smiled, making his way outside, awaiting his tipple.

Sara pondered whether to reveal what had taken place in the abbey, but thought better of it for now. 'We can't be too long,' Sara called through the open door, remembering the invitation for aperitifs at six o'clock at Jean-Michel's. She brought out a bottle and two glasses. The wine, a rather tasty, robust St.Chinian seemed to help them both relax. For a few precious minutes, they entered into a deep reflective silence, absorbing all that had taken place on the bridge and in the abbey. Sara glanced at her watch. 'Time to make a move,' she said patting Alex on the thigh. She got up and went inside; he could hear her busy in the bathroom, presumably restoring her makeup before their date with the old man.

Looking down the dark blue barrel of his Maverick 88 pump-action shotgun, the hunter confidently lined up his target. The wild sow twitched her nose and looked anxiously around, suspecting something wasn't quite right. Before she could act, the unforgiving stalker let rip, and with one last squeal, the wild boar fell to the dusty ground, killed outright. Her three piglets ran panicking, but straight into the line of fire. One by one, they too were fair game in the minds of their executioner. De Vlinder smiled. '*Ja ja ja* ... three little pigs... now there's plenty to eat at the braai!' he said, delighting in his kill.

At the entrance to L'Hermitage Alex raised his hand to knock, but the door opened as if by magic, to reveal Jean-Michel wearing a beaming smile on his healthy looking, tanned face. 'Welcome, welcome... come on in, come on in,' he beckoned as if speaking to them individually. Pamplemousse barked twice, extending the invitation.

'Oh he's so sweet,' said Sara stroking him. 'How old is he?'

'He's fifty-five now,' replied Jean-Michel

'Okay, that's dog years, so that makes him about eight in human years,' calculated Alex.

'No, he's fifty-five,' repeated Jean-Michel adamantly. Alex looked at Sara as they followed him into his home, and made a gesture to suggest that Jean-Michel was perhaps a little eccentric.

The little house was much bigger than outward impressions would have you believe, and a tangible warmth filled the place from top to bottom. It was a simple home, with the semblance of a rustic beamed chalet, expertly finished in dry, honey-coloured, rendered stone, and handmade wooden panelling. The two front windows had no curtains, but functional robust chestnut shutters, with small diamond shaped spy holes. Towards the back of the room, a partially opened and rather grubby curtain revealed what looked like a kitchen area, with pots and pans hanging from the beams, and a large jug holding an assortment of kitchen utensils.

Hand-whittled carvings, and a salmagundi of artistic creations hung from the walls and beams. A ready-laid, delightful stone fireplace, with a large supporting dark oak beam above, showed signs of frequent use. To the right of the chimney breast, a neatly stacked pile of split logs sat beneath a third window, as the glass pane gleamed and glimmered with vermillion and golden light, silent evidence to the finale of the stunning Languedoc sunset. A beautifully carved and engraved walking stick stood alone in the corner. A dreamcatcher turned slowly backwards and forwards above a robust looking farmhouse table, which sat in the middle of the room surrounded by sturdy rustic chairs and padded benches. The table invited you to sit down, relax and open up, as if it was a useful tool for greasing the wheels of intimacy and sharing. At first impression, one would have thought that the humble house was a little empty, because it was void of many of the modern day expectations, but in fact it was full of something inexplicably valuable and magical. All in all, it felt safe, homely and very peaceful.

There in front of them was an unexpected mini-banquet. Not quite what they had imagined. Jean-Michel had clearly taken time and effort. There were several different bottles; one looked like it contained water, others wine. A plate of assorted sliced dried sausage, a bowl of olives, a second bowl full of topped and tailed large radishes sitting next to a small flat container full of salt, a half demolished large round cheese, and a selection of breads completed the simple but impressive display.

Jean-Michel ushered them to sit on the solid wooden chairs which looked as though they were a hundred years old. 'What would you like to drink?'

'I'll go for a glass of red,' replied Alex impatiently.

'And what about you Sara?' Jean-Michel smiled warmly at her, and gestured to the wines.

'White for me, please.' She smiled back.

He poured the two glasses of wine and prepared a *pastis* and water for himself. The pungent aroma of the aniseed flavoured aperitif filled the room. Before long the conversation, as well as the wine, flowed. Alex and Sara quickly felt at ease with Jean-Michel, the frosty first meeting now long forgotten. As if reading their minds Jean-Michel confessed, 'I am sorry for yesterday. It's just that recently I have been broken into, and so I'm very careful with visitors and security now.'

'A break-in? Is there much crime here?' asked Sara.

'Apart from children messing about, it's the first time ever, but I guess there's a time for everything... anyhow enough of that... how is Lucette?' he enquired, with a real twinkle in his eyes.

'She's very well, sends her love and is hoping to come out and see us later in the month,' responded Alex rather matter-of-factly.

'She's a very special lady, really special. Tell me, is she happy in her life?' Jean-Michel seemed to allow a little mist of emotion to overcome him, as he stared off into the distance.

'Yes, she is' replied Alex 'but ever since she lost grandad five years ago she's been a bit lonely. She doesn't say it, but I know. I can feel it. But otherwise she's fit and healthy...'

'And spritely!' added Sara.

'She's one of a kind, that's for sure,' said Jean-Michel still looking towards the light streaming through the window. Once more, Sara was sure she could see the glint of a tear or two in his eyes. She noticed his radiant blue eyes appeared to be full of life and light, and a palpable magnetism seemed to emanate from them, which intrigued her.

A pregnant pause filled the room, broken by Jean-Michel with a complete change of subject. 'So tell me... what have the two of you been up to today?'

Alex explained about their visit to St. Guilhem, and what a lovely place it was. 'But it was a bit weird,' piped up Sara, unable to contain herself, perhaps the wine getting the better of her.

'Weird, in what way?' Jean-Michel was intrigued.

'Well because some strange things happened...'

'Tell me more.'

'Well first we were on the bridge ...'

'The old bridge, Le Pont du Diable?'

'Yes, Alex took us there, and then he had a funny turn...'

'And?' Jean-Michel was becoming more interested as he shunted his chair closer.

'And his eyes glazed over. He seemed to lose track of reality.'

Jean-Michel turned his attention to Alex, who had distanced

himself a little, and was tugging his ponytail tight again. 'Mmm... so what happened to you Alex?'

'I still don't know. It all seems like a bit of a dream. It was as if I was there but I wasn't there...' he trailed off, still not quite sure what had gone on, nor whether he should really be discussing it right now.

'Well, where were you then?'

'No idea, but I wasn't aware of Sara at all. I just can't remember what the hell happened.'

Alex was getting a little stressed now, tightening his ponytail again, but Sara seemed oblivious to her husband's growing discomfort as she interrupted, 'And that's not all. When I went into the abbey....'

'The Abbaye de Gellone?' Jean-Michel butted in flipping his gaze now back to her.

'Yes, when I went inside I had the most awful feeling that something terrible had happened there. That... that at some time in the past men, women and children were put to death in that godforsaken place. Well, not just put to death... but slaughtered, cut to pieces, mutilated, drowned ...'

Sara stopped short; she was shaking and thought she might just burst into tears.

Alex was a little disconcerted that Sara hadn't shared her shocking story until now, but carried on listening attentively to what was being said. However it was now Jean-Michel's turn to reveal a few things himself. 'Yes Sara, what you have said is very true,' he confirmed, 'terrible things *did* take place in the abbey, but that was over seven hundred years ago.'

Sara felt the hairs on the back of her neck stand up and she shook. 'God, that's bizarre! And I knew, I saw it all...'

Alex was now both concerned and intrigued. Leaning over to his wife to rest a calming hand on her knee, he looked at Jean-Michel and asked, 'So what exactly did happen in the abbey at Gellone?'

'I think you probably know more than you realise. You see what happened on the Pont du Diable and in the Abbaye de Gellone are closely linked. They happened on the same day, and within hours of each other,' revealed Jean-Michel, which only fuelled more curiosity.

Sara and Alex looked at each other, equally perplexed, both now desperate to know more. 'Well?' asked Alex impatiently, having had no memory of what happened to him at all.

Jean-Michel leaned back a little; as if considering how to break it to them he finally came out with, 'What happened that day changed our world forever.' Alex and Sara glanced at each other, thinking that Jean-Michel was referring to the life of the villagers and nothing more. But they hadn't fully understood what he meant. Jean-Michel was a man who said what he meant, and meant what he said. 'Before I tell you more, I need to make sure you're ready. I need to ask you both some questions.'

'Okay, shoot,' said Alex looking and nodding at Sara as if to reassure her everything was alright, suspecting that it was all a little bit odd.

'Who wants to go first?' asked Jean-Michel. Sara jumped up to volunteer. 'Okay, you come and sit directly opposite me. Alex you get up and move around to the side.' They did as he requested. Another long silence was broken as Jean-Michel coughed deliberately to attract Sara's attention, before looking deep into her eyes. He didn't just look at her eyes; he looked *into* her eyes, right through her, seeming to penetrate deep into Sara's innermost self. 'Now, Sara relax. Concentrate on your breath.' Jean-Michel asked them both to close their eyes and be still as he proceeded to guide Sara into a deeply relaxed state. When he sensed she was ready, he began. 'Now open your eyes, Sara, and look at me.' As she did, Jean-Michel's eyes appeared more mesmerising than ever. 'Tell me… what is your true vocation or service?'

Sara hesitated at first, but with comfort and encouragement seeming to radiate from the old man's kindly eyes, the answer flowed naturally, 'To be free, to liberate and to be love.'

The answer surprised Alex, but not Jean-Michel, who appeared to recognise its meaning and nodded his head gently. 'And what role can you undertake in this life to do so?' said Jean-Michel, all the while holding mesmerising contact between his eyes and Sara's.

'I am here to do what I must do,' came the puzzling but effortless response.

'And what must you do?' asked the persistent Jean-Michel.

'We are here to help you, to support you and to continue in your place.'

By now Alex was a little frustrated, as he couldn't really grasp what was occurring.

'And who is "we"'?' continued Jean-Michel, ignoring Alex's clear agitation.

'Alex and I are here now, you need look no further,' she validated.

Jean-Michel clasped his hands together, turned his gaze away from Sara, and let out a long deep breath.

Sara was coming back to her senses, semi-conscious of what had been said, but she had seemed to have had little control of the answers she gave. However the response was enough for Jean-Michel, who now knew for sure that these two were the ones he had been waiting for. Safe in that knowledge, he looked over at Alex. 'Sara has answered for you both, so there's no need for you to respond to my questions.'

Alex was in two minds. He was disappointed not to have his 'turn', but also relieved, as he didn't like the idea of being questioned, let alone in such an intimate manner.

Jean-Michel got up from the table and lit the fire. The dry kindling, gathered from the scrubland, caught alight easily, the small seasoned oak log slices burst into life, and within a short while the room was comfortably warm and well lit. Jean-Michel turned to them both. 'I'll be one minute,' he said, and left the room.

'What was all that about?' Alex whispered to Sara.

'About life, about truth, about us,' she replied softly.

'When you said "continue in your place" what exactly did you mean?' he persisted, dissatisfied with her generalised response.

'It will all become clear in time.' Another lofty reply, which only stoked Alex's curiosity more.

'What happened when he looked in your eyes?' His voice was above a whisper now.

'I was opened up... my fears seemed to fall away. I felt safe, and had no reason to pretend or protect myself. I simply told him the truth.' Sara, looking right at her husband was now deadly serious.

The old cotton curtain rustled, and Jean-Michel re-entered the room, 'Yes, you did speak your truth Sara, and in time everything will make sense.' Jean-Michel refilled the glasses and sat down.

'I'd like a bit of "sense making" now,' Alex piped up.

'Ahhh... all in good time, my friend, all in good time!' Jean-Michel raised his freshly filled glass and, with a complete change of mood, proposed a toast. 'To love, light and truth!' Not wanting to spoil the jovial tone, Sara and Alex agreed and a very merry evening was had by all. On leaving Jean-Michel invited them back for supper again the following night, to which they both happily agreed. As Alex stepped out into the mild night air, Sara took Jean-Michel's arm; giving it a little squeeze she thanked him most sincerely, with a look of true appreciation in her eyes.

With that, Jean-Michel clasped Sara's shoulders firmly, 'Be very careful. Tell no one. Trust no one. They're watching and listening. Lock your doors.' Sara gazed deep into his intense eyes and nodded inexplicably, before following after her husband.

As they approached the cottage, Sara turned to Alex. 'What was that?' She thought she heard muffled voices in the shadows. Alex listened, heard nothing, and shrugged his shoulders. Then a few more steps ahead, the pair became rooted to the spot as they saw the smashed lock and open door of their cottage.

Sara gasped. 'Shush...' said Alex, pulling Sara in close behind him. Slowly making his way into the cottage, with Sara clinging on tightly, he headed for the kitchen drawers and grabbed the biggest knife he could find. 'Just in case,' he whispered over his shoulder.

'Come out wherever you are. We're armed!' Alex managed to shout out, repressing his fear. Nothing.

As they entered the living room, Alex turned on the lights and found the furniture scattered. The sofa cushions lay separated from their covers on the floor, and the lamp on the small buffet had fallen behind the wooden sideboard. Further investigation upstairs revealed that the bedroom had also been completely ransacked. Clothes were strewn here and there, and the interior wooden drawers from the large commode lay scattered about the room. Even the mattress had been upturned, touching the floor as it hung partially suspended between the wall and the bed frame.

Alex disappeared back outside to check around before coming back to the bedroom. 'Well, whoever robbed us has gone now.'

'But Alex, that's it, I don't think anything's stolen,' said Sara who had made a quick check of the places where they'd stashed their cash and valuables. 'God, what a day, we've seen strange things, heard bizarre stories and now... we've been broken into. Jean-Michel was right. He warned me, we need to let him know.'

'What? He warned you? When? What else did he say?' Alex demanded.

'To trust no one and tell no one,' Sara replied, recalling as best she could the odd warning word for word. 'He grabbed me before I left, just after you'd gone out.'

'And that includes the police?' Alex asked, genuinely unsure.

'Well, nothing has been stolen...' Sara was almost pleading.

Alex thought for a few seconds. 'Okay, but we'll have to let

Madame de Morreze know.' He pulled out his mobile and called the number on the information sheets. There was no answer, so Alex left a calm message, clearly explaining what had occurred.

'Alex, I want to go back to Jean-Michel, he knows something about this I am sure, otherwise why even say it? Please let's go back, he'll still be up, I know he will.'

Alex went over to his wife, put his arm around her and agreed to head back, to reassure her, if nothing else, that it was all just an unfortunate coincidence.

Sara was not at all surprised to see Jean-Michel standing in his doorway as they greeted him for the second time that evening. In silence they all sat down, and it was Alex who spoke first. 'The cottage was broken into, Jean-Michel. We don't think anything was taken, but it does seem very suspicious... and with what you said to Sara, well she insisted we come back and talk to you... Do you know more than you have told us, Jean-Michel?' Alex leaned in, half-expecting the old man to smile and tell them it was all just a very unlucky coincidence, and they should go home and sleep.

But no, instead Jean-Michel's manner was firm and, looking long and hard at them both, he too leaned in and calmly spoke. 'Now listen, there is a covert, global conspiracy being orchestrated by an extremely powerful and influential group called "Der Vierte Kreis", or the DVK for short. It's German for "the fourth circle". The secret organisation has cells all over the world, and its members are reputed to include some of the world's wealthiest people, leading politicians, and corporate elite. Their agenda is to establish a One World Government, stripped of nationalistic and regional boundaries. Their intention is to develop complete and total control over every human being on the planet and, more worryingly, their demented cabal aims to reduce the world's population to five hundred million people.'

Alex rolled his eyes, mocking what he had heard, as Sara, now rather confused, looked on, slightly embarrassed.

Jean-Michel could see they were not taking him seriously at all. 'Do you really think it's funny?' The couple sat there like naughty children who had been caught red handed misbehaving in a classroom.

'And just how are they planning to reduce the world's population?' enquired Alex, barely able to contain his bemusement.

'They're already doing it, Alex. Their methods include orchestrating conflicts, introducing lethal bioengineered disease organisms via 'friendly' vaccines and the infiltration of mind-altering chemicals through the food chain. And that's only part of what we know. There's much more. That's why they mustn't get their hands on the shell.'

'I'm sorry... the shell, did you say shell?' Alex was beginning to lose his patience now.

Jean-Michel, ignoring his guest's blatant incredulity, wandered over to the window and peeped out suspiciously from the house, which only served to make matters worse. Alex looked on thinking the old man really *was* losing his marbles. 'There's an ancient shell, a golden shell of mystical powers and origin. If the DVK get their hands on it and utilises its limitless power for their own ends, then the world will tumble into a dark abyss of conflict from which it will never recover...' Jean-Michel's words trailed off, his voice quavering.

'Really? Gold, mystical shells... the end of the world?' scoffed Alex, his blood now beginning to boil at the thought that he had been taken in by this old-timer.

'Jean-Michel why are you telling us this?' said Sara trying to defuse the increasing tension between the two men.

Undeterred, he replied, 'Because I was chosen to be the guardian of the shell, and now it is the two of you. You are to be the next guardians of the shell.'

'Us! Guardians of a shell? Well, where is it then?' Alex enquired, almost through gritted teeth, tightening his pony tail for the umpteenth time, his agitation clear.

'No, the shell is for you to find,' Jean-Michel tried to explain.

'You're crazy, do you know that?' snapped Alex, leaning toward their host once more, and pointing his slightly shaking index finger inches from Jean-Michel's nose.

'Alex!' squawked Sara trying to rein him in, before he really lost it.

'No Sara,' continued Alex, turning back to Jean-Michel. 'So you are now telling us that you have a golden shell in your possession, which dark forces are seeking to capture in order to fulfil their monstrous desire for world dominance?'

'Correct,' replied Jean-Michel matter-of-factly.

'And somehow we're meant to believe this from someone who claims he has a fifty year old mongrel?' Alex was fuming.

'Alex, please!' exclaimed an embarrassed Sara.

'Fifty-five, he was born in 1961,' corrected their host calmly.

'I can't take any more of this. Come on Sara!' snapped Alex as he pushed up from his chair, giving his wife a prolonged and determined 'time to go' look with over-exaggerated raised eyebrows.

'Please, let me tell you more about the powers of the shell. Ask your grandmother, she knows,' Jean-Michel pleaded.

'PPhhttt… what would Lucette know about golden shells? Leave her out of this, in fact leave us all out of this, you're completely bloody mad!' barked Alex mockingly, shaking his head in a derisory manner and leaving the front door of L'Hermitage wide open as he stormed out.

Jean-Michel called after him, 'You must learn how the dark forces of the world came here, how hell came to heaven!'

But his words drifted without purpose, falling on deaf ears. Sara got up and wriggled past Jean-Michel who was now standing in the doorway staring after Alex. 'I'm so sorry, Jean-Michel,' she said avoiding eye contact.

Outside, Alex was muttering away and stomping over the

scattered white stone and gorse. Sara ran to catch up with him. 'What did you do that for? There was no need to be so rude.'

'Magic shells, dark powers, apocalypse. He's nuts... bloody crazy!' said Alex in a raised voice as they walked past a stone building which had the name 'Élan' hanging from the door.

'That still gives you no right to treat someone like that in their own home,' said Sara, her shoulder barging Alex who then collapsed forward with a crash, hitting the earth rubble and gorse. Sara helped him to his feet. 'Too much to drink eh, serves you right!' she attempted to lighten the mood.

'No.' Rolling up his trousers Alex revealed grazes and cuts to his leg. 'I think I'm stuck in a hole.' He shone the torch to where his right foot had become trapped. As he did, the torchlight shone down the hole and he could see what looked like a stone construction and a hollow beneath. 'What the hell is that?'

But a rapidly tiring Sara showed little interest. 'Listen it's really late. We need to get back to the cottage and I need to put some antiseptic on your leg and knee.' The female voice of reason won out and they set off.

Back at the chaos of the over-turned cottage, Sara went to find some antiseptic to treat Alex's cuts. There was nothing much at the cottage in the way of medical supplies, apart from a few plasters in a faded old green plastic first aid box. Sara used the next best thing she could find, even if it was Alex's favourite tipple. Alex felt the cleansing sting of the alcohol as the Armagnac went to work. Sara wanted to talk, but her brain was numbed from the goings-on earlier in the evening, and she was more than aware of the upset it had all caused Alex.

'I've got to get to bed Alex, are you alright?' she said looking at him. Alex nodded. With a huge yawn Sara made her way upstairs to the bedroom. Still unable to relax, Alex decided to sit for a while in the comfy chair, looking out over the terrace and the hillsides contemplating all that had taken place throughout the day. He didn't know what to believe. He just knew that his beliefs were changing so rapidly he was struggling to rationalise what was really going on. Maybe Sara was right. Perhaps what Jean-Michel was saying had some truth to it after all. For his own peace of mind now, Alex was determined to find out, one way or another.

In the private rooms of the large white house adjoining the ruins of an old chateau, De Vlinder gazed down at the all-too-real polar bear rug at his feet and then back at the two passports on his desk. 'And nothing else of importance you say, Wicky?'

'Nothing,' replied Fritz sitting opposite, intently watching his boss's face for any crumb of satisfaction or appreciation.

'Something's going on, I'm sure of it. And we're running out of time. The old man's the key, but these two may well be part of it somehow. I want to know everything about them, their families, the colour of their eyes, and even what they're planning for their next meal. Apply full surveillance and report back immediately as soon as anything happens... anything at all.' Fritz nodded and rose up from the chair, but before he got to the door De Vlinder spoke again. 'Wicky, you're bloody well paid to do a bloody good job right, and you better... or the shit will hit your fan my friend!' A tense Fritz Wicky nodded and left the room.

Waiting outside in the corridor was Alina. 'Well... how did you get on?' she asked nervously. In response to which, he reached out, grabbed her throat and pinned her against the wall. His face right up against hers, his breath reeking of spirits and stale smoke, he looked at her, full of rage. 'I'm sick of you asking your stupid questions, just leave me alone'. He dropped her to the floor and walked off. Alina, dazed and head in hands, struggled to hold herself together.

But she managed. Years of violence at the hands of the man she once so admired and longed for had taught her one thing – resilience. However, it fuelled her desire to seek out other sources of 'comfort', and now she wanted to ensure De Vlinder was still one such source. Standing upright, tidying her hair and adjusting her top to make the most of her assets, she knocked confidently on the door.

'Christ! What is it now, Wicky?' De Vlinder said, hardly flinching when Alina sauntered in. Her full lips were parted slightly, her head tilted a little to one side, her curves clear beneath her clothing, but none of it stirred his loins anymore. But he did smile at her nonetheless. And he could see she took it as a glimmer of hope, when really he just found her pathetic, empty, and only good for one thing, and it wasn't sex... 'It's you acting like a *doos*... well you can turn around and leave. I have no time for... you... any more Alina. Might I suggest you find yourself another good looking bastard to play with.' He gave her a broad, meaningless grin.

'You utter shit, Zarco. For years I have satisfied your every twisted and perverted little whim and now you think I won't want my place by your side when all the glory comes to pass? Well, fuck you! I will have my time in the light, just as much as you. You'll see!' With that she turned and stomped out.

De Vlinder smiled smugly, shook his head and pacified himself in the best way he knew how. Turning to the laptop screen, he removed a black ledger from his desk drawer and methodically cross-referenced and ticked off the monthly deposits he could see on the screen, against the well-known names in his ledger. And just as they had done for decades, he saw that the revenue streams flowed in steadily from near and far; Italy, Switzerland, England, Russia and the Americas. De Vlinder was long past caring whose money it was, or whose it had once been, deriving great satisfaction from the fact it was now all in his hands, to use as he saw fit.

'It's our...' a moment passed, 'no... *my* time' he whispered through a self-satisfied smile. Closing the ledger, De Vlinder strolled over to an upright, stone-carved hand in the large, deep alcove of his office, which held a golden shell. He placed his hand on top of the shell and smiled knowingly, like a man confident of his inevitable success.

Four

Jean-Michel

Back at L'Hermitage, Jean-Michel was immersed in his dreams, reliving his earlier life, and so unfolded the tale of how he became the guardian of the shell...

It's 1945, at the end of the Second World War, and following the subsiding of the floods at St. Guilhem, a group of speleologists from Montpellier begin to explore the newly accessible extensive caves of Clamouse. The excavations create great excitement among the locals, some of whom labour on the site, removing vast quantities of stone to make the caves more 'visitor friendly'. Some of this stone is then also used to renovate local agricultural buildings and barns. The excavation works carry on for several years. And it is during this time that Jean-Michel is born, a happy-go-lucky child, living with his farming parents in the family house at St. Guilhem, working the land and trading their goods at the local markets. Life is simple, almost dreamlike until tragedy strikes, when his father dies suddenly in the late 1950s. Jean-Michel's mother is brokenhearted and passes a few years later.

So by the mid-1960s, the teenage Jean-Michel is pretty much alone in the world, apart from a couple of cousins nearby in Lodève, and his little dog Pamplemousse – his closest and dearest friend. In fact he is far more than a dog. Jean-Michel is convinced it has an all-too-human quality about him. At times Jean-Michel is almost certain he is looking into the eyes of a boy... a special boy at that, from another time and place... Jean-Michel continues to live in the small stone family house in St. Guilhem, and work the family's small olive farm up on the plateaus of the scrubland, just outside the village. The income from the olives coupled with growing his own vegetables and

49

making his own pickles and jams, means that he has just enough to get by.

One day, after walking on the hills surrounding the village, Jean-Michel arrived home and noticed Pamplemousse was missing. A few minutes passed, with still no sign of him at all. 'Mousse, mousse... where are you boy?' shouted the young Jean-Michel, giving the special high-pitched whistle his friend always responded to. But there was still nothing. Jean-Michel decided to sit on one of the rocks on the scrubland perched on the hillside overlooking L'Hermitage, and wait a while longer. Perhaps Pamplemousse was hot on the trail of a rabbit or two. He waited and waited, calling out occasionally and whistling, but still no sign of the dog. Then, just as his concern grew into worry, he heard a faint bark; as it grew louder Jean-Michel recognised it as the voice of his friend.

As if by magic, less than one hundred metres away, the little dog's dusty head appeared out of the rocky hillside. Jean-Michel ran over towards him. Though the dog's head was out, his body was now firmly wedged between the two sides of a small hole. Carefully removing a large stone, then another, Jean-Michel gradually freed the relieved Pamplemousse from his hillside prison. His friend thanked him with an excited, slobbery lick. In removing the stones Jean-Michel could just about make out that the opening led deeper down into the hill. It was there, on his family's land, to the side of the ruined walls of a small ancient outbuilding he found the secret second entrance to the caves of Clamouse, hidden and unknown to anyone else alive. Little did he know, but it was the same secret entrance Sebastian Cavalles had used to enter the Grotte de Clamouse nearly seven hundred years earlier.

With Pamplemousse now ferreting about happily, safe and well, Jean-Michel investigated further, and discovered the small entrance was in fact a small cave in some disrepair. He decided to come back with the old SNCF railway lamp of his father's. With the light, he was able to see that it wasn't just a small cave, but that via another small opening in the far right hand corner it led deeper into the mountainside than expected.

Over the following months, in the company of his canine companion, Jean-Michel worked hard clearing the area around the entrance, and spent many more hours exploring the caves. He never told another soul. As they began to navigate their way around the underground wonderland in the upper chambers of Clamouse, Jean-Michel even found a spot in the cave where he could look down at the visiting tourists who had by then flourished in numbers. The only downside of these frequent expeditions were the regular scratches and scrapes he collected squeezing between the tight crevices. So, when he felt inclined to, he would chisel away with a bolster and mason's mallet at some of the sharper edges. Sometimes, because of the dampness from the water he would slip over too – more nicks and knocks.

However one day, while working inside the main cave he had a bad fall and suffered a deep, nasty gash to his left leg. Being far inside the cave and finding it painful to move, cleaning the wound was top priority. With great difficulty and discomfort, he scrambled down to a small pool in the cave and sat bathing his leg.

The small lagoon was full to the brim. White crystal reflections appeared to dance and swim as they became caught by the beam of the old lamp in Jean-Michel's hand. At one point he was so transfixed by his surroundings he completely forgot the deep gash to his leg, which by now was bleeding profusely. Gigantic stalactites, majestically loomed down from the ceiling, high above his head. The distant lights and voices from the cave tours below him provided an eerie backdrop as he sat there, the lamp by his side, his back now supported by a large boulder, and both legs dangling in the crystalline liquid.

Though rather cold, the water was refreshing as he cupped it in his hands and let it gently wash his wound. The blood was now trickling into the pool; it was blatantly obvious he'd need stitches. Putting his right hand over the cut he focussed on his breathing, calming himself down, sedating the anxiety of the thoughts flowing through his mind by focussing on being still and peaceful. As he did, a strange but familiar feeling came over him – profound love! Bursts of electromagnetic energy pulsed through his body. Looking down at his leg he was astonished to see that the gash had closed, and the bleeding had completely ceased. 'The water!' exclaimed Jean-Michel, 'the water is miraculous!'

From that day on, with the help of a trail of homemade lamps that burnt his very own olive oil, Jean-Michel gathered water from the pool, both to drink and for more medicinal purposes. In time he became known as the local *guérisseur* or healer, all the while keeping the healing waters a secret. Expanding his knowledge intuitively, using natural remedies from the local flora and fauna, he became a knowledgeable and gifted herbalist too. In the early days, he healed and cured the villagers of St. Guilhem, but after a while, people came from farther afield to seek his help.

Inevitably, because of the nature of his work and the growing rumours of miraculous results, some of the locals feared him. They simply didn't understand who he was, and what he did. Perhaps they didn't want to know. Jean-Michel decided to sell the family house in the village, and to use the money to renovate the farm and buildings on the hillside. He would then be able to live in greater peace and seclusion, close to the cave and the healing powers of the pool. It made perfect sense, and felt like the right thing to do.

To sell the house, he employed the services of a local *Notaire* – a lawyer specially qualified and appointed for estate transactions, rather than an estate agent from the city. It took little time to sell his place as properties in St. Guilhem were very sought after, and the sale provided Jean-Michel with the necessary funds to undertake the renovations of his parent's olive farm. Planning permissions were passed without any problems as the Napoleonic *'plan cadastrale'* map indicated all the footprints of the buildings clearly. Most of the semi-ruined stone buildings were small, bar one which was destined to become Jean-Michel's new home. He planned to restore two more outbuildings; one for storage named La Cabane, and the other located near the secret cave entrance, which was christened Élan.

The main house, which he fittingly named L'Hermitage, didn't take long to come together; Jean-Michel was very handy and delighted in this work. The ground floor of the house consisted of a large main room with a central fireplace, and a small kitchenette set off to the far end. Out the back, the small extension housed a shower, basin and toilet. He also built a covered terrace, which extended the living space considerably. Upstairs, he created a simple bedroom which had a stunning, panoramic view of the valley. He spent many hours making intricate wood carvings, including a beautiful hard wood fire surround which added a unique flavour to the building. L'Hermitage oozed character, yet at the same time remained functional and practical.

During this time Jean-Michel discovered he could dowse, not only for water, but for virtually anything he set his mind to. It was another string to his gifted bow, and one which the locals employed from time to time. He became known as the local *sourcier* (dowser or sorcerer) because of this new found ability. He never charged a fee for this service, but would accept food and drink or monetary donations in exchange for any work he undertook. Utilising this gift of divining to locate a bountiful source of fresh water on his land, he employed a local company from Béziers to drill a well which provided him with a free, endless supply of potable water. Over the years, as solar panel technology improved, he improvised the power supply so that he had mains as well as his own free electricity supply. All in all, with the garden produce as well, L'Hermitage was pretty much self-sufficient and virtually 'off grid'. Jean-Michel lived a way of life which fed and nourished him in many ways.

Alex's grandmother Lucette, and her family were local villagers, their ancestors having lived in St. Guilhem for centuries. One day, Lucette, then a beautiful teenage woman, was involved in a traumatic car accident. Returning from a visit to the Lac de Salagou, the car she was travelling in at high speed hit a tractor. Her best friend Marie-Claire, who was driving the car, was killed instantly, and Lucette was rushed by ambulance to the local hospital at Clermont-l'Hérault. The farmer escaped unhurt, though he suffered for many years before his death, having never come to terms with the tragedy. Following several days of intensive care, Lucette's condition stabilised, but with one devastating outcome; she failed to regain her vision. Following several days of comprehensive medical examinations, the doctors at Clermont gave the prognosis that she would never be able to see again.

Jean-Michel knew the family and soon heard the tragic news. Lucette's devoutly religious parents (who were suspicious of healers and all things mystical) wouldn't even entertain the thought of approaching him for help. Then, some weeks later, on a beautiful Sunday afternoon, Jean-Michel found Lucette perched on a large stone at the 'beach' of the gorge beneath the Pont du Diable, basking in the sun. The beach beneath the bridge was in a dramatic setting, with the mountains and scrublands towering over the visitors, as if watching over them. The turquoise water glistened in the sun, and a group of youths were taking turns jumping off the rocky sides of the gorge beneath the bridge.

Hidden from view, Jean-Michel looked on as Lucette gently shook her head, clearly enjoying the warmth of the late spring sunshine. A white stick sat by her side, standing upright in the gritty sand of the riverside beach. *How brave*, he thought to himself. Jean-Michel was drawn to the blind girl who didn't appear to have a care in the world. She gleamed with life as she bathed in the warm sunshine. Jean-Michel watched her attentively as she stood up and tip-toed slowly towards the water's edge. Feeling the cool water with her toes, her mouth opened in response to the sensation as she gradually became immersed in the water, and then she began to swim. Jean-Michel marvelled at the courage of the beautiful girl who now looked more to him like a divine water spirit or mermaid. Following a few minutes swimming, with the now completely captivated Jean-Michel watching her every move, she safely navigated her way back to sit cross-legged on the same stone again, face up, basking in the healing rays, with every inch of her wet skin glistening in the sun.

Jean-Michel moved out from behind one of the bushes lining the water's edge and, ever so slowly, walked toward her. She turned as if to look directly at him, but Jean-Michel could see the light in her eyes had gone. 'Hello... may I help you?' asked Jean-Michel.

Lucette recognised the voice of the healer. 'Help me with what?' she replied, a little wry smile escaping the corners of her mouth.

'With your eyes?' Jean-Michel clarified, timidly.

'But there's nothing you can do, there's nothing anyone can do,' came the response heavily tinged with a sadness that moved him deeply. Lucette bowed her head.

'Please, just let me try...' said Jean-Michel, captivated by her face, enchanted by her voice, and now more determined to do all he could to change her fortune.

Lucette bit on her lip as she hesitated, realising her parents wouldn't be happy about it. But knowing Jean-Michel from their schooldays, she liked and trusted him. 'Ppphhh... Why not, give it a go. See what you can do...' With nothing to lose she finally gave in, though from the skeptical tone of her voice, Jean-Michel could tell she really didn't think he would be able to help her.

'But Lucette, you must really believe I can help you,' Jean-

Michel blurted out, his hand moving to touch hers to make the point.

Her hand now squeezing his, she leaned her face slightly closer to his and said reassuringly, 'I trust you and I'm sure that whatever you can do will be from the depths of your heart.' With that, he gently pulled her forwards from where she was perched on top of the large rock, steadied her, touched both her arms gently, before bending down and making a symbol in the ground. Lucette didn't panic, but filled with expectation as she could sense he was busy at work. She liked his voice and felt comfortable in his presence, and, unlike her parents, she trusted him. Gathering some of the silty sand from beneath him in one hand, he dampened it with his own spittle a couple of times, then placed both of his hands together, mixing the sand with his own saliva as he did so.

'Now keep your eyes tightly shut,' he instructed her firmly. Then, ever so gently, he smeared the damp mixture over her eyelids, and softly whispered some foreign sounding words Lucette didn't recognise. The mixture covering her eyelids tingled so much it almost made her laugh. 'Now go back into the water and wash your eyes,' he said, gently nudging her towards the water in the gorge.

Lucette walked into the water, with her head slightly tilted backwards so as to hold the muddy sand in place. It all felt so unreal and dreamlike to her. She kept going until the water covered her waist. Then she took a deep breath and let herself fall backwards into the water, submerging her entire body. As she rose to her feet in the shallow waters, she washed the residue of the muddy mixture from her eyes. But nothing seemed to be happening. After three submersions, and trying to hide her disappointment, she turned around to head back to the shore. However, with each step, glimpses of light appeared shimmering in front of her, until her eyes became bathed in bright sunlight. At first she thought it was her imagination, but now an amazing display of vibrant rainbow colours glistened and danced before her like a thousand tiny angels. When she finally made it out of the water, she was overcome with joy, and was crying hysterically because she could see! She looked at the world for the first time since the accident, and searched for Jean-Michel, but he was nowhere to be seen.

Lucette was so overjoyed, so full of energy, that she ran all the way back to the village, shouting out loud that it was a miracle, intent on telling the whole world she could see again. Arriving home, she ran into the house and blurted the story out. 'Maman! Papa! I can see! I can see! Jean-Michel healed me. It's a miracle, a real miracle!' Her parents tried to calm her down to find out exactly what had taken place, as an inquisitive crowd gathered at the front door, which Lucette had left wide open. Sitting her down at the kitchen table, Lucette's mother gave her a glass of water, noticing her daughter's hands trembling with excitement and trepidation.

With a crowd amassed by the doorway, Lucette's father asked what had happened, and how it was that her sight had returned. 'He put mud on my eyes, Papa,' Lucette replied beaming, 'and told me to bathe them in the waters below the bridge, and now... now... I can see!' She turned her face to look up at her father, who was standing over her with arms crossed, and with a disapproving gaze.

'But we told you not to have anything to do with him, he's dangerous, you know... not right in the head. He's mad,' her father retorted forcefully.

Lucette stood up from the table to reiterate what was really important here. 'What does it mean to be mad? Whether he's mad or not, you decide, but I don't care. The one thing I do know is that I was blind but now I can see!'

By now the babbling crowd of friends and neighbours had swelled further and again one of them asked Lucette, 'What did he do to you, how did he heal your eyes?'

'I've already told you what happened, and you must have heard me. Why do you need to hear me say it again? Don't you believe me? All I know is… I can see, I can really see!'

'Who does he think he is? He's not God, he's used witchcraft, he's a warlock, he's evil…' came a voice full of fear and ignorance from behind the crowded doorway. Lucette was angered by the nescient words, and shouted aloud so that all could hear, 'If this man was not moved by God, he would not have been able to do such a wonderful miraculous thing. For doesn't it say in the Bible 'The Lord opens the eyes of the blind?' Lucette's impassioned response caused a hush of awe to descend on all present. Even her parents were stunned into a prolonged silence. And back at the water's edge, the white stick, still standing upright in the sandy spot where Lucette had firmly placed it, quivered and shook as if it were alive and rejoicing at the good news.

A few days later Lucette, now strictly forbidden by her father to visit Jean-Michel, decided that she must, regardless – after all she wanted to look him in the eyes and thank him personally for what he'd done. So she told her parents she was going for a swim, and secretly went in search of her healer. She found him working on the plateaus of his olive farm and they began to talk. She thanked him, and he explained that 'he' had done nothing and was merely a vessel. Over the coming weeks and months, Lucette visited often, sharing many interesting conversations. They became close, and fell in love. One afternoon, while lying on a rug on the hillside with his arms wrapped around Lucette, Jean-Michel dozed off and spoke aloud in his sleep of the magical waters of Clamouse. When he awoke, she quizzed him about the pool, and the golden shell he had also mentioned. Jean-Michel openly shared the story, but explained he had no idea about any shell, and put it down to a symbolic dream. Lucette knew better, and suggested it was something he would actually find one day. This was how she learned, or rather intuited the secret of the golden shell.

Then one day, quite out of the blue, Lucette was informed that her father had been offered a 'once in a lifetime opportunity' and the family were to move almost immediately. The well-paid job, with its new car and free accommodation, tore Jean-Michel and Lucette apart. Not quite seventeen years old, she had little choice but to go.

A devastated Jean-Michel struggled to come to terms with their separation. Lucette was the love of his life, and in his heart and mind he could never envisage loving anyone else. After several days of grieving, followed by a night's bout of heavy drinking, Jean-Michel made a rash decision to leave. The very next day, still perturbed and angry, he left Pamplemousse with his cousins in the nearby town of Lodeve, and travelled to Aubagne to take part in the pre-selection process of the French Foreign Legion.

Being physically and mentally fit, and somewhat embittered, Jean-Michel was in many ways an ideal candidate, and soon became a welcome addition to the Legion. The promise of anonymity attracted Jean-Michel strongly, and he enlisted under a false name, as was permitted. At just twenty years of age, he travelled the world, and by 1969 found himself posted abroad to Chad, in central Africa, where he witnessed countless atrocities.

It did little to nourish his soul, but during his time with the Legion, he had the opportunity to learn hand-to-hand combat, self-defence and martial arts, including Jujutsu and Zen Do Kai, all of which he found rewarding. But he loved nothing more than getting up early in the morning and practising Tai Chi, a gentle slow practice of breath work, body movements and postures which improved his balance and general psychological health, and, as his fellow legionnaires found amusing, he also developed more than a healthy interest in the Chinese philosophy of the 'Supreme Ultimate' state of infinite potentiality. In time, the barbaric realities of war turned him away from violence, teaching him profound spiritual truths. Following completion of his five year contract of service, Jean-Michel was sure that his time was up. So with a large FFL kit bag strapped to his back, and through force of habit singing 'Le Boudin', (the official march of the Legionnaires), Jean-Michel returned home to the plateaus above St. Guilhem, retrieving his now much older friend Pamplemousse from Lodeve along the way. In his absence, Jean-Michel's cousins had done their best to look after the farm, visiting as and when they could; but it was still a little run-down and overgrown. There was much to do.

Jean-Michel moved back into L'Hermitage and committed his energy into getting the farm productive again and finishing all his renovations. Each morning he practised Tai Chi, and read as much spiritual philosophy as he could get his hands on. Over a period of several months he worked relentlessly, creating a short but deep stone tunnel connecting the now renovated small stone outbuilding he'd named Élan to the cave entrance. He then re-covered and camouflaged the freshly built stone ceiling with dirt and rocks. In order to keep it completely secret, he disguised the hole inside the rustic shelter to look like another well. What made the well inside Élan different was that at the bottom there was the opening to the tunnel which led into the cave.

He worked every day, and in all weathers, fully dedicated to the work ahead. With time, he began to mellow and come to terms with his life to date, a maturing which was greatly helped by meditation, Tai Chi, and living immersed in nature. As the restorations on Élan continued, Jean-Michel covered the entrance to the cave that Pamplemousse had uncovered, using stone, lime and sand he had left over from the main works. All in all, it was quite a feat of masonry. He even poured water into the base of the interior 'well' so that it reflected the light. Then, if somebody was nosing around, they would assume it was a well, but to the one side (difficult to see in the poor light) there was the secret entrance covered with old hemp sacks. As if that wasn't enough, he installed security grills over the door and windows of the building, making the property into a rustic Fort Knox.

With the restorations of L'Hermitage, Élan and La Cabane now complete, Jean-Michel loved nothing more than visiting the caves every day. He updated and expanded the homemade olive oil lamps in the stone arched tunnel and cave, placing them at twenty paces apart, a form of lighting which worked far better than candles. He discovered that a few ounces of oil burned for several hours, and Jean-Michel had an endless supply. He crafted lamps from white clay dug from a small section on one of the plateaus, making the wicks from old shredded cotton tea towels. He stored two large barrels of olive oil inside Élan so that he didn't have far to go to refill the lamps. Empty plastic containers, once thoroughly cleaned, were an ideal way of carrying the liquid to refill the lamps, especially the larger five litre ones with built in handles. For relighting, he used his father's old dented embossed lighter and a few boxes of tapers he kept stashed in one of the hessian sacks which hung from the large brown rusty nails embedded in the stone wall of the little outbuilding. The old flash lamp was now always kept there too, as a preliminary aid for lighting up the steps down inside the well.

Unlike Jean-Michel's building work, which had gone from strength to strength, his dear friend Pamplemousse was evidently suffering the consequences of old age. He was a smallish mongrel with a great beard and moustache, and had the most intelligent and loving look in his eyes. Jean-Michel, now in his mid-twenties had increasingly noticed the ageing of the dog, and accepted it as best he could. However his best friend's breathing had now deteriorated alarmingly and Pamplemousse would often decide to stay home rather than go walking with his beloved master.

One mid-morning as Jean-Michel was meticulously crushing a specific measure of herbs in his pestle, he was distracted by a crash. Looking around he found Pamplemousse sprawled on the floor, in trouble – his legs had given way, and his breathing was very erratic and shallow. Jean-Michel rushed over, lay down on the floor and looked his friend directly in the eyes. He saw the normally white cataracts turn a luminous emerald green, and intuited that the soul of the dog was in the process of leaving his body.

Picking him up and wrapping him in an old towel, Jean-Michel went outside heading to Élan. He arrived at the door hot and sweaty, and remembered that he'd forgotten the keys to get in. He gently lowered Pamplemousse to the ground and sprinted back to his house, picking up his small set of keys, and returning at speed to the side of his old friend, who lay there breathing sporadically.

Jean-Michel unlocked the grill and door, and picked up Pamplemousse. Strapping him to his back in an old cloth sack he had used to carry him many times before, he took the old SNCF flash lamp, lighter and tapers and descended. They went through the disguised well wall opening, Jean-Michel lighting the olive oil lamps one by one with the tapers as he ventured deeper into the cave, making his way down to the pool.

By now Pamplemousse was barely breathing and his eyes were glazing over. But Jean-Michel was determined not to lose his friend without doing everything he possibly could. Laying him down beside the crystal clear pool, Jean-Michel scooped some water in one of his hands and, carefully holding his friend's head with the other, deliberately dribbled the water into the dog's mouth. 'Come on Mousse. You can do it... live... live... live!' he shouted defiantly.

A last deep breath exited the dog's lungs followed by an eerie silence. Pamplemousse had gone. Jean-Michel sat on the cave floor, head in hands, overcome with grief. Now, all alone in the world, without his beloved friend, he broke down in tears. He cried and cried, so much so that eventually he fell asleep next to the lifeless body of his companion through sheer emotional exhaustion. Waking from his sleep, Jean-Michel felt water on his face.

There was something else too, something warm. Opening his eyes his vision was almost completely blocked by a fleshy, wet tongue. And then he heard a bark. 'Pamplemousse!' he exclaimed. The dog, tail wagging, was licking Jean-Michel's face, very much alive and now appeared considerably younger. He looked, acted and sounded like he'd been reborn. Jean-Michel cuddled the little dog and spoke with him, knowing that Pamplemousse understood every word he said.

Feeling grubby and dirty, and in need of some refreshment Jean-Michel decided to bathe his face in the pool. He bent down, putting his entire head underwater. It was cool, refreshing and invigorating. In order to get himself back up he pushed on the bottom of the shallow edge of the pool with both hands, but one of his hands slipped and he nearly fell in. He'd felt something give way and, knowing every nook and cranny of the pool, was keen to discover what had come loose. He studied the pool wall carefully, but nothing seemed dislodged. Leaning back into the water, his hands wandered freely around searching for the loose stone.

And then he found it. He was unable to see what it was, but he held it carefully in his hand and drew it out. It was neither a stone nor a crystal. Now out of the water, he could see it was a shell, not just an ordinary shell, but a golden shell which glistened in the half light of the secret cave. Lucette's intuition of the incredible find had been right after all. In that brief, timeless moment, Jean-Michel changed. Although he knew nothing about the shell, he sensed it was something very special, uniquely powerful, a feeling most people would call magical. Just being near the shell was both soothing him and filling him with elation. Not one to announce his newly discovered treasure to the world or to be overcome by such matters, Jean-Michel decided to keep the shell hidden in the pool, because there, surely, it would be safe...

On that day Jean-Michel's heart and mind had been blown wide open, revealing a myriad of unspoken possibilities and hidden truths. The real meaning of life and death was turned on its head. He started to see the world, and everything within it, in a new light, and began to receive incredible visions. Once, Jean-Michel was sitting on the hillside contemplating the intelligent and artistic quality of nature. And as he closed his eyes, he saw the same mountain panorama, but with one new addition, a man, floating slightly above ground height. Jean-Michel blinked but the image remained.

As Jean-Michel relaxed into this possibility, simply allowing it to be, he saw that the bearded man was wearing a simple tunic with a woven braided belt. The sun, directly behind his head, created the illusion of a halo. The man then opened his arms as if to invite Jean-Michel to speak. Intuitively, Jean-Michel stood up, with his two arms wide apart, reciprocating the gesture. The energy was intense, the air charged with a potent, intelligent force as the man asked Jean-Michel what the reason for his life was. Without hesitation, Jean-Michel replied, 'To be free, to liberate and to be love.'

'And to what lengths would you go to in this life to make that happen?' asked the man.

And it was at that point, Jean-Michel gave a solemn oath, 'I give my life to serve humanity, to support and serve the rebirth of a Golden Age, when human beings will see the light within all life; a time when the Divine will be known to be within us, and we will be known to be within the Divine. I freely give my life to this sole end. I am here to continue in your place.' The words flowed out of Jean-Michel's mouth as if he had always known them. When the dialogue finally came to an end, he felt a great sense of relief, all his doubts put to rest, and somehow, now he was ready to go to work in the world.

The anonymous man would regularly appear. He told him stories of the shell, how it came to St. Guilhem and more. This man was a teacher, just not in the way you would ordinarily imagine a teacher to be. Jean-Michel told no one of these encounters, and never asked the man his name. In time the spiritual entity revealed that he was Armand Cavalles, no longer present in the physical dimension, but able to access the earthly human realm to secure the passing on of the guardianship of the shell to its next guardian.

From Armand, Jean-Michel learnt that the healing pool was called 'La Source Vitale' meaning 'The Lifeblood' and it was part of a sacred site used by a Gnostic spiritual community once living at St. Guilhem called the Liberae. He explained that by the late thirteenth century, their philosophy and altruistic way of life, coupled with rumours of a miraculous golden shell, had attracted growing numbers to St. Guilhem.

The majority of the Liberae were so called 'heretics' who had fled the persecution of the Vatican, these included; Bogomils (from Eastern Europe), Albigensians (Cathars), members of the Brethren of the Free Spirit, Beguines, Henricians, Waldensians, and a small number of Franciscan monks or 'Spirituals' who were later to become known as the Fraticelli.

The common ground they all shared was threefold; they rejected the corrupt hoarding of wealth by the Church of Rome; they believed that God was present within each and every human being by virtue of a soul; and that, in order to realise their divine heritage, they believe each individual was free to find and follow their own path, doing their own work as necessary. And so the population of St. Guilhem grew. The caves at Clamouse were an ideal place for the Gnostic families of ascetics, contemplatives, healers and mystics to meet hidden away from the prying eyes of the Church. So it was in the caves of Clamouse and not the abbey that the Liberae gathered conducting sacred ceremonies and healings at La Source Vitale many hundreds of years ago. In time, the entire village, including the priest, became part of the Liberae community, and the abbey, now seen as a symbol of extortion and extravagance, a sad, lonely husk.

As these experiences continued, Jean-Michel encountered an increasing number of new phenomena. He saw orbs of energy surrounding birds of prey as they circled above the mountainside. He seemed able to communicate telepathically with his 'resurrected' Pamplemousse, and with many other animals. Colours would appear surrounding people, and he could see auras and energies of indescribable beauty. Jean-Michel's consciousness was expanding beyond the limits of the physical senses; beyond ordinary smell, sight, vision, touch and taste. Since finding the shell he seemed able to touch inexplicable dimensions of being no one had ever told him about. And each time he did, he also touched on a feeling of unconditional love from the core of his very being. He learned how to 'read' people; their minds and more. One day, he experienced the complete dissolution of the individual self into 'The All', 'The One' or 'The Self' so that nothing 'else' or 'other' exists. In that timeless moment, Jean-Michel consciously dissolved into the totality of the Universe. From this, a sacred, unshakeable sense of harmony and equality filled his consciousness as he realised the truth of 'who' and 'what' he really was.

From the spirit visitations of Armand, as well as insights, dreams and intuitions, he not only discovered he was the guardian of the shell, but was told that one day two people would come to him as the new guardians, and the two would become one. Jean-Michel was told by the spirit of Arnaud that the new guardians would be a man and a woman from across the Northern seas; that they would discover a mystical connection with the village of St Guilhem and authenticate their legitimacy by finding the shell themselves. They would be silently called by the vibration of the shell. He was shown that when the time came he would be able to identify them, and once he had done so, he would intuitively know when to share what they needed to know, as Armand had with Jean-Michel.

But not all was such plain sailing. Jean-Michel also learned that the new guardians would require help. An ancient malevolent power was hell bent on recapturing the shell. And should it fall back into their hands it would open a second destructive cycle of ownership, resulting in a war to end all wars. The DVK covertly used religion, business, and politics coupled with occult practices to fulfil their dream of establishing the kingdom of the master race. Its members were convinced of their superiority as direct descendants from a single progenitor, the mythical high priestess Hekate. She was said to have lived thousands of years ago, at the time of Atlantis. But, and it was a big but, Jean-Michel knew that if he could find the next guardians, two would become one, and they would hold the key to opening the shell, which would bring the about the very real possibility of entering a second Golden Age – the second age of the Soul...

Five

Darkness & Light

Early next morning, having hardly slept, Alex rubbed his eyes and answered his phone. It was Madame de Morreze who had been shocked to hear the news of the break in, but was relieved to know that nothing had been stolen. She assured the couple that the locksmith was on his way so that the damage would be repaired as soon as possible.

Within the hour there was a knock at the door. A large man dressed in overalls, holding a toolbox stood at the entrance, and introduced himself as Pascal Bonnet, the local locksmith. Pascal rolled a cigarette and went to work. He unleashed an impressive blend of expletives with Gallic vigour as his head smashed against the old metal doorbell fixed against the outside of the door frame.

Twenty minutes later, the lock was successfully repaired. Pascal handed Alex two new keys and a small plastic item, about the size of a ten pence piece, insisting it must belong to Alex, who thanked him as he went on his way. Once back in the kitchen area, Alex went to get the orange juice, and, as he did, the circular plastic item in his hand leapt and stuck fast against the fridge door. Now Alex could see it also had small holes in one side. *Magnetic... and a mic?* Alex thought to himself, deducing the unsuspecting item was a bugging device. With that, he wrapped it in several layers of aluminium foil, took it outside and placed it on the stone wall.

Returning inside, he moved his index finger over his lips to warn Sara as she climbed down the narrow stairs. They took breakfast together outside on the stone terrace where Alex gave her a whispered update on the discovery of the small bugging device. On hearing the news, Sara raised her eyebrows in surprise, but didn't seem that shocked. Maybe Jean-Michel was telling the truth after all, and they were under surveillance. Sara wanted to return to L'Hermitage, and Alex promised he'd be on his very best behaviour. He retrieved the silver foil and its contents from the garden wall, which by now was warm to the touch.

Approaching Jean-Michel's house, they watched as the grey-haired old man went through the motions of his Tai Chi moves on the sunny terrace. He looked so at peace that they waited a while, studying his graceful moves, until eventually his eyes opened and met theirs. He smiled and beckoned them towards him. They approached, Sara immediately recounting the break in, and then a slightly embarrassed Alex apologising for losing his temper the previous night, unwrapping the silver foil and holding out his hand containing the bugging device.

Jean-Michel took the disc, gave it the once over before wrapping it back up in the foil, placing it in a chequered handkerchief and putting in his pocket, 'We need to talk. But first, why don't both of you join me for a few minutes; it'll help you relieve the stress...' It seemed a strange response to them, but they went with the idea, and spent a few minutes copying Jean-Michel's slow, graceful moving meditation, which the couple found made them feel surprisingly relaxed and help to calm their racing thoughts.

Jean-Michel silently invited them into the house, where all sat down at the kitchen table. He then retrieved the disc from his pocket and placed it carefully on a log in the fireplace, before picking up the poker from the side of the fireplace and smashing it down on the small listening device, crushing it. 'Look,' he said as he produced another identical squashed device he'd discovered at L'Hermitage.

Repeatedly curling his forefinger towards himself as if to beckon them closer Jean-Michel lifted a small rug exposing a wooden trap door. Led by a now inquisitive Pamplemousse, the three climbed down the short wooden staircase into a gravel floored cellar measuring about four metres long and three metres wide. It was dimly lit by a single bulb, and contained wine, jars full of pickles and preserves and a stash of old wooden crates. Upturning the crates Jean-Michel continued in hushed tones, 'It's clear we're all being listened to and we're probably being watched. I'm afraid there's no going back for either of you now. Whether you believe this is real or not, you're into it up to your necks. For your own safety you need to listen, and listen very carefully…' With Alex and Sara nodding in silence he continued, 'I'm pretty sure my house is clean of bugs, but I will make a thorough sweep with a pipe detector later. And then we better sweep your cottage too. There is more…' He looked at them both, searching for permission to continue in their eyes, but he intuitively knew now was the time, whether they were ready or not, 'and when you hear what I've got to tell you it'll change your world and your beliefs forever.'

Alex and Sara nodded again, anxious to hear more, and Jean-Michel obliged. Sitting on the makeshift chairs, he explained the history passed on to him by Armand Cavalles – that from around 800 AD to the late thirteenth century, the village of Saint-Guilhem-le-Désert and the Abbey of Gellone had become a place of spiritual truth, a vibrant symbol of purity and a shining example of human potential. Beautiful miracles happened, people were cured, healed, and phenomena took place which no one could fully understand. He explained that Vatican mercenaries came to St Guilhem in search of heretics in possession of a sacred artefact which supposedly contained untapped power or limitless potential. It was said that whoever held this artefact, held the fate of humankind in their hands.

In those days, the village was home to good people who were free to find and follow their own understanding of the Divine. The label of their spiritual search had little importance, but the level of authenticity with which they lived their lives did. They lived in peace, love and harmony and treated each other as equals, men, women and children alike.

Jean-Michel continued, 'These people known as the Liberae, simply called themselves 'Bons hommes' and 'Bonnes Dames' and because of their good deeds, were also referred to as the 'Children of the Light'. They held sacred ceremonies and meetings in the 'Cathédrale du Temps' in the local cave called Clamouse, and followed a line of teaching which went from France, all the way back to the Holy Land and beyond. To them, 'Christ' was not an individual, but the core loving consciousness within all people. In many ways, they were the true 'Christians'. Like the Essenes, and the Therapeutae before them, they believed it was the birth right of all human beings to 'cleanse' themselves by purging their minds and bodies to experience their true perfect nature, making them sons and daughters of God. This was a direct challenge to the Church of Rome, which renounced such 'satanic' teachings as heresy, forcing the Liberae underground.

'Then the darkest of days befell them. Following a gathering in the "Cathédrale du Temps" the villagers came out of Clamouse to find armed mercenaries waiting for them. Next, the dark robed "Élu" (the inner circle of holy leaders) were marched down to the Pont du Diable and asked to hand over the artefact. They were threatened with death. Still not one of them said a word, giving nothing away. The commander of the soldiers, now filled with rage, ordered the twelve to be lined up on the bridge. They were spaced out at intervals of several metres, and their hands tied behind their backs. Ropes were then passed through the small holes at the base of the bridge wall, and back over each of the heads of the twelve. Small blocks of wood were fixed to the other ends of the ropes. Then, one by one, the twelve (two of whom were women) were dropped off the bridge wall, their necks broken outright. It was a horrific scene.'

'But I... I knew that. That's what I saw on the bridge when we went to the village,' Alex interjected, struggling to contain himself and nearly coming off his crate as he threw his hands up in a real 'lightbulb' moment.

Jean-Michel, totally unfazed, continued, 'And yet still, the soldiers had not found what they were looking for. So they marched the remaining crowd back up into the village of St. Guilhem, gathering strays and bystanders on the way. They made it absolutely clear that if the artefact was not handed over immediately, then more deaths would follow. They rounded everyone up in the village square and asked again. Still, no one uttered a word.

'The commander ordered the soldiers to put all the people, all two hundred and sixty five of them, into the abbey. Still the "Children of the Light" refused to capitulate. Within minutes of the order being given, they were all massacred. Men, women and children were tortured, limbs sliced off by swords, beheaded, and babies and children small enough to fit in the baptism font were drowned in full view of their mothers. No mercy was shown that day at the Abbey of Gellone, but still not a single person told the mercenaries where the shell was. And so the artefact remained hidden.'

'God...that's exactly what I saw in my nightmare and what I felt in the abbey!' Sara spurted out as Alex looked on in curious disbelief.

'Yes Sara, but there's more to tell you, much more,' Jean-Michel carried on, 'you see there was one young boy, Sebastian Cavalles, who managed to escape the massacre because he had not gone with his family to the caves that day.' Pamplemousse looked up at his master and whimpered. Jean-Michel smiled lovingly at his companion and continued, 'He'd had a terrible dream the previous night, and so frightened was he that he feigned illness to stay home and not attend the cave ceremony. So upon hearing the commotion, scared and bewildered, Sebastian looked down from the upper opening of his family house in the square of St. Guilhem.

'He watched and listened as the savage end to chivalry unfolded before his young, innocent eyes. He saw the villagers rounded up and forcefully herded like animals into the abbey, before the large doors slammed shut, and an eerie silence unfolded. From the direction of the prison-like building, blood curdling screams cut through the air, spreading far across the market square. Ripples of suffering rolled across the water of the village fountain.

'Sebastian ran down the wooden staircase and hid behind the enormous granite fireplace, on the verge of panic and unable to think clearly. Then something most wonderful happened. His father, one of the twelve who had been put to death on the bridge just one hour earlier, appeared before him. Not only that, he spoke, "Sebastian, don't be afraid, I will always be here for you. There is little time. Now listen carefully. There is a task you must undertake, and now only you can do it."

'Sebastian's father, Armand, was the guardian of the shell. It was his sole and sacred responsibility to protect it and only he knew where it was hidden. "Pull up the small light coloured flagstone on the left of the fireplace," he instructed his young son. Sebastian moved to the left hand side of the fireplace, located the smaller light coloured stone, and using a metal poker from beside the fireplace as a lever, just managed to get his small fingers underneath the terracotta stone. He quickly and carefully lifted it and placed it to one side. Underneath, wrapped in cloth, he found a small dark wooden box with a golden clasp in the shape of a scallop shell. Sebastian heard his father's voice again, though this time he was nowhere to be seen, "Now take it to the Cathédrale du Temps, and you'll know what to do when you get there."

'Full of hope yet riddled with fear, Sebastian picked up the box, replaced the flagstone, and moved the dirt with his shoe to cover the tracks. He looked outside in the market square. As the din of the merciless slaughter in the abbey came to an end, the door flew open and out came the soldiers, their faces splattered with the blood of their victims. They now targeted the houses, trashing and pillaging every single one.

'Sebastian shoved the box down inside the belt of his breeches. The soldiers were now just a few metres from Sebastian's house. He didn't know what to do. Should he go this way, should he go that way? Should he simply hide in the house? With his father's words still ringing in his ears, he decided to make a run for it. And run he did. He ran so fast that he shot past the soldiers posted to block the exit of the main square. He ran out onto the main exit road of the village. He ran so fast, that although he had little time to think, he was still surprised by the incredible speed he'd managed to reach.

'As Sebastian reached the main entrance to the cave, he heard soldiers' voices. He decided to enter the caves via the secret entrance on the far side of the hill. Bending low down in an attempt to hide and blend with the small trees, bushes and stones, he made his way to the hidden entrance point. Now completely out of breath, he clambered down through the small hole and into the cave, the higher levels of the *Grotte de Clamouse*. As his father had asked, the brave youngster nervously made his way in the blackness through to where the villagers normally conducted their weekly celebratory ceremony, a place they called La Cathédrale du Temps.

'Approaching the main section of the cave, he emerged from the darkness of the small entrance. Occasional oil lamps placed in small cubby holes still lit the way. The caves were full of magnificent stalactites and stalagmites, incredible natural architecture, made all the more mysterious by the flickering glow coming from thousands of sparkling crystals. Rock formations appeared like melted cheese, almost edible. This was the Cathédrale du Temps. Closing in on the roughly carved cuboid stone altar to the rear of the large chamber, he passed by the transparent water of La

Source Vitale on his right hand side. Removing the box from his frayed leather belt, he moved towards the scallop shell shape carved into the cave wall, when just at that moment, a powerful arm grabbed him pulling him backwards, making him crash down to the floor which his head hit with some force.

'"I'll take that boy," said the darkly clad soldier towering over Sebastian and nodding towards the box. Sebastian didn't know what to do. His father wasn't there and he was alone and terrified. "C'mon, give it to me now," growled the soldier. "Hand it over, boy!" Closing his eyes, Sebastian cried out, "Father, Father help me!" but his father didn't appear. Instead, in a moment that seemed frozen in time, he heard his comforting voice. "Be strong. Love them for what they do..."

'Sebastian held the box even more firmly, close into his chest now. The soldier drew his large sword and, without hesitation, plunged it through the boy's heart, twisting the embedded blade and withdrawing it in one brutally fluid motion. The last thing Sebastian remembered was watching the soldier prise the box from his clutching bloodied hands, as the last breath left his body.

'As his blood flowed across the cave floors, and the first drop entered the baptism pool, Sebastian found himself transported. He found himself in a dark tunnel, but the pain and the fear, like the fatal wound, were gone. A golden light shone in the distance, which drew him in like a powerful magnet. Coming closer to the golden rays Sebastian felt more at peace than ever before in his entire life. Reaching the edge of the light, he hesitated as a hand reached out from the glow and his father's voice said aloud, "Welcome home my beautiful son. You have done well". And with that the joyous, smiling young boy disappeared into the light, to re-join his loved ones.'

Pamplemousse barked excitedly as if to corroborate the entire story.

Alex and Sara, who had listened attentively to Jean-Michel for some fifteen minutes, were by now totally gripped by the story. 'But what happened to the shell in the box?' asked Sara, putting her hand out to Jean-Michel in some sort of last ditch attempt to keep him talking, as though she sensed it was all they would be told today.

'Yeah, and where did it come from?' Alex blurted out excitedly.

'There is more to tell, and much to learn,' replied Jean-Michel. He looked at them both and decided against his initial plan... for it was safe now. He could see into their hearts and souls, and knew it was time to finally pass on what he knew. Much to Sara and Alex's relief, Jean-Michel cleared his throat and announced, 'Perhaps it's best to go back to the beginning.' And so he did...

'A great many years ago, in a different land, there was an ancient civilisation living on a most beautiful island in the Mediterranean Sea. They were more advanced than any other peoples in the world, not materialistically, but spiritually. Theirs was a utopian society that had evolved a profound wisdom. As a way of life, they practiced equality, meditation, healing, and encouraged the opening of the heart-mind in all people. They were ahead of their time. This evolutionary step in human beings was known as the first "Golden Age of the Soul". It was a great and wonderful place and time to be. 'But it was not all peaceful. One day a young girl was washed up on the shores of Atlantis. Adopted by a kind Atlantean family, the girl grew up to become an ambitious sorceress named Hekate (commonly pronounced Heck-ah-tay). She was different from the islanders, who in time increasingly noticed a strange red hue coming from the depths of her eyes.

'In time, discovering that she was furthering her over-ambitious personal desires of power by using mind-altering drugs, necromancy and sacrifice, she was placed under house arrest by the direct orders of the council. According to the myth, she escaped by leaping from a cliff, and upon plunging into the water, morphed into a three-headed sea snake, and left the island.

'Settling back in the old world she had come from, Hekate plotted her revenge by casting a dark spell over the entire land of Atlantis and all its inhabitants. And so the fear of Hekate's revenge hung in the ether. In time, the high council (made up of elders, priests and priestesses) became aware of an impending catastrophe, and, as seers – attuned to knowing what was, is and will be – this was not taken lightly. They knew that their civilisation was going to be wiped out. They watched as the violent storms increased in number and strength, and how the animals and birds became increasingly panicked into irrational acts. It was all proof of what they already knew... the end was coming.

'So they convened an urgent council meeting. In all, a group consisting of twelve priests, priestesses, elders and council members came together in the Great Hall. They listened to each other and carefully deliberated the options. As to their own survival, there were no options, what was coming was a natural devastation more powerful than anything man-made, but because they were evolved and advanced, they came upon a way of retaining their wisdom for future generations of humankind.

'They conducted a sacred ceremony. The ceremony involved offerings, pure intention and universal energy. Each of the twelve brought the offering of a small crystal to the final meeting, placing them one by one into a scallop shell on the white stone altar. In the centre of the hall was the "eternal flame" which burned all day and night as a reminder to the permanent presence of the Divine. As they circled around the sacred flame they held hands and chanted. The energy they had built up manifested as swirling golden light circling above them.

'As each one of them surrendered totally to the flow of Universal Intelligence, small radiant orbs left each of their bodies and entered the vortex of golden energy present in the room. As they continued the ceremony, the floating orbs merged with the swirling golden energy, all the while moving faster and faster. Then, in a powerful explosive climax, the golden vortex of energy shot into the crystals held in the shell, and the transformation happened.

'The crystals were melted by the intensity of energy, and a sea of liquid crystal filled both halves of the shell. As the liquid began to solidify, the shell itself alchemised. Under intense heat, pressure and a blending of human will and universal energy, the scallop shell was transformed. It was spiritual alchemy of the highest degree. The shell was now gold on the outer layer, while the inside solidified crystal had become a strange but beautiful mirror. The molecular change to the crystals produced an iridescent play of vibrant colours; blues, blacks, gold, green, turquoise and silvery grey.

'Then the shell slammed shut. And it was done. A solid golden scallop shell was all that could be seen. Knowing that the end was approaching, the shell was placed by the high priestess in the stone offering bowl to the side of the 'eternal flame' in the centre of the council chamber. The twelve hugged one another and calmly made their way out of the hall.

'Within hours the greatest natural catastrophe in human history took place. Violent earthquakes, tsunamis and cataclysmic flooding occurred with such force and to such extent that within a single day and night the island, and all trace of the advanced civilisation, disappeared into the depths of the sea. The explosions that occurred were so powerful that debris of all kinds was thrown forty miles into the earth's atmosphere. Hekate had taken her revenge.

'But the Universal Intelligence in the shell was still alive. The shell was shifted and moved by the sands of time until thousands of years later it washed up on the shore of the Holy Land. And it was there around 250 BCE that Adameil, the Essene, would find it. Being an Essene, Adameil had little interest in property or money, but like the others in his community, he led a sacred lifestyle which included immersing in water every morning, eating together following prayers, and devotion to charity and benevolence.

'In those days, the Essenes lived throughout Palestine in their own spiritual communities. Preferring to reside in the wilderness, they believed they were cutting themselves off from the impure animalistic minds of the world and at the same time cleansing and purging their own. Their wilderness communities expanded rapidly as people sought to escape the war-torn madness of the world. They dedicated their lives to the seeking of the promise of old. There was belief, preparation and dedication of each of the sect to prepare their bodies and minds to act as vessels through which the Divine could enter into the earthly realm.

'Adameil was a good man who sought and shared the love within his heart. One day, strolling along the seashore, his attention was drawn to what appeared to be a flashing light. For few quick seconds the reflecting golden light could be seen, and then it would disappear for a short while. Like a stranded light-house. It was as if somebody or something was trying to grab his attention. Adameil was intrigued by this mysterious phenomenon, so decided to investigate further. As he approached the light, the tide washed over his feet, and the light disappeared once more.

'For a while he stood mystified. As the water retreated, the light appeared once more. This time he was close by it. Now he could see it was a shell, a golden seven-fingered scallop shell. He reached down hesitantly, but as his fingers stretched to pick up the shell, the water covered it and it disappeared once more. Yet, this time he could feel the weight and shape of the shell held in his hand. It seemed that when the shell was covered by the water, it became invisible to the naked eye.

'Adameil was in awe, he could feel it in his hand and yet it was without doubt invisible! It must be sent from Heaven he thought. Adameil sensed the immense significance of the ownership of the magical shell. He sat on the rocks holding it, trying to decide what to do with it. Should he keep it, sell it, bury it? Then, the answer came to him clearly like a bolt out of the blue. Adameil returned to the Essene encampment and took the shell to the chief priest named Pinchas.

'The Essenes governed Adameil's community by a system called "1:3:12 and the Many", drawn from the principles of sacred geometry. The number "1" referred to the chief priest, the "3" to the highest-ranking priests of the community and a Council of "12" – twelve overseers. Daily affairs of the community were a harmonious blend of experience and evolving consensual democracy.

'The main role of the spiritual hierarchy was to uphold the secret esoteric teachings, and not to actually "govern". So they had formed what was known as a "holarchy" – a true democratic society functioning within a highly disciplined hierarchical order. Like cogs in an old pocket watch, each person played a vital part in the movement of the whole.

'So Pinchas, the "1", received the shell from Adameil (one of the Many). Thereafter the Essene community flourished, and their simple, open lifestyle and sacred ways attracted more and more people who were disillusioned with the apparent wickedness of the world. Many healings took place, which were attributed to the power and presence of the shell.

'In that same community, some years later, a mysterious young man called Yohanan joined the desert sect. Yohanan was the son of a priest who came from the line of the famous prophet Zadok. His family line was said to have held the privileged office of high priest since the time of King David. People believed that this made Yohanan who and what he was, but Yohanan was who he was because he followed no man.

'He became a compelling orator; thousands would cross the desert to visit the Essene community just to hear him preach.

Yohanan became the most influential Essene of his time. His radical and direct honesty gave him popularity and prominence in the Essene community, and his fame quickly spread. In time he became the guardian of the shell, and unbeknown to others, carried it in a leather pouch firmly tied to a belt around his waist. But all was not well.

'As more and more people flooded in to join the community, their numbers swelled, and Yohanan began to witness escalating contradictions, inconsistencies and jealousies, so one night he decided to leave the desert community for good. Crossing the wilderness, he emerged from the desert and began his principal practice of baptism, the traditional and symbolic Essenic rite. Regular meetings drew ever-increasing crowds who gathered to see and hear the so called prophet of the wilderness, the Essene who had emerged from the desert. But one day there was to be a meeting which changed the face of history as we know it.'

On that note Jean-Michel put his hands on his thighs to push himself up on his feet and said, 'Now let's get you something to eat.' Without hesitation, and despite the risk of leaving his captive audience sitting on a knife-edge, the old man climbed the stairs, returning in his own time with a tray full of bread, cheese, pâté and three tumblers. Putting them down on another wooden crate, he uncorked a bottle of red wine from the cellar and invited his guests to tuck in. 'Water ...' muttered Jean-Michel as he disappeared again. 'This is the strangest lunch invitation I've ever had,' Alex finally managed to say, smiling as he looked into Sara's eyes to check she was alright. She closed her gaping jaw, and smiled back. Just then Jean-Michel returned with a large carafe full of chilled water, shutting the trap door behind him once more.

Six

Yeshua & Miriam

'Are you still happy for me to continue?' asked Jean-Michel looking first at Alex, then at Sara to see if they were taking in the enormity of what he was saying.

'Yes, yes, please do,' replied Sara, who like Alex, was completely captivated.

So Jean-Michel continued. 'Yohanan received an increasing number of prophetic dreams concerning his own future demise, and intuitively knew that his end was approaching. And yet his sadness was accompanied by an elated sense of joy at the forthcoming arrival of the next guardian of the shell. Yeshua was no Essene, and adhered to no fixed belief, for he was a liberated soul. Consequently he was free to interpret his direct experiences, as well as the sacred laws and the prophets in his own way as Spirit moved him.

'In his mid-thirties, the dark-skinned Yeshua came across as an person unusual in several ways. Being taller than average height, this was embodied by a slightly awkward walk, and a modest stoop. Viewing him side on, it was apparent his shoulders dropped forward. He had a well-proportioned body, neither heavy-set nor thin, a largish head with a long face and a straight nose. On first meeting, his piercing blue-grey eyes seemed to look right "into" you, displaying an occasional luminescence which came and went with his mood and manner. A mole, which resembled a beauty spot, was clearly visible on his left cheek. His chestnut coloured hair (bleached by the sun) was parted in the middle and always worn shoulder length.

'Women found him attractive, as he was a handsome man with looks verging on the effeminate, looks inherited from his beautiful mother. A short masculine beard from ear to ear was shaped into two fork-like strands at the ends, which were well-cultivated and carefully preened. When he was deep in thought, he twisted the forks of his beard one after the other, as if it was a way of focussing his mind. He appeared youthful and yet spoke words of wisdom which were beyond his years. He enjoyed his food and wine, rarely laughed, and often wept. There was something delicate yet evidently powerful about the man. A small group of devotees followed him wherever he went, as did his wife, Miriam.

'One day, Yohanan was baptising and preaching on the banks of the River Jordan. Over his bare, sun-tanned skin he wore a camel-hair cloak; symbolic of the non-materialistic lifestyle he lived and loved. Yeshua arrived unannounced and unrecognised.

'Yeshua heard rumours of Yohanan's powerful preaching and, accompanied by a growing band of his own followers, came to listen to his message. Yohanan stood on a large rock above the river and spoke to the crowd, *"Do not think you will be saved by your rituals in the temple, for it is not the sacrifices of bullocks and lambs that the Lord, thy God, demands, but complete repentance within your hearts. Open your heart to Him, and He will listen. Repent all your sins, allow His light to enter you, and only then, will you be truly forgiven. You cannot truly forgive others until you have first forgiven yourself. The Kingdom of God is at hand, and you must prove your worthiness now in order to receive His love. Who so ever has two shirts, must give one to the man who has none. And who so ever has more than enough, must share it likewise. Do not take money by force, and do not accuse anyone falsely. Be content with what you have, for all that you have was given you by the Lord, thy God, so that you would come to know and love Him in your heart."*

'People were drawn to his powerful words and the convincing manner in which he delivered them. Around sunset, Yohanan's helpers beckoned the crowd to move towards a small cove on the water's bank. Many were baptised that day. Eventually, Yeshua stepped forward and waded into the water, moving towards Yohanan. Then, with one hand on the back of Yeshua's head, and the other on his lower back, he gently lowered his body into the water. Just a few seconds was all it took.

'When Yeshua came back up and out of the water, Yohanan recognised the unconditional love emanating from his eyes and was moved to tears. Yohanan saw some kind of energy around Yeshua which was astounding. It looked as though there were rays of sunshine emerging from Yeshua's head, almost blinding. The startling rays of light appeared in the shape of a golden scallop. At that time, only Yohanan could see the striking vision. But it was the same light that would be visible at the later "Transfiguration of Yeshua" on the mountain witnessed by Peter, James and John.

'Yohanan knew he had encountered the next guardian of the shell. Taking Yeshua's hand, he pulled it towards him and, removing the shell from his pouch, placed it firmly in his hands. 'You are he... you are the one I have been waiting for,' said Yohanan.

'Yeshua's followers assumed that this was a reference to the long awaited Messiah of the Jews, but Yohanan simply meant that he had found the next guardian of the shell. Yeshua took the shell. After putting their arms around each other, Yeshua turned and disappeared with his companions. Yohanan looked on as they disappeared in the distance. And it was from that time that Yeshua went to work in the world.' Jean-Michel paused.

'Please don't stop...do carry on,' begged Sara.

'Yeah...Wow... Amazing, I don't know what to say!' exclaimed Alex, now totally on board, all doubts and sarcasms exorcised.

Urged on by Alex and Sara, Jean-Michel continued by explaining that following the meeting with Yohanan, Yeshua disappeared into the Judean desert alone, where he fasted and underwent a prolonged and deliberate process of self-enquiry. 'This was similar to the process that Siddhartha Gautama (Buddha) went through when he faced the demon "Mara". The demon Mara who tempted Gautama, and the Satan who tempted Yeshua, were one and the same.

'In time followers of Yeshua witnessed many miraculous events. During these "miracles" Yeshua seemed to draw inspiration and energy from the presence of his beloved Miriam. They met in Bethany near Jerusalem, where being of darker skin than the locals, she was persecuted and described as a prostitute or as a carrier of evil spirits.

'Nothing could have been further from the truth. Miriam was descended from Ethiopian royalty, and more recently from a line of priests and healers. The name "Magdalana" literally means "of Magdala", and this was in reference to the town of Magdala in Ethiopia, today known as Amba Mariam, the "Hill of Mary".

'Ethiopia was also the homeland of the Mekada, the Queen of Sheba, who, according to the Bible and the Koran consorted with King Solomon some thousand years before. To this day, Amba Mariam points to the true identity of the woman from Magdala, and the depth of relationship she shared with the man named Yeshua.

'Yeshua often entered an altered state of consciousness, a type of trance, at times becoming completely unaware of his own body. He became famed for his healings and miracles. Prior to each miracle occurring, he would make a symbol with his hand in the sand or in the dust, or on the entrance to the house he was visiting.

'The symbol worked in the same way as any sacred mantra or chant. When Yeshua drew the symbol, or meditated on it, it set a clear intention and helped bring about positive results. The use of the symbol was all about Yeshua being in alignment with the Universal life force, and merging with that energy to bring about healing, allowing him to transcend the individual mind and to directly experience the natural flow of Spirit.

'Most people in the crowds who saw Yeshua draw the symbol thought it was simply a fish, others, well versed in knowledge of the astrological age, believed it was a sign of the newly arrived Piscean Age. Only Miriam really knew what Yeshua drew in the sand. It was not a fish, but a lemniscate, the symbol for wholeness, completion and infinity. She knew because she played an intimate, powerful and important role in the earthly embodiment of Yeshua's authentic soul. For Yeshua and Miriam, the sign of the lemniscate epitomised the union and of "two becoming one", just as their ancestors had and just like the appearance of an open escallop shell.

'Following three years of healing, speaking and carrying out his work, Yeshua knew that his earthly life was to be cut short, and looked to pass the shell on to the next guardian. At first Yeshua thought the new guardian was likely to be one of his closest initiates; Peter, John or James. But in the fullness of time, he realised it was none of them, but rather his best friend, lover and wife – Miriam. In one intimate moment he saw the golden light in the eyes of Miriam and knowing his earthly life was coming to completion, gave the shell to her to safeguard.

'So Miriam, the muse, teacher, healer, alchemist, lover and wife became the guardian of the shell. You see, Miriam played the most important role in the earthly embodiment of Yeshua's authentic soul. Only that's not, all for Miriam and Yeshua were lovingly intimate knowing that he was about to be arrested and killed. They wanted to preserve his seed. And that child born out of the love shared by Yeshua and Miriam was to become known as "The Holy Grail". Most think of the Grail as a goblet or cup, or even a treasure, but would not a child of Yeshua and Miriam be a true vessel of Spirit?

'As lover, wife and soon to be mother, the fulfilment of the sacred feminine role of Miriam was the final, vital stepping stone in Yeshua's soul-realisation, allowing him to fully live every critical stage of human existence, and to sanctify it. Through Miriam, Yeshua experienced the path of the perfect matrimony, the secret of alchemy. Together, they lived and experienced the holistic meaning of love.

'Then the soldiers came, Yeshua was taken away, beaten beyond recognition and put on trial. The traditionalists within the Sanhedrin, frightened by Yeshua's blatant heresy, had plotted to get rid of him. He was openly spreading a heretical Gnostic philosophy. He taught that divine truth, power and wisdom lies within. He talked of a force far greater than anything created by man, a universal intelligence ever-present in all forms of life, and that realisation of our innate divinity was the route to heaven and the liberation of the soul.

'Yeshua spoke in parables and often in paradox because in that way he could secretly convey his revolutionary message. So for those who were ready and willing to receive the deeper meaning of his stories, an exchange or transmission took place, but to "outsiders" his teaching remained either simplistic or nonsensical. This was so that 'they may be ever seeing but never perceiving, and ever hearing but never understanding' – Mark 4:11-12. The parables and Gnostic teachings Yeshua shared were consciousness-expanding, permitting people to see, feel and sense beyond the accepted ways of the time. Yeshua knew that all people were able to perceive the existence of this pure energy consciousness – and that the energetic vibration brought about through connecting with it would resonate throughout their entire being, resulting in a profound and lasting awareness.

'To the Sanhedrin, Yeshua was an extremely dangerous man, for he was a provocative character, rapidly spreading teachings strongly at variance with the religious establishment and the beliefs and customs of the time. Following his death, and with the fourth century legalisation and adoption of a "Christianity" as a useful power base by the Romans, words, passages and events from the gospels were altered and rewritten to converge with other popular belief systems, establishing an easy shift to "Christianity" – the new profitable religion of Rome. This new hybrid religion offered spiritual comfort and the prospect of salvation on the one hand, with attractive new career paths and riches on the other.

'To ensure this the first Bible was commissioned, paid for, inspected and approved by Rome. That's why we end up with an Old Testament God who is vindictive and inconsistent; making a world and then drowning it, then repenting for what he had done, before promising not to do so again; a God who was quite the opposite to the compassionate, loving, all-forgiving 'Father' of Yeshua.

'Complete texts or codices were hidden, discarded and destroyed, especially those pointing to any suggestion of a non-divine Yeshua, and the truth of the healthy, loving, sexual relationship he shared with his beloved Miriam.

'With the tragic end of Yeshua's life on the cross, Miriam knew she was also in grave danger, for, if the Sanhedrin discovered that she was carrying their child, they would surely want her dead. Following Yeshua's crucifixion, his wife, fearing the likely desecration of his body and burial place, paid for the corpse to be removed from the tomb at night, in complete secrecy. It was then Miriam who revealed to the distraught and fearful disciples that the tombstone was rolled away, and his body was missing, which also fulfilled the messianic prophecies.

'You see, there was no physical resurrection. On the other hand, it is entirely possible to see a person after their passing, and to talk with them, but then the physical body is no longer inhabited by the light of the soul and so it becomes simply an empty vessel. Following the burial, the disciples saw and spoke with Yeshua in the form of his non-physical spirit body, and their false conclusion that this was his "resurrected" physical body has led to two thousand years of ineptitude and ignorance. Physical "death" is a fact, as is "life" after death. Life and death are one.

'Once we see through the idea of death, the window of eternal life opens. Again, the confused facts of Yeshua's "resurrection" were adapted and manipulated by the Roman Church in order to claim that Yeshua was uniquely divine, and the only son of God. Think about it, if that was so, why would he himself have taught people the Lord's Prayer, and to say "Our Father"; sharing his truth that all people (including himself) were children of God? We are all children of God, and in this respect Yeshua was, and is, your brother. It's one of the greatest ironies of world history that those ultimately responsible for his demise used the example of his life to sustain the fear, separation and control he openly opposed.

'So the pregnant Miriam Magdalana, Mary Salome (the mother of Yeshua's followers John and James) and Miriam of Clopas (the sister-in-law of Yeshua's mother) were part of a group of evacuees who were smuggled away on a merchant boat which, following a treacherous stormy voyage from the Holy Land, arrived on French soil. They disembarked at a place which became known as Saintes-Maries-de-la-Barque (Saint Mary's of the boat) a town which was renamed in the nineteenth century, and better known today as Saintes-Maries-de-la-Mer, in Provence.

'Rumours of the arrival of a "Black Madonna", an ancient pagan goddess, spread like wildfire. You see, in those days, there were numerous expat communities from the Holy Land established throughout the trade routes in France, with many evacuees and free-thinkers looking to escape harsh Roman legislation and control. And so it was here in southern France that the son of Miriam and Yeshua was born. Time passed. The secret was kept well hidden and the bloodline of Yeshua thrived, spreading throughout France, Scotland, England and beyond.

'Now, the world population has multiplied by thirty times in the last two thousand years. What this actually means is that hundreds of millions of people are descended from Yeshua through genealogical lines, and have his DNA in their cells. It's ironic to think that the "unique son of God" is the ancestor of the majority of people living on Earth today.

'And there is another problem for the Catholic Church here. If Jesus was a family man, a husband and father, then the idea that celibate priests are somehow closer to God is totally false, and the practice of sexual abstinence completely unnecessary. Their ignorance of the real meaning of "purity" and "innocence" was completely at odds with the wholesome, loving, holistic example of Yeshua's life and concealed the catalytic role Miriam played in his spiritual awakening and evolution.

'*Et voilà!* So you can see... Yeshua was a real man after all. He did not die to save our sins, rather he lived as an example of true self-knowledge or Gnosis. The powers-that-be – including corrupt elements within the Vatican – infiltrated organisations, constructed hoaxes, manipulated cover-ups and deliberately manifested seemingly far-fetched stories in order to confuse and exaggerate the truth about Yeshua. They deliberately suppressed the truth of his human nature and the importance of the role of the Divine feminine, in order to keep people controlled, in fear, and themselves in power and riches.

'Miriam Magdalena spent the last thirty years of her life in France. She was revered as a great healer and sage, and continued to perform many miracles. When she finally passed away, she was laid to rest with the shell in a small secret tomb at Rennes-le-Chateau.'

'Well bloody hell, would you believe it,' spurted out Alex 'It's all becoming clearer and clearer, like I'm remembering the truth as you tell it to us.'

'Now, I am not forcing you to believe anything, and neither do I have anything to sell you,' replied Jean-Michel 'It is for you to recognise that which is true, for only those who can truly listen with their hearts will know the truth when they hear it.'

'Well it not only sounds true, but it feels true too,' quipped Sara.

Seven

Charlemagne & Guilhem

'Have you ever heard of the Emperor Charlemagne? Charles The Great, I think you call him?' asked Jean-Michel. Alex and Sara nodded in such a way that it suggested they knew the name but little else, so Jean-Michel carried on...

'In the eighth century AD, with his empire uniting most of western Europe, he led a dedicated and unrivalled search for religious artefacts. Not since Constantine's mother, Saint Helena of Constantinople, journeyed to Palestine in the fourth century had there been such an arduous effort to recover Holy Relics. Charlemagne collected a variety during his lifetime, some of which are still kept in Aachen Cathedral in Germany. The four most important are the cloak of the Blessed Virgin; the swaddling-clothes of Yeshua; the loin-cloth worn by Yeshua on the cross; and the cloth on which the head of St. John the Baptist was placed following his beheading.

'By the late eighth century, Charlemagne's highly trained and dedicated soldiers, following leads, myths and rumours, finally uncovered the tomb of Miriam Magdalana in a cave at Rennes-le-Chateau. Several personal belongings were buried with her, including the golden shell still clasped between her hands. She never found the next guardian, so requested it be buried with her. Perhaps the most remarkable thing was that when her body was discovered – because it had been embalmed with oils – it was hardly decomposed.

The shell was taken to Charlemagne, who ordered that Miriam's body be secretly re-buried within the secure private walls of the nearby Benedictine Abbey of St. Hilaire. Her empty stone sarcophagus remains there to this day, opposite the twelfth pillar of the cloisters, unmarked and unnoticed, just as she would have wished. However on the twelfth pillar, the scallop shell which marked her new burial place has been removed.

'And so the real shell was taken to the court of Charlemagne where it caught the interest of his first wife, Gerperga, nicknamed "Desiderata", as she was the daughter of Desiderius, the last king of the Lombards. On holding the shell, she became entranced, and wrote the following words...

Let grace be your guide through the chaos; forget not the peace which underlies silence. Bring no quarrel to others without good reason. Speak your truth with quiet clarity and listen to others speak theirs. Let not aggression be a drain on your spirit. Draw no comparisons to others, for there will always be some greater and some lesser, this measurement may not serve you well. Enjoy your successes. Be diligent in your work, however humble, in time you will see the wolf among sheep and the virtues of those who strive for high ideals. Be yourself, do not love falsely, for love is what sustains the soul and conquers all.

Embrace the counsel of the years, recognising well the time to surrender the things of youth. Nurture strength of spirit to shield you in sudden misfortune, but stress yourself not with dark thoughts, born of fatigue and loneliness. Do all things in moderation, but paramount is to be gentle in spirit. You are a child of the universe, no less than the trees and the stars; you have a right to be here and the universe is unfolding as it should.

Therefore, be at peace with your Creator, whatever you conceive it to be, and whatever your labours and desires, in the cacophony of life listen to and keep peace with your soul. With all its failings, it is still a world of great beauty. Be the joy in your heart, be the miracle of your life.

'Within a few months, and with no sign of children on the horizon, Gerperga's politically arranged marriage to Charlemagne was annulled, and she spent the rest of her life in exile within the walls of the monastery of San Salvatore in Brescia in northern Italy. Then one day, a few years later, the great warrior and conqueror of the Moors, Guilhem D'Orange, Count of Toulouse, Duke of Aquitaine and cousin to the King, discovered the writings hidden in one of the royal chambers. He was so deeply moved by the words of Desiderata, that he turned his back on a lifetime of war, and at the age of forty-nine lay down his arms to seek God.

'At first Charlemagne was annoyed and disappointed, but soon realised that Guilhem was single minded and would not be deterred in his decision. Faced by that unshakeable determination, and coupled with the fact Guilhem had served him so faithfully for many years, Charlemagne granted him the freedom he desired. On leaving the King's service, Charlemagne gave Guilhem two holy artefacts as a powerful sign of his blessing; a piece of the actual cross on which Yeshua was crucified, and the golden shell of Miriam.

'In 804 AD, and with a handful of loyal friends and followers, Guilhem set off to Aniane, here in the Hérault. Time spent at the Abbey of Aniane, accompanied by deep contemplation of nature allowed him to experience the beauty and calm of the area, and to become aware of the silence within. In a wild isolated spot, he discovered a haven of peace, a place where the air, water, stone, wood and earth called out to him, naturally feeding and nurturing his soul. It was there he found a magical stillness which profoundly fed his prayer and contemplation. It was his "desert" – a remote place and an idyllic spiritual retreat. And it was there, with the help and support of the Abbey at Aniane, that he established a monastery which became known as the Abbey of Gellone.

'But Guilhem never fully realised the power of the shell, even though it had changed his life in the most dramatic of ways. When he passed away a few years later, he was buried beneath the Abbey of Gellone, entombed with Charlemagne's gifts. As rumours of the power of Guilhem's Holy Relics spread, they became the cause of thousands of pilgrimages. By around 820 AD, the secret sign of the scallop had become carved in stones, on trees, wells and even on houses to point the way, and so the road to Gellone became marked by the coded symbol of a scallop shell. The sign of the shell was in use well before the supposed discovery of the body of the apostle James, and the pilgrimage route to Santiago de Compostela.'

Alex raised his eyebrows, attempting to catch Sara's eye and remind her of his original master plan to walk the Way of St. James to Compostela, but by now, Sara was so engrossed in the story, she didn't even notice his comical attempts for attention. Alex, slightly embarrassed he was being overlooked, coughed a couple of times.

Jean-Michel looked over towards him, before continuing, 'The Abbey of Gellone increasingly gained a reputation for healing, and the legends of the shell exploded. There was increasing concern that the artefacts would be stolen from Guilhem's tomb, and so the friends and followers of Guilhem, who had witnessed the golden age of miracles and prosperity at Gellone, came up with a secret plan.

'In order to draw attention away from the abbey and the shell, they invented a brilliant cover story. They would make up a tale allowing pilgrims to still visit Gellone, but also sending them farther away on a pilgrimage elsewhere. They would use the sign of the shell to mark the route, leading attention away from Gellone. To do this they adopted a rumour from Galicia in Spain to disguise the truth. According to Spanish legends, James (one of the twelve apostles of Yeshua) had seen a vision of Yeshua's mother Miriam on the bank of the Ebro River while he was preaching the Gospel in Iberia. Following that apparition, James returned to the Holy Land, where he was beheaded by King Herod Agrippa I.

'The Benedictines of Gellone fabricated the rumour and began the myth that following James' death, his disciples had shipped his body back to the Iberian Peninsula. Off the coast of Spain, a heavy storm hit the ship, and the body was lost to the ocean. After some time however, it washed ashore undamaged, covered in scallops. From there it was taken inland and buried at Santiago de Compostela. It had all the elements of miracles and the link to Yeshua, so it could work. They would claim and reveal the discovery of a burial site full of shells, and that could work too. And it did. Perhaps better than they had imagined.

'These creative inventions became the pilgrimage route, The Way of St. James, first established in the ninth century, and led to the construction of a shrine dedicated to James at Santiago de Compostela, in Galicia in Spain, becoming one of the most famous pilgrimage sites in the Christian world.

'The route became known by many names, including "The Way of Arles" or the Latin name "Via Tolosana", meaning via Toulouse. It had a destination in both directions, Compostela one way and Rome the other.

'As the legend grew the Abbey of Gellone remained an important stop for pilgrims traveling the "Via Tolosana" even though it required them – most unusually and with some difficulty – to abandon the most direct way to Spain, instead heading up into the rugged hinterland of the Languedoc. So the Abbey at Gellone seemingly became just another part of the route for pilgrims visiting Santiago de Compostela. The plan had worked, to a degree. But the healings and miracles continued, for hundreds of years, spreading rumours far and wide that there was something miraculous at Gellone, which had now become known as Saint-Guilhem-le-Désert. More and more people came. The Pont du Diable was built out of necessity because of the increased numbers of pilgrims in around 1030 AD.

'In time the community on the other side of the valley at Aniane became jealous of the stories of the miracles at Saint-Guilhem-le-Désert, and the relationship disintegrated. The monks at Gellone Abbey asked to be released from the tutelage of Aniane, and following years of conflict and ill-feeling, Gellone remarkably received its independence from the Pope in 1090 AD. Still the rumours of miraculous healings persisted, so the Vatican kept watch on the small idyllic town.

'From the beginning of his reign, Pope Innocent III attempted to use diplomacy to end any "heretical" groups and dealings, but in the year 1208 AD his papal legate, Pierre de Castelnau, was murdered while returning to Rome after preaching the Catholic faith in southern France. The Pope declared him a martyr and launched what was effectively the genocide of an entire way of life. And so despite their wise, peaceful and loving ways, the "healing collective" or "heretics" as the Church now unashamedly branded them were systematically hunted down like wild animals.

'The Vatican lead crusader army (made up of various mercenary groups) came under the command, both spiritually and militarily, of the Cistercian abbot-commander, Arnaud-Amaury, the Abbot of Cîteaux. During the first significant "battle" in the war against the Cathars, the town of Béziers was besieged on 22 July 1209. The Catholic inhabitants were granted the freedom to leave unharmed, but many opted to stay and fight alongside the Cathars. When Arnaud-Amaury was asked how to tell Cathars from Catholics, he replied with the infamous words *"Caedite eos. Novit enim Dominus qui sunt eius."* – Kill them all, the Lord will recognise his own.

'The doors of the church of St Mary Magdalene were broken down and the refugees dragged out and slaughtered. Reportedly, 7,000 people died there alone. Elsewhere in the town many more thousands were mutilated and killed. Prisoners were blinded, dragged behind horses, and used for target practice. What remained of the city was razed by fire. Arnaud-Amaury wrote to Pope Innocent III, "Today your Holiness, twenty thousand heretics were put to the sword, regardless of rank, age, or sex." Many other such massacres were carried out by the Church of Rome, including the episode in the aAbbey of Gellone.

'The Vatican remained very concerned about the heretics, especially the Cathars, so much so that the Inquisition was primarily established to uproot any who remained. Operating throughout the Languedoc during the thirteenth century, it succeeded in crushing Catharism and driving its remaining adherents underground. Cathars who refused to renounce their beliefs were hanged, or burnt at the stake. This was how from the mid- to late-twelfth century onwards, large numbers of the fleeing Cathar community came to the Liberae sanctuary of St. Guilhem, where they were given safety, compassion and welcomed as equals.

There is solid historical evidence that villages in the south of France continued to house secret communities of Liberae type 'heretics' until the ending of the first quarter of the fourteenth Century. In the Ariège department, Jacques Fournier (the Bishop of Pamiers from 1318 to 1325) personally interviewed and interrogated hundreds of locals, recording the interviews in intricate detail. Bishop Fournier personally supervised nearly all of those operations. The resulting punishments he gave out were as diverse as imprisonment, being forced to wear a yellow cross on one's back, fines and outright confiscation of individual property. Those refusing to renounce their "heresy" were burnt at the stake. The "Fournier register" is considered by historians to be one of the most remarkable and insightful documents to survive medieval times. With the final purging of the last few heretics from the farthest corners of southern France (or so the Vatican presumed) Fournier was made Bishop of Mirepoix, and, only a year later, a cardinal. By 1334 he received an unexpected reward, becoming better known as Pope Benedict XII. The register he had compiled followed him to Rome and was placed in the Vatican Library, where it remains to this day.

'So today, we only have a partial, biased view of these "heretics" as their writings were almost entirely wiped out because of the doctrinal threat perceived by the Vatican. For example, much of the existing information we now have about the Cathar ways comes from those who opposed them, from Inquisition documents like the "Fournier register". Fortunately, another document, entitled "The Cathar Creed", was discovered at Rennes-le-Château in 1891 by the Catholic priest François Saunière. And it is this which provides authentic insight into their real beliefs and practices.

'Saunière, who made some of his discovery known to the Bishop of Carcassonne, was subsequently paid huge amounts of money by the hierarchy of the Church for handing over the "heretical" parchments. They rewarded him, but at the same time suggested that he keep silent or else. However, he wisely only handed over a fraction of what he had discovered in an ancient crypt beneath the church. He found Templar treasures and coins hoarded from the Holy Land. Yet perhaps one of the most astonishing items he discovered was a manuscript, a Gospel written by Miriam (Mary) the wife of Yeshua and secretly hidden by the Cathars in the thirteenth century. It was clear from reading this document, that Yeshua and Miriam not only treated each other as equals, but were a loving, married couple who had conceived a child.

'Many copies of this and other Gnostic Gospels had been destroyed on direct orders of the Orthodox Church in Rome, but inevitably some copies were saved and hidden away. These textual variations and rediscovered Gospels cast real doubt on the accuracy of the Bible, and were an obvious danger to the Vatican. The "Gospel of Miriam – The Wife of Yeshua" was unusual and significant, because it gave prominence to the leading role Miriam played as a dark-skinned teacher of equal standing, a muse-like catalyst to Yeshua's transformation, and the mother of their interracial child.

'The shocking revelations the priest Saunière had discovered were obviously powerful and dangerous; for the papers and scrolls contained sensitive information capable of completely undermining the word of the Orthodox Church. He uncovered written testaments which clearly indicated Yeshua did not "rise from the dead", so was never "resurrected", and was no less human than anyone else. A panicked Saunière secretly ordered the ancient crypt, or the "Tomb of the Lords" as it is referred to in the old parish registers, beneath the church at Rennes-le-Chateau permanently sealed so that no one else would be able to gain access.

'Following these mind-blowing discoveries, rumours abounded, as Saunière spent his new found wealth dedicating expensive new constructions at Rennes-le-Château to Miriam Magdalana. He gave the buildings names such as "La Tour de Magdalana" and the "Villa Bethania", after Bethany where Miriam intuitively prepared Yeshua for his approaching death, anointing his feet with the aromatic essential oil spikenard. Shortly after this event, a humbled Yeshua evoked the same process, bathing the feet of his own disciples before being arrested and crucified.

'From one parchment recovered from the crypt, Saunière pinpointed the exact location of the original burial site of Miriam in a nearby cave. Saunière never discovered her body, for although he uncovered the location of the cave, as I've already explained, the body of Miriam had been removed several hundred years previously when Charlemagne attempted to hide the truth of her origins, and ordered a brisk, secret reburial within the walls of the Abbey of St. Hilaire. Reading the manuscripts he had discovered, Saunière now knew the shocking truths about Yeshua, Miriam and more.

'With further study of Miriam's teachings from Rennes-le-Chateau, it became clear that she was a master healer. There were meticulous records of her use of essential oils and their effect on the limbic system. Utilising specific blends of aromatic oils, she was not only able to heal, but to activate the higher end chakras, altering the brain's frequency. This meant she could induce an elevated state of consciousness simply by applying the right blend of oils to the appropriate part of the body.

'According to Miriam, the symbolism of the two palms touching in prayer was of greater significance than he'd realised. It not only reflected the unification of the Divine with the individual, and the feminine with the masculine, but was a way in which positive and negative energy forces in the left and right hands become neutralised when placed together. Pressing your hands together stimulates the vagus nerve, which leads to a reduction in heart rate and blood pressure. This response alters our brainwaves, and puts us into a different frequency of thought, or altered state of consciousness.

'In an attempt to resolve things quietly, in 1909, the then Bishop of Carcassonne ordered the priest to be transferred. Saunière's refusal to leave Rennes-le-Château and continue his priesthood anew in a distant parish incurred a lifetime suspension. From then onwards, he was subject to mounting accusations of financial impropriety by his superiors. Having spent enormous funds on the buildings at Rennes-le-Chateau, the ironic outcome was that he became a debt-ridden, independent priest without a parish, who no longer received a stipend or salary from the church. From once being a very affluent, wealthy man, Saunière was now so broke that he traded furniture and personal belongings just so he could buy provisions to eat. Throughout this time he continued to pray and celebrate mass using an altar constructed in a special conservatory joined to the Villa Bethania.

'One day in January 1917, Bérenger Saunière was found collapsed and dying at the foot of "La Tour de Magdalana" by his housekeeper Marie Dénarnaud. Rumours that he had consumed a potent infusion of hemlock following the visit of two Catholic priests were quickly silenced. In the end, he saw his enemy was not the so-called heretics of the past, but the Church of Rome itself. Unable to disclose what he knew, like many before him, he provided an abundance of clues where he could. For Saunière the signs he left were not only in the secret architecture and the names of his expensive buildings, but also in the small church at Rennes-le-Château. The fourteenth station of the cross normally depicts the laying of Yeshua's body in the tomb. However, the one on display in the Church at Rennes le Chateau clearly depicts the night time removal of Yeshua's body from the tomb.

'Also, near the entrance to the little church, dedicated to Miriam, is the figure of the Devil supposedly carrying a holy water basin in the shape of a seven fingered golden shell. Directly above it you can see his initials "BS" and above that, the inscription "By this sign you will defeat {him}". The building is littered with clues, if you look without bias and with an open mind.

'What Saunière passed on over the years, in code and clues, was done in the knowledge that all will be revealed to the world when the time is right. He realised that real change and transformation of human beliefs could be possible, but it would take time. He knew that there is little point in giving the truth to people when they aren't ready to hear it, or are unable to accept it. It profoundly changed his attitude and beliefs, understanding that the Church had manipulated the truth, wiping out tens of thousands of peace loving men, women and children in the process, all in the name of Christ, when the "heretics" acted in a far more Christ-like manner than their persecutors. So we could understand, Saunière left us a copy of the Cathar creed.'

With that Jean-Michel vanished into a corner of the cellar only to reappear with a piece of folded worn paper, that he gave to Alex for them both to read, and upon which was the following...

This church is without walls or members save those who know they belong recognising each other by their deeds, their being and by the light in their eyes. No one is greater than any other. It is without rivals, being a family of men and women. It seeks only to serve the whole, which is without boundaries or division. It acknowledges all sages who have lived the truth of love, and those who participate and practice this truth. It seeks not to preach but to be. It recognises the shift from separation to wholeness and proclaims itself with the subtle whispers of the Beloved. It offers no reward, save that of the ineffable joy of being. Each shall seek to advance the cause of understanding, teaching only by example. They shall heal their neighbour, community and our world. They shall not fear, nor know shame and their witness shall prevail. It has no secret, no initiation, save that of the true understanding of the power of love. All those who belong, simply belong; they belong to AMOR – the Church of Love.'

Jean-Michel fell silent, then, realising Alex and Sara were still hanging on his words said wearily, 'Next it's the massacre on the Pont du Diable, which you already know about. So I think we better stop there for now.'

Alex and Sara were dumb-struck. Time had slipped by unnoticed.

'I'll tell you more soon' said Jean-Michel as he stood up and stretched. 'Come back tomorrow.' A little dazed and confused Alex and Sara reluctantly made their way out of the cellar, bidding a fond farewell to Jean-Michel and Pamplemousse.

Eight

666

The piercing love song of countless *cigales* was at long last fading in the warm Languedoc evening. High above the valley, a giant hornet-like hum could be heard approaching, drowning out the dying chorus of insects completely. With a whirr from the slowing engines and an unforgiving repetitive machine gun-like noise, the unmarked black helicopter appeared, hovering like a giant bird, before touching down safely in the grounds of the old Cathar Chateau. A lone figure exited the aircraft. Under cover of the fading light, a dark hand moved over the small red scanner, turning it green, as the door opened and the smartly dressed man entered the building.

A weary-eyed Jean-Michel went to bed that night with Pamplemousse snuggling down in his normal space on his favourite worn blanket at the end of the bed. Jean-Michel knew in his heart that Alex and Sara were in the throes of becoming the new guardians of the shell, and, as those before him, instinctively knew that his guardianship would soon be coming to an end. He was filled with a bizarre mixture of relief and concern. The two of them would now need to find the cave and the shell themselves, that was about as much of the future as Jean-Michel was sure of.

That night was filled with visions. In a series of film-like dreams, Jean-Michel saw how the shell was taken by the Church's mercenary death squad at Saint-Guilhem-le-Désert in 1278 AD, bringing about a dark cycle of ownership lasting 666 years. Throughout that cycle the people who 'possessed' it didn't carry out wondrous beautiful acts or healings at all. What they misunderstood as their ownership of the shell (which belonged to all or none) made them potentially delusional and a danger to those around them, their society and the world they lived in. Their time with the shell was ended not by some amazing act of heroism or divine intervention, but solely by the selfish desires of their own super-inflated egos.

From St. Guilhem, Jean-Michel watched as the shell was moved to the Byzantine emperors' chapel in Constantinople. The then emperor, Andronikos II was so plagued by economic difficulties that in time he was forced to sell many of the valuables and holy relics in his possession (including the shell) to a Venetian bank. The shell, still in a dark mahogany box with a golden scallop clasp, was kept locked away for many years, until one day the bank was required to make heavy payments to the newly installed Pope, Alexander VI (Rodrigo de Borja). And from that time the golden escallop was in the hands of a new family, the infamous house of the Borgia's. Over the years they carried out many crimes including adultery, theft, bribery and murder, making numerous enemies and coming to a sticky end. By the late sixteenth century, as the Borgia's influence gradually dissolved, the shell (now seemingly a family heirloom) passed into the hands of Francisco de Borja, an important official in the Spanish court who was also Viceroy of Peru until 1621.

In 1622 Francis Bacon, the disgraced English statesman, visionary, philosopher and prolific author met with Francisco de Borja and others at a secret Rosicrucian meeting in Paris, where they exchanged ideas of revolution and enlightenment. This rapidly growing Rosicrucian movement caused waves of excitement throughout Europe by declaring the existence of a secret brotherhood of alchemists and sages who were preparing to transform the arts, sciences, religion, commercial, political and intellectual landscape of Europe. It was an anonymous threat to the powers that be.

Jean-Michel looked on through the eyes of Bacon as he witnessed how the two men became unlikely friends. And it was during one private meeting in Paris that Bacon encountered the shell. That fateful rendezvous led to his writing of *New Atlantis* – a novel which told of a mythical island discovered by the crew of a European ship after they find themselves lost in the Pacific Ocean somewhere west of Peru. The book was a master plan of Bacon's vision for creating a Utopian Order in the newly established colonies of north America. Within a few days of each other, several mysterious Rosicrucian order posters appeared on the church doors of Paris in 1623. The first read, *'We, the Deputies of the Higher College of the Rose-Croix, do make our stay, visibly and invisibly, in this city, by the grace of the Most High, to whom turn the hearts of the Just. We demonstrate and instruct, without books and distinctions, the ability to speak all manners of tongues of the countries where we choose to be, in order to draw our fellow creatures from error of death. He who takes it upon himself to see us merely out of curiosity will never make contact with us. But if his inclination seriously impels him to register in our fellowship, we, who are judges of intentions, will cause him to see the truth of our promises; to the extent that we shall not make known the place of our meeting in this city, since the thoughts attached to the real desire of the seeker will lead us to him and him to us.'* The posters echoed the liberated Gnostic heresy of the Cathars that the Vatican had painstakingly tried to exterminate. The 'secret doctrine' pointed to the real meaning of the words 'the Kingdom of God is within you', awakening people to the fact that Christ is not an individual, but the core consciousness of every single person.

By 1696 Sir Francis Bacon's *New Atlantis* went on to inspire a cult-like section of Rosicrucians previously known as 'The Hamburg Group' led by the German mystic Johann Jacob Zimmermann. Zimmerman died in transit as he and his followers prepared to travel to North America, leaving Johannes Kelpius in charge as the new leader. The radical group which became known as the 'Woman in the Wilderness' were to leave the 'sinful world' behind in an attempt to re-establish the original state of the 'True Church' and to prepare for 'The End of Days' and the second coming of Christ. Kelpius and his followers expected the world to end in 1694. The prophecy passed, as did Kelpius, but the core of the group went on to form the inner sanctum of a variety of evangelical churches, controlling the hearts and minds of their congregations. Bacon's dreams of an idealistic New World were never fulfilled in the Americas, but his philosophy was later destined to bear some fruit in the form of the Napoleonic code.

By the late eighteenth century, as the shell continued its journey through time, it came into the hands of a wealthy Frenchman and courtier Arnaud II De La Porte. During the French Revolution, as Louis XVI's trusted collaborator, De La Porte was arrested in 1792 for distributing secret funds and bribes on behalf of the King in an ill-fated attempt to moderate the Revolution. He was tried, convicted of treason and sentenced to death, becoming only the second political victim of a fiendish new killing device – the guillotine. In a macabre gesture, his severed head was presented to King Louis XVI as a grisly birthday gift, and his belongings were ordered to be confiscated by the Republican hierarchy.

In his vivid dreams, Jean-Michel was next transported to a sunny April afternoon in 1795 to the auction house at Marseilles, where François Clary, the ex-mayor, a wealthy local trader and merchant was sitting patiently awaiting lot 242. It was bound to be expensive, but after all, it was his engagement present to his daughter Désirée who was betrothed to wed a successful and ambitious captain in the French army. François Clary was delighted to be the highest bidder and gave his daughter the golden shell in the mahogany box as a gift as he had intended. She liked the shell, but someone else was even more entranced with it, her husband to be, a certain Napoleon Bonaparte. The engagement was cancelled and Désirée never married Napoleon, but she eventually became Queen of Sweden and Norway, adopting the name Desideria.

When they parted, Napoleon ensured he had ownership of the shell. He believed that it had magical powers and was able to communicate with him. His power and luck seemed enhanced by being in contact with the shell so he kept it with him day and night. But eventually, having failed to listen to sound advice, he was consumed by his own ego. Napoleon's luck ran out.

In June 1815, Napoleon's spies made him aware that the approaching Prussian troops had orders to capture him dead or alive. Fleeing for his life, he escaped to Rochefort, a port on the Charente estuary, intending to flee to the United States. It was in the Americas and guided by the *New Atlantis* of Sir Francis Bacon, that Napoleon intended to establish a French Caribbean Empire. However, with British ships blocking every port, and escape impossible, Napoleon formally demanded political asylum at Rochefort from the British on HMS Bellerophon on 15 July 1815.

Imprisoned and exiled to the volcanic island of Saint Helena (named after Helena of Constantinople the mother of the first Christian Emperor Constantine) in the Atlantic Ocean, Bonaparte lived in a large pavilion on the Briars estate. The pavilion was in the garden of William Balcombe, an English merchant who became a purveyor to Napoleon. His fourteen year old daughter Elizabeth Balcombe was the only family member who spoke fluent French and she became the family translator.

Moving to the purpose-built Longwood House, Napoleon regularly received the Balcombe family as his guests. It was on one of these trips that Napoleon spoke to the young daughter Betsy Balcombe in private, telling her that he would be killed by his British captors and that his life would end on the island he hated. Bonaparte offered Betsy one of the few valuable personal belongings he still had, the golden shell. She just had to act as an intermediary for Napoleon's clandestine correspondence with Paris and beyond.

Because of their closeness to Napoleon, the Balcombe family eventually attracted the attention of Governor Hudson Lowe, and in 1818, suspecting them of smuggling secret messages out of Longwood House, the Balcombes were ordered to leave the island and return to England. Napoleon died in 1821, apparently from a stomach ulcer, but some say the English poisoned him with arsenic. At the age of just 51, he was laid to rest in a nameless tomb in the Valley of the Willows on St. Helena. It wasn't until many years later that the French obtained permission from the British to return Napoleon's decomposed remains to France.

Jean-Michel's visions now carried him forward in time to 1830, several years after Napoleon's death on St. Helena. Joseph Bonaparte (Napoleon's elder brother) visited Betsy Balcombe in London, and the shell disappeared once more. Betsy, a peaceful and kind soul, realising the value of the shell to Napoleon's family, gave it to Joseph. And so the shell was returned to the Bonaparte family, who considered it as divine intervention and verification of their immortal dynasty. A turn of fate and desire led to the shell being used as collateral for bank loans from De Rothschild Frères, the French branch of the Rothschild Family Bank. Vast sums of money were lent to the Bonaparte family, which were mostly used in their futile attempts to restore their bloodline to the throne of France. Years later, Emperor Napoleon III (Bonaparte's nephew and the first President of France) intended to reward Betsy Balcombe with five hundred hectares of Algerian vineyards in memory of her kind services to his uncle. Unfortunately, Betsy didn't live long enough to receive the incredibly generous gift, as she died in London in 1871, aged 69.

In the same year, a novel, *The Coming Race* was published by the Rosicrucian author, Edward Bulwer-Lytton. Lytton's novel tells of an intrepid explorer who discovers an advanced race of humans living within a vast subterranean world, beings that formerly dwelt on the planet's surface until a global catastrophe forced them to take refuge deep under the Earth. The survival of this evolved society was facilitated by their use of universal energy he called 'Vril', the energy associated with the power of the shell, and these rumours circulated the secret chambers and offices of the rich and powerful.

Leading esoteric sources were convinced that the fictionalised Vril was based on a real magical force. Helena Blavatsky, the founder of Theosophy, endorsed this view in her book *Isis Unveiled* (1877) and again in *The Secret Doctrine* (1888). She was not alone, for William Scott-Elliot author of *The Story of Atlantis* (1896) accepted the understanding of Vril as being close to the truth, as did the esoteric philosopher Rudolf Steiner.

The early part of the twentieth century saw the arrival of the First World War with millions of casualties. Jean-Michel's visions dragged him through the horrors of the trenches, the blood-soaked fields and past the vacant stares of the dead and dying young men of this turbulent living hell. Following the end of the war in November 1918, he was witness to the quiet rise of occult societies and organisations in Germany, a nation desperate to elevate itself from its sombre, humiliating, post-war ashes. Neo-radicals sought to establish '*die Neuordnung Europas*' (the New Order of Europe) to counter what they saw as the injustice of the post-World War I international order dominated by Britain and France, which tied in well with the idea of the arrival of 'the new age of Aquarius', by then an increasingly popular belief in European culture.

Rudolf von Sebottendorf founded the Thule Society, a secretive group of occultists who fervently and conveniently believed in the coming of a 'German Messiah' to redeem Germany following their demoralising defeat. They hoped that if an untapped power did exist, the mastery of an occult force such as Vril would not only assure future German dominance, it would ultimately unleash a new source of energy capable of regenerating the aspirations of the Aryan race. This society sponsored the establishment of a mainstream political party, the German Workers' Party. This party was joined in 1919 by Adolf Hitler, who was to transform it into the National Socialist German Workers' Party or Nazi Party. And in the same year, inspired by Bulwer-Lytton's novel, spiritual medium and channel Maria Orsic formed another group the 'Vril Society', effectively an inner circle of the Thule Society, whose leading members included a small group of young women, essentially gifted channels and mediums, whose focus became a search to master the secret of Vril energy.

When the highly influential politician and journalist Dietrich Eckart (a 'Thule' member) met Hitler, he was convinced that this was the prophesied German Messiah. Eckart exerted his considerable social and political influence grooming and promoting Hitler. No one else had such an impact and influence on Hitler's life. Hitler dedicated *Mein Kampf* to his colleague and mentor, also later naming the Waldbühne amphitheatre in Berlin the 'Dietrich-Eckart-Bühne' (the Dietrich Eckart stage) when it opened at the 1936 Olympics.

Eckart died in 1923. To establish contact with Eckart, Sebottendorf organised a séance with the gifted Vril Society mediums. Sebottendorf found it uncomfortable watching as Maria Orsic's eyes flickered and rolled as she rocked forward and backwards in her chair, mouth wide open, as if having a fit. However his manner changed to amazement when the voice of the deceased Eckart was clearly audible in the room. After a short while the voice of Eckart announced that he was going to let someone else come through who was carrying an important message for the German people.

A strange, female voice identified itself as Hekate, the Atlantean witch, who retold the story of Atlantis and the golden shell. The powerful yet unnerving voice explained how ownership of the secret powers of the shell wouldn't just pave the way towards the rebirth of a new Germany, but how, with the shell in their possession, the Aryan master race would rise like a phoenix to their rightful position of world dominance. A transcript of what had taken place at the séance was passed directly to Heinrich Himmler.

In the weeks leading to Adolf Hitler's appointment as Reich chancellor of Germany in 1933, his success was looking very unlikely. In the 1932 November elections the Nazis suffered significant losses and Hitler began to doubt himself, breaking down in front of colleagues and openly mentioning the possibility of suicide. Witnessing his erratic emotional state, others in the party now questioned his suitability as a leader. Some even went as far as to profess that his very existence could prove too great a liability...

Jean-Michel was transported now to see through the eyes of one of the most powerful men in Nazi Germany. Heinrich Himmler was a boyish small bodied weasel-faced man. With his hair cut short to hide his receding hairline, he resembled an innocent boy scout, but his sneering smile was most unnerving. In his trusted position of *Reichsführer* of the SS, Himmler had established many powerful connections. He put Hitler in touch with a renowned channel and medium, Erik Hanussen. Hanussen was rapidly becoming known for 'fortune-telling', but he was also gifted with telepathy, clairvoyance, precognition, mediumship and mind control. Himmler discovered the trance medium in 1932 when he came across a newspaper article in which Hanussen delivered a prediction that within one year's time Adolf Hitler would become Reich chancellor, the Chancellor of Germany, head of the government.

The Nazi Party were desperate to use any and all opportunities at their disposal, and so a private séance was arranged by Himmler in one of Hitler's rooms in the Kaiserhof Hotel in Berlin. On a bitterly cold morning in January 1933, Hanussen arrived, as Jean-Michel looked on from above. Hitler was pacing the room, agitated, concerned about the mystic's predictions. Footsteps could be heard climbing the stairs. On his arrival, Hanussen was searched thoroughly by the guards before entering and flamboyantly removing his camel wool coat and white silk embroidered scarf to study the room in silence. Without making eye contact with Hitler, he dragged a robust and ornate carved wooden chair from the side of the large hotel suite and placed it in the middle of the room, then walked to the windows and, with some force, drew the curtains tightly shut. He produced a small candle and a stand from his jacket pocket and placed it on the wooden hexagonal table. Still without speaking he gestured to Hitler to come forward and be seated.

Hitler somewhat reluctantly approached the mystic and sat down. 'You must not say a word. Whatever happens, please remain silent,' requested the charismatic and handsome Hanussen, putting his forefinger to his lips to make the point. Then reaching out, he took Hitler's hands, and examined them carefully, nodding once or twice. Next Hanussen held Hitler's chin and with a slight upward movement moved Hitler's head so as to be at a slight angle to keep eye contact. Hanussen ran his fingers through Hitler's hair three times, as if gently stroking him, all the while maintaining direct eye contact.

Visibly shaking, Hitler struggled to contain his agitation and angst. What if he was destined to fail? Hanussen's eyes became glazed as he sank into a deep trance. Hitler agonised as the doubts crept in and the lack of control became all-consuming. Beads of salty sweat ran down his face, stinging his eyes and splashing to the floor as he repeatedly mopped his face with his dampening shirt sleeve. The extended poignant silence only served to increase his obvious discomfort. Then at last Hanussen spoke, 'I see victory for you my Fuhrer within thirty days... It cannot be stopped.'

Hitler was so impressed by Hanussen, and his ego so buoyed by his words, that in a period of just a few weeks, he asked to meet the mystic several times more. However, Hitler was not Hanussen's only client. For so was Himmler, who recorded hours of their one-to-one private, undisclosed séances on early prototype Dictaphone using the then new magnetic tape technology being developed by BASF...

As his fame grew, Hanussen found himself once more in the presence of Hitler and Himmler, but this time in the company of an impressive group of high ranking Nazi officials and assorted VIPs at a private dinner in Berlin. He was invited as a guest speaker to foretell the glorious Nazi future. Hanussen captivated the influential audience when he claimed to see a 'great house in flames' during the post dinner séance. Again he was proved right, as literally only a few hours later, the Government's Reichstag building was engulfed by a devastating fire. The Reichstag fire in the February of 1933 was a crucial historical event which handed absolute power to Hitler. Following this event, he became head of state, leader of the army and Chancellor of Germany. Hanussen, the unorthodox but intoxicating trance medium had seemingly predicted the event.

However, rumours were rife that Hanussen had something to do with the fire and had somehow participated using his mystical powers. What actually happened was that Hanussen, under direct orders from Hitler, had hypnotised the young Dutch council communist Marinus van der Lubbe (the 'patsy' subsequently convicted and executed for starting the Reichstag fire). This clever underhand move not only assured an on-going public belief in Hanussen's powers of prediction, but also meant the German people would blame the communists for the entire event.

Predicting the Reichstag fire before such a large and important assembly was Hanussen's most famously publicised feat of clairvoyance. He was now a superstar. However, Erik Hanussen was not destined to be famous for long and on March 25 1933 he was led away by a group of SS soldiers. Himmler had become increasingly jealous of Hanussen's place as Hitler's new favourite, and as a direct rival for the Führer's attentions. Himmler had also discovered an incredible secret. Hanussen, the handsome charismatic mystic who had made Hitler sweat, and the very same man who had run his hands through Hitler's Aryan locks, was, in fact, a Jew. So Hanussen was thrown in the back of a small lorry, driven out into the German countryside and executed.

Unbeknown to others, the secretly ambitious Himmler had personally benefitted greatly from Hanussen's trance and channelling gifts. Utilising Hanussen's remarkable abilities, Himmler was provided with a constant stream of channelled information, prophecies and clairvoyance including the whereabouts of several historical and religious treasures of powerful significance. These included articles such as the Holy Grail, the Ark of the Covenant, and what is known as the 'Arma Christi' (a number of articles associated with the crucifixion). If the Nazi's recovered items such as these, they believed it would give them an unmitigated hold of supernatural powers and ensure the future of the Third Reich. Hanussen also spoke of Atlantis, Hekate, the golden shell, the importance of France and more.

The Nazi's had also drawn inspiration from the writings of Helena Blavatsky, a Russian aristocrat who had lived in England, becoming a well-known author. It was Blavatsky, amongst others, who brought the Nazi Party's attention to the idea of a pure root gene, the possible existence of an advanced 'Aryan race' descended from the Atlanteans. Himmler was deeply entranced by the thought of the power he could gain through the occult. But he sought the type of absolute domination of others that only truly deluded men dream of.

He believed himself to be the reincarnation of Henry the Fowler (Heinrich I) the first king of the medieval German state. More importantly, and behind the back of Hitler, he also considered himself the true guardian of the Nazi vision, and in reality was far from the faithful servant Hitler considered him to be. He had his own aspirations of leadership, and was determined to live them.

In 1933, as a direct consequence of Hanussen's trance recordings Himmler was given the authority to set up an 'SS School' at Wewelsburg castle in Germany. A thousand year lease was agreed. Wewelsburg was no ordinary school, not even by SS standards. To Himmler, the castle would one day be viewed as the most important place on Earth, naming it the 'Centre of the World'. And for the purposes of future propaganda, a Nazi pseudoscientific research unit was officially created on July 1 1935, named the Ahnenerbe Institute. Its purpose was to both uncover and create the archaeological and cultural history of the hypothesised 'Aryan race' which traced all the way back to the days of Atlantis. It was founded by Heinrich Himmler, Herman Wirth, and Richard Walther Darré. The organisation was handed a virtually unlimited budget by the Nazi party (heavily funded by International Oil companies, Motor giants and American 'banksters') and was charged with the mission to rediscover 'the secret power of the forefathers.'

The official line of the Ahnenerbe was that it was created to unearth 'new evidence of the accomplishments and deeds of Germanic ancestors using exact scientific methods.' The unofficial mission was to hoard as many historically significant, sacred, occult and holy relics as possible to support and fuel their sense of power and dream of domination. They would also have a complete hold over the Vatican, who would not speak out against the horrific acts of the Nazis until near the end of the Second World War.

From their centre at Wewelsburg, scholars, spies, archaeologists and those who had a keen interest in occult relics were hand-picked to take part in the operation. Himmler was setting up a new religion, a Neo-Pagan cult which was to travel the world seeking sacred relics to enhance their occult power. They travelled the world looking for historical proof to confirm that the Germans were indeed the master race, in direct line from the Atlanteans.

On one particular expedition, a group led by the SS recruited Arisophist Otto Rahn (who had written two books on the Cathars) was sent on a mission to southern France. He had uncovered historical documentary evidence from the secret Vatican library which made it apparent that in the early thirteenth century, a sacred relic which contained insurmountable power was in existence in the Languedoc region of Southern France. The unnamed item was said to contain the gift of healing and to give human beings the power of immortality, allowing them to be 'born again'.

Himmler, wildly hoping it was the Holy Grail, sent Rahn off to southern France, where, begrudgingly aided by the French mystic and historian Antonin Gadal, his team excavated several caves, uncovering some evidence that the story was indeed true.. At each attempt to progress, Gadal, with the covert support of members of the Lectorium Rosicrucianum (a mysterious Gnostic Rosicrucian movement with strong links to the Cathars) led Rahn's men on a series of wild goose chases. They invented stories and spread confusing rumours to baffle the Nazi's, a plan which worked so well and to such an extent, that in the end, the Occitania expedition was called off, and an empty handed Otto Rahn was summoned back to Germany in disgrace. Back home, disillusioned and confused, he resigned from the SS, becoming isolated and snubbed. Offered the option of taking his own life or else, Rahn's frozen body was discovered near Söll on the Austrian Tyrol in 1939. Himmler, the Nazis and most people failed to recognise that the True Grail was not a thing at all, but rather the wisdom of a very different way of being. You see, the Grail very much exists, not as a visible 'form' but as a knowable vibration of consciousness.

With virtually unlimited funding, and a mass of information

and research (including the clues and readings given by the Vril society and the Hanussen séance recordings), in time Himmler and the group discovered many items, including the golden shell which was taken by the Nazi's along with other treasures, to Chateau Lafite, on the Gironde estuary near Bordeaux.

As a matter of strange interwoven coincidence, Château Lafite (now property of the Rothschild family) was once owned by Madame Barbe-Rosalie Lemaire, whose husband, Ignace-Joseph Vanlerberghe, was a leading arms supplier to Napoleon Bonaparte. It was there, at Chateau Lafite the Germans uncovered a secret storage room, hidden behind large armoires in the cellar, where Himmler ordered the crates full of treasure to be kept. A German garrison was entrenched for the entire length of the occupation at Château Lafite Rothschild. In that time, the Rothschild properties (including Château Lafite) were placed under public administration.

The war raged on, but holding France was becoming untenable for the Nazis. In early August 1944, shortly before Paris was liberated by the Allies, a train loaded with artefacts, paintings and treasures (including the golden shell) and a handful of Himmler's loyal SS troops, secretly left Chateau Lafite via train from Bordeaux. The plan was to cross unoccupied Vichy France, continuing on to Toulouse, down and across to Narbonne and then along the coast into Italy. The security, anonymity and privacy of the Vatican Bank was an assured safe haven, for they had accepted huge donations from Hitler's close ally Mussolini in 1929 for Papal recognition of the fascist regime. Himmler gave orders to move the treasure trove himself, withholding this information from Hitler. Allied spies got wind of secret rail movements, passing their surveillance details to the British, which led to a team under the command of a British Captain William Small contacting the Maquis (French resistance fighters) to request support in wrecking a Nazi supply train known to be heading from Narbonne to Montpellier.

Now Jean-Michel saw the Maquis lay bundles of high explosives in a tunnel and derail the train south west of Montpellier. A fight ensued with the SS guards, who were all eventually overcome and killed. What the resistance fighters discovered on the train shocked them all, for in the crates stamped with swastikas, they found treasures beyond their wildest dreams. The secure wooden crates contained valuable works of art, as well as rare coins and ancient artefacts. Orders were given to move the immense stash immediately and securely store it in complete secrecy. And so a small group of Maquis drove a dispersed convoy of unmarked lorries into the remote countryside of the Hérault, far away from the scene of the train's derailment. One of the leaders of the Maquis, Serge Fayette, whose family were from Saint-André-de-Sangonis, knew the whereabouts of a secret cave in the Hérault valley, where it was agreed they would hide the treasures. The cave was the Grotte de Clamouse, and the shell was finally back at Saint-Guilhem-le-Désert. Exactly 666 years since the shell had been taken in 1278 AD, the dark cycle had finally come to an end.

As the war also drew to a close Himmler's SS secretly liquidated the Vril Society mediums, fearing that their secret knowledge and ability would fall into the hands of the Red Army, SS officers killed them all. As Jean-Michel witnessed their execution he felt the ground beneath him shake and in an instant he was transported to St. Guilhem.

An earthquake was taking place, powerful enough to cause several stalactites to fall from the ceiling of the cave he was standing in. As one of the stalactites fell, it crashed to the ground with such force that it dislodged a mahogany box, which then fell into the newly formed cavity created by the mighty stone arrow. The box was now damaged, but kept its shape because it was being held together on each side by the two faces of the crystalline rock. There the box remained secretly hidden from the world, trapped deep in the heart of Clamouse. A small group of

Maquis returned to retrieve the hoard, some of which was lying strewn across the floor of the cave. They took the boxes away, oblivious to the one left behind.

A few years later, severe flooding hit the area. The locals knew all about the power of water, as the village had suffered severe floods in the past. The caves of Clamouse, a small part of which were now open to the general public, were closed as a safety precaution. In the cave, the water rushed in with such power and at such a fast rate that it caused a compressed explosion of water. As the water rushed past where the treasures had once been, and through the crevice which still held the box, the immense pressure caused the damaged box containing the shell to shatter into pieces.

This released the shell, now invisible in the cascading water, and it was carried down through the cave, on the flood's tide, eventually coming to rest in a small pool; the same pool that had been used by the Liberae community hundreds of years ago; the very pool which the young, courageous Sebastian Cavalles died beside – La Source Vitale. And there it stayed, waiting for the next guardian to bring it to life in the world...waiting for Jean-Michel.

Nine

The Soul of Clamouse

Waking mid-morning in the bright shimmering light of yet another beautiful day in the Hérault, Alex and Sara got out of bed, showered, and dressed, before tucking into a delightful French breakfast; *pains au chocolats* and delicious and invigorating arabica coffee, lots of it. They sat a while longer at the picnic bench on the timeworn stone terrace, sensing the warm scented mountain air caress their faces, silently bathing in the pleasurable uncomplicated moment. 'Well, what did you make of all that?' asked Sara referring to the previous night with Jean-Michel.

'I don't know what to make of it, but I think we need to be careful, take each day as it comes and see what opens up. There's little point in trying to get our heads around it all, we're in it and we have just got to go with it. Whatever it is.' Alex stood up and went inside to make yet another sweep of the cottage, anxiously making his way around the rooms to see if he could uncover any other bugs. He couldn't.

So it was back to the village of St. Guilhem to see what else they could piece together. Leaving the white faced cottage they noticed several cars pass by on the country lane. Across the opposite side of the hill, they could see an empty, parked, red convertible sports car, which Alex had noticed several times recently. They continued to make their way back down the track, out of the gates and into St. Guilhem, keen to see what more they could find out about the local history for themselves.

Stopping at the *Office de Tourisme* in the village, they enquired about the Cathars coming to St. Guilhem. 'No, the Cathars were never here,' said the lady who was sat behind the information desk. 'That's weird,' thought Alex. Sara and Alex looked at each other, and sensing something was not right, left the office together.

Glancing back, Sara noticed the lady behind the desk had immediately picked up the phone and dialled. Sara was uneasy, but put it down to her vivid imagination.

Alex and Sara spent the morning discovering St. Guilhem, finding scallop shell signs all over the village. While Alex explored further, Sara popped in and out of a cute little shop and bought a book on 'Mary Magdelene'. In addition to the numerous signs of the shell, they found stone symbols or Yantras embedded in the pavements.

Alex stopped quite still and spoke. 'Yantras are mystical symbols used to focus the mind on spiritual concepts, an artistic wordless code which feeds the expansion of consciousness. The act of concentrating on a Yantra has transformational consequences.' Alex's imagination was on fire, like the light in his eyes. Why were these signs here? Strange but true, the two of them were walking through a village in southern France, looking at the pebble Yantras they had found embedded in the cobbled pavements. Alex studied them, like a time-travelling detective, as if he knew what he was looking at. 'This one is a symbol about becoming a whole human being,' he commented on the circle made up of hundreds of individual pebbles '...and this one concerns the next dimension, the consciousness of the Soul.'

'How do you know that?' enquired Sara gently.

'No idea... I just... know,' shrugged Alex nonchalantly. They sat down at the bistro tables in the market square and waited for the waiter to serve them. It was a hot day again, and they both fancied cool refreshing drinks.

'Just what exactly do you know about this next dimension of the Soul?' Sara said, quizzing Alex about what he had just said.

Alex began to think, but as he did, what he planned to say slipped his grasp. However, when he relaxed his train of thought and opened his mind, words simply poured from his mouth like a cascading waterfall. 'Physical awareness is three-dimensional. It is limited because it is dependent on the physical senses alone. If we continue to think we are the individual body-mind alone, then that remains our experience. Three-dimensional awareness concerns time, space and matter, which create the experience of separation, body and mass. As we step through the window of the fourth (awareness) and into the fifth dimension of human consciousness, we can be said to be awakening to the presence of the Universal human being. In that dimension of wholeness, the past and future simultaneously coexist. Without thinking what to do, there is a sense in the here and now of a timeless, permanent state of being. That sense is not of material things, or memorised thoughts and patterns, but of subtle intelligent energies. The present moment is the gateway to the next dimension. That dimension is the dimension of the Soul.'

Sara was excited, but somewhat gobsmacked. 'Bloody hell love where did all that come from?'

'By not thinking about it and by letting go of the desire to seek an answer, enables the sensing and feeling of subtle intelligent universal energy to be expressed.' Alex continued, 'Most people in the world are not ready for this dimensional shift, and for many it will not be an easy ride. However, such a dramatic change need not be such a difficult one. For once you accept and allow the reality of the evolutionary leap that human consciousness is going through, your own evolution becomes increasingly natural and effortless. You just let go and get in the flow. No true dimensional shift is for one person, one group, one religion or one school of thought, because it is available to all. In simple terms, the present dimensional shift is the universal intelligent process of growth.'

The waiter interrupted, asking what they would like. Sara ordered two Diet Cokes with lots of ice and lemon. 'Sounds a challenging process for us all to go through...' she remarked '...so how do we deal with the old patterns and beliefs that we are firmly convinced of as being true?'

Alex leaned in, resting his chin on his hands, elbows propped on the table. 'If you watch and listen to your thoughts and observe them with an unbiased and open transparency as they manifest, it becomes apparent that they are temporary obstacles and blockages arising from your life-programming and in some sense, self-induced ghosts of the mind.' He went on, 'But if you continue to identify with these self-limiting patterns, if you continue to insist they are true and get carried away with them, then you remain addicted and deny yourself the very freedom you seek.'

The waiter returned, placing the two drinks on the bistro table. 'Thanks' said Sara, taking a sip from the glass then looking back directly at her husband, now apparently turned sage, 'But when we enter the next dimension will we still see the world as it appears to us now?' she asked, keen to keep Alex flowing.

'Material physical form will continue, but the fundamentals of separation will dissolve. Such old patterns of the mind are dense and, if seen as absolute, stop us from evolving. All thoughts are essentially electromagnetic frequencies which directly affect our surroundings and those around us, which is why each person must be responsible for their own thoughts and emotions. Once we let go of our dependency on the physical senses, and dive headlong into the awareness of the heart, we begin to glimpse the joyful intelligence we all share. Increasingly seeing this you will begin to live in each moment with focus and awareness, and participate authentically in the full mysterious beauty of life', Alex smiled raising his glass of Coke in a little toast and took a good swig.

Sara, thinking aloud, asked, 'If it's going to happen anyway, can't you just wait and hope that everything will turn out alright in the end?'

As he removed his sunglasses and reached for his glass, again Alex seemed to lose his flow. 'Mmmmm… I don't know.'

Well life was certainly becoming more interesting day by day thought Sara. Better just go with it. She was getting used to weird things happening now. It felt like a lucid dream. Accepting what she had just heard and allowing enough silence to absorb the words, they continued to sit in the square, bathing in the palpable peace.

'This is a timeless place,' said Sara, 'and this plane tree is the biggest and oldest in France.' She pointed at the huge tree which dominated the market square.

With eyebrows raised, Alex looked quizzically at her 'And how exactly did you know that?'

'I read it in the guide book back at the cottage!' replied Sara, as they first broke into smiles, then laughter.

They stayed a while longer in the comforting shade of the huge ancient plane tree which dominated the village square. Sara noticed how the narrow streets seem to radiate out from the tree, and disappear into inviting corners filled with shops and tall, amber stone houses of times gone by. It was as if the tree was the Sun, the source of life itself, she pondered.

As they slowly got to their feet and headed back out of the village, a few hundred metres on the right hand side of the road they saw the entrance signs to La Grotte de Clamouse – the cave Jean-Michel had spoken about. Deciding to take a closer look, they headed up the steep tarmac walkway.

It looked worthwhile investigating, so they entered the shop area. The shop was stacked full of crystals, trinkets and books. Alex found several books on the mysterious Cathars, which struck him as strange because of what the lady at the tourist office had said. He held up two of the books and showed them to Sara. 'Look,' said Alex as Sara tightened her eyebrows and looked upwards in an expression of disbelief. At which point they were accosted by a short, mousey but determined middle-aged lady named Estelle, inviting them, or rather urging them, to join the tour of the caves. They purchased their tickets, and were taken into a small dark room with fifty chairs set out in theatre style. Accompanied by twenty or so other visitors, they sat down to watch a film about the formation of caves, with particular reference to Clamouse.

From there, they passed through a solid metal door, and were taken on an amazing journey through time with the very informative guide Estelle. She explained how the caves were first discovered in the mid 1940s by a team from the Montpellier Caving Club. How the main entrance to the cave was just above the spring which fed a crystal clear, beautiful pool.

Estelle explained that following an exceptional summer drought in 1945, the main entrance to the cave became passable for the first time in hundreds of years, as the water level dropped enough to allow entry on foot, and that was when the true extent of the Grotte de Clamouse was officially discovered. Estelle pointed out that in Occitan 'Clamouse' means a woman who shouts or screams. It was said that a young boy died in the cave, and a female family member wandered the caves in despair screaming for months afterwards.

'I wonder if that's Sebastian she's talking about,' Sara whispered to Alex.

In all, over three miles of passages and rooms were uncovered, including rare white crystal deposits, and strange prehistoric looking cave lizards which were on display for all to see in the glass reptilarium. 'They look like aliens,' quipped Alex to Sara. As well as the usual stalactites and stalagmites, there were several other strange rock formations in the grotto, including aragonites, spiky concretions that resembled sea urchins, and helictites which made Alex hungry because they looked like a bright jumbled mass of spaghetti.

In the distance, there was the faint bark of a dog. At another point in the tour, they stopped at the top of a plateau in the cave and watched and listened to a rather an unusual music and light show. The hypnotic combination of sacred music, lights and the beautiful natural surroundings made them think of the stories they'd heard from Jean-Michel, and all that had taken place in the caves and the village of St. Guilhem in the past. The other visitors to the cave couldn't help but notice the serene English couple, standing there silently listening and watching the music and lights in the depths of Clamouse.

At the end of the hour long tour, they came out of the caves and back into the bright sunshine. Sara and Alex thanked Estelle, and walked hand in hand along the tarmac footpath which criss-crossed its way down to the main road to the village. From there, they turned right and walked past the parked cars on the far side of the road, down past the Pont du Diable, and within a few short minutes they were back at the cottage.

As the light of the sun was beginning to descend behind the backdrop of the stony hillside, they ate a simple late lunch, using up leftovers. They decided to pop in at Jean-Michel's earlier than expected to tell him all they'd been up to, and to ask about the strange incident with the hole that Alex had fallen down. They walked up the hill behind the cottage, passing right by the spot next to the small stone outbuilding where Alex had fallen the previous night. Only there was no hole, the cavity he had tripped in had completely vanished.

Looking closely, Alex could see it had been covered over and concealed. The metal security grill of Élan was open wide, folded back on its hinges, the force of the cool wind making the metal bang against the golden stone pointed walls. Alex lent forward to enter. The door creaked open, but there was no sign of Jean-Michel. As the light was now poor, Alex shone the torch from his mobile phone towards the back of the building. All he could see was a few old sacks and an interior well, but as he snooped around, he caught the reflection of a faint light down in the well, 'There's something down here. There's a light… Do you know what, I think he's gone down the well.'

Sara peered down the well. 'Let's follow him,' she suggested.

Alex needed no further convincing.

They clambered down, using what they discovered were a sequence of strategically placed footholds. As they reached the bottom, with their feet on the small lip of the cylindrical concrete tube, they realised the water had no real depth. Pulling back the hessian makeshift covers, they could clearly see the open tunnel. And so with the oil lamps lighting the way, they entered.

In the tunnel, they noticed a patch of recently repaired stone, with some loose dirt on the floor, exactly below where Alex had fallen. Then the stone built tunnel led to a rock face before entering into another opening. As they followed the tunnel they discovered more oil lamps lighting the way farther into the depths of the cave. 'This must be a higher level above Clamouse,' Alex remarked. 'Yeah, that's why I heard Pamplemousse barking earlier' Sara remarked keenly.

The light began to flicker and change as it reflected the white shining crystal stalactites and stalagmites which now seemed to surround them. At a junction in the caves they decided to go left, but discovered the way led upwards but to a dead end.

They headed back up between the rock faces and back to the junction now heading the opposite way. Up and down the passage wound and turned, eventually coming to an opening which revealed what seemed like a very large room. The walls and ceilings looked as if they had been designed by a new age visionary architect, and yet it was all the wonder of nature. Millions of years of the movement of water through the limestone plateau of Clamouse had created an amazing array of intelligent sculpture, which was mind-blowing. The flickering lights danced, water trickled, and they felt as if they were in another world.

They manoeuvred along the route lit up by the oil lamps, entering a low narrow passage. Following a sharp ninety degree bend, they found themselves in an open space aglow with several more lamps. Jean-Michel was nowhere to be seen. 'It feels like we're in some sort of sacred space, like a church, or meeting place,' observed Sara.

As they ventured further still, they noticed a pool of water; it looked so pure and cleansing. The crystals sparkled, and the small lagoon appeared almost alive in the unusual reflective light. Set some way back to the left hand side of the pool was a huge solid chiselled block of stone. It looked like a table or altar. Alex could just about make out what looked like a fossil in the wall of the cave, behind the massive stone slab. It was poorly lit, so he approached the fossil and ran his fingers over it. 'Saz, come and check this out.'

Not being able to get a clear view, Sara ran her hands over the area. It wasn't a fossil, but the indented sign of the scallop. It was similar to the ones they'd found throughout the village, but this was an upright indented open scallop, resembling the number eight.

Underneath they could just make out the engraved words *Liberae sunt nostrae cogitationes.*

'Latin?' proposed Sara.

'Yeah, it's something like 'Free are our... thoughts,' Alex replied remembering his schoolboy Latin. Still no sign of Jean-Michel.

Jean-Michel was already back at L'Hermitage, and after checking the olive trees on one of the plateaus, had remembered he'd left the dwelling unlocked and returned to shut the door, close the metal grill, and secure the hefty padlock. There was no need to return to extinguish the lamps, which were nearly empty anyhow. He was aware his memory was beginning to fade a little, an idea which amused him.

Alex and Sara spent a couple of hours exploring the main part of the caves and discovered that, although they were at a lower level, there was a section where they could overlook the visiting tourists, which Alex thought could be a bit of fun. But it was mid-evening and there were no visitors to be found. Having completed their exploration, they decided it was time to head back.

On their way they noticed the lamps were getting very low, so they used Alex's mobile to light the way. They exited the cave, entered the short tunnel and climbed up the circular wall of the well. At the top, the solid wooden cover came off easily. Alex helped Sara by pulling her up from the well. Once safely back inside the little stone building, they tried the front door, but it was locked tight. Banging on the door and shouting for help was fruitless. No one could hear them. It was getting late and their muffled cries were absorbed within the thick walls of the solid stone building.

'I guess Jean-Michel has locked up and gone home,' remarked Alex with a little wry smile.

'So what are we going to do now?' asked Sara, not thinking it quite so funny.

'Well... we'll just have to make the most of it... I'll have to find a way to keep you warm,' Alex flicked his eyebrows suggestively as he grabbed the old sacks hanging on the wall, and made a makeshift bed for them both. They snuggled down and began to run through all that had happened. With the moonlight streaming through, and in the quiet romantic solitude of the stone building, they kissed passionately and made love, finally falling asleep in each other's arms.

Sometime later, in the early hours, Sara nudged Alex and whispered, 'Alex wake up, wake up.'

'What?' said a semi-conscious Alex.

'Shhh ...'

Sara put her finger to her lips, rising to her knees and looking about her, ears peeled.

A rapidly moving light streamed through the narrow gaps in the solid oak wooden door. Voices mumbled. Alex was sure there were at least two people. They had a torch, and were trying to force their way in, as the distinct noise of metal on metal rang out. The potential intruders were struggling to get past the padlocked robust metal door grills which Jean-Michel had installed for security. 'Robbers...' whispered Alex as Sara, increasingly worried, clung tightly and silently to him, gripping his arm and waist.

Various failed attempts to enter were made with what sounded like keys and a heavy metal object, before the robbers spoke. They were just a few feet away. As Alex listened carefully he made out that the voices were definitely not French, '*Betg avunda*' said the male voice. They didn't recognise the Swiss German words of the Romany language, meaning 'not enough'. The torch light began to fade, as did the footsteps. With the natural calm of the hillside restored, it still took a while for them both to get back to sleep, but in the end they did.

Early the following morning, Alex and Sara were woken by a metallic clunking noise, followed by the sound of a key being rotated in the lock of the solid door. The door opened, the sun poured in, and in rushed Pamplemousse followed by the figure of Jean-Michel, with the sun directly behind him. The golden rays seemed to radiate from behind his head, giving him a golden glow. 'No wonder you didn't make it to me last night...' chuckled Jean-Michel. 'How did you get here?' he asked, looking at the two exceedingly tired faces in front of him, their bodies still covered in hessian sacks.

'We, we found our way down the well last night. We were trying to find you, but couldn't,' said Alex apologetically.

'Yes, and we found the cave, it's amazing!' said an excited Sara. Jean-Michel looked disappointed.

'We're sorry.' Alex offered up his rather embarrassed but well-meant apology.

Jean-Michel was remarkably calm. 'Ah, it's okay. It was obviously meant to happen this way.' He paused. 'Now, I expect you've got more questions. You better come and have some coffee.' They removed the hessian sacks, quickly dressed and hung the sacks back on the metal hooks fixed into the wall.

'Someone tried to break in last night,' said Alex.

'Could be kids messing about,' said Jean-Michel not wanting to cause panic. 'They did that last time, and sprayed graffiti over the door.' Shaking his head, then locking the door and grill, Jean-Michel whistled to Pamplemousse who barked back intelligently as if to let them know he was coming too. Then, all together, they made their way back across the hillside. As he walked, Alex thought to himself it couldn't have been 'kids' trying to get in the stone building, because the voice was much older, and anyway there was a vehicle involved.

'I've done a clean sweep with the pipe detector. It's all clear,' said Jean-Michel. Pamplemousse barked, 'Oh, yes and Mousse helped too!' he added. The little dog had followed the scent of the two broken audio bugs and come up with a blank also. They entered the front door of L'Hermitage. Jean-Michel reached for the glass cafetiere in the lower cupboard of an old wooden buffet. He went to the sink and ran the tap, filling an old fashioned whistling kettle which he placed on his small Aga-style cooker. Jean-Michel used everything in nature, and even fuelled the cooker with a varied assortment of wood and cuttings gathered from the hillside. He took a seat with Alex and Sara at the old kitchen table, and they began to talk once more.

'You must have many questions?' prompted Jean-Michel.

'So it must have been you who repaired the hole in the tunnel?' asked Alex the detective.

'Yes, that was me,' said Jean-Michel.

'And that's what all the noise was in the last few days... you were cutting new stones to fit the domed ceiling of the tunnel...' deduced Alex.

Jean-Michel nodded, but then added... 'I built the tunnel many years ago.'

'You mean you built the secret well and the tunnel which lead to the cave?'

'Exactly...'

'But why... to hide the cave entrance?'

'Yes, but more than that, it was because I was chosen to be the guardian of the shell.'

'Chosen by who?' asked Sara.

The old metal kettle began to whistle, so Jean-Michel got up from the table and spooned freshly ground coffee into the cafetiere. He then added the hot water. Remembering that the English often take milk with their coffee he brought out a carton of UHT milk along with the cups, spoons and brown sugar cubes, and placed it all in the middle of the table. 'You will know more as you need to know more,' replied Jean-Michel in a response which appeared more of a riddle than a fully blown answer. Jean-Michel knew that Alex and Sara were the new guardians of the shell, but remained very aware that in order to fulfil what had been revealed to him they would still need to find the shell themselves. It was how it was supposed to be, and Jean-Michel didn't question that. 'Why don't you go back to the cottage, catch up on some rest, and then come back to the caves with me late morning?' he suggested. Pamplemousse barked in agreement, as they gladly accepted his invitation.

Ten

Exposed

Returning to his private chambers in darkness, De Vlinder sat down at his desk, thinking it odd that the door was still ajar. He then noticed the warm, spicy scent in the air. He tilted his head, his keen hunter instincts aware of something foreign present in his room. Out of the corner of his eye he could see a white glare reflecting in the glass table top. Very slowly he rose to his feet, pistol in hand, and in a few silent strides whipped the door back, exposing his 'guest'.

The imposing figure moved forward, the white of his teeth breaking through the shadows. 'Kingston', said De Vlinder in surprise, flicking the lights on.

'Ah there you are, De Vlinder. I was just on my way to the Swiss Meet. Thought I ought to stop by and catch up with you.' The tall, large frame of the smartly dressed figure loomed imposingly over De Vlinder, the pair just inches apart. Jared Kingston, the Afro-British rising star of British politics, hailed as the European Obama, destined for great things, now commanded the room. 'So what news?' he enquired, adjusting his gold 'coat of arms' engraved cufflinks. '*Ja*, we are very close to completion. Just waiting for our window of opportunity,' replied De Vlinder, clearly pissed off at this intrusion, but mindful not to bite the hand that feeds.

Kingston shook his head as a menacing smirk crept across his face. 'Right then, my colonial friend… one way or another, I want this operation finished ASAP… and I mean "job done". This is only one part of a far larger puzzle. If this *thing* really is what some suggest, then it's mildly interesting and somewhat entertaining at best. Personally, I have my doubts. And if it's not what they say, then we're all wasting our time and some of us are wasting our money, aren't we?'

De Vlinder stepped back a little. 'I understand Kingston, and I will get the job done, I stake my life on it.'

'How perceptive of you,' remarked Kingston as he opened the door and disappeared.

Back at their cottage Alex and Sara, tired from their night spent locked in the little stone outbuilding, fell quickly and soundly asleep, but it didn't last as they were soon woken by a loud repetitive banging. Someone was knocking on the glazed front door. A naked, dishevelled Alex quickly made himself presentable, and thinking it was Jean-Michel rushed down the tiny stairs to unbolt and unlock the front door. There, to his surprise, was their host Madame De La Morreze. 'Is everything alright?' asked Marianne inspecting Pascal's new lock installation.

'Yes, great thanks,' replied Alex.

'I'm so sorry about what happened the other night. You say you had nothing stolen, so we're guessing its more than likely drunken youths fooling about. I've reported it at the local *gendarmerie*, but they don't need to take statements, because there was nothing stolen. Anyway, we wanted to make up for it somehow, so we were wondering if you and your wife would like to come over to our place and dine with us tonight... We have another couple of friends here, and thought we could make an evening of it?'

'That sounds very nice. Can I let you know in a little while?'

'Well, the only problem is that I'm going out to buy fresh provisions from the market, so I really would like to know now...' she said, pausing, gently pressurising Alex into making an on-the-spot decision.

'Oh I'm sure in that case we'd very much like to join you, thank you. What time do you want us?'

'Shall we say eight o'clock?'

'Lovely, see you then.' Alex closed the door and went to

explain to Sara, but there was no need as she'd overheard the conversation. Alex got back under the duvet and they cuddled up.

Having rested well, they reorganised themselves and made their way back to L'Hermitage, where they found Jean-Michel working on his olive trees in the sunshine. Although no gardener, Alex was intrigued by the way Jean-Michel worked, because he seemed to be so completely focussed on the olive trees. Alex asked about growing olives and what Jean-Michel had to do to look after them.

'All olives are green to begin with, and turn black as they mature. These olive trees flower in May, and by July the fruit is large and the inner nut has hardened. From September harvesting of the green varieties begins. In October the oil is harvested for use directly in the kitchen. At the beginning of November the fruit begins to turn yellow, and then darkening shades of red. At this stage the olive is harvested for the first olive oil. From mid-November growth stops and the fruit turns black.' Jean-Michel explained that the harvesting of certain varieties continued until January.

He told Sara and Alex the history of how millions of olive trees had died in the south of France in 1956 because of the extended cold winter and hard frosts.

'And what about pruning and taking care of them?' asked Sara.

'Younger and older olive trees need to be pruned differently. These here are more established taller trees, so in spring I cut away the suckers from around the roots to provide space for the central branches, or *charpentes*, and then use secateurs to remove unwanted branches which are growing into the middle of each tree. Thinning and opening the olivier out in this way lets the sun in – and olive trees love the sun.'

Alex and Sara joined in and helping Jean-Michel with the harvesting some of his autumn crop of green olives, with the use of baskets, ladders, a rake and nets. They learnt that Jean-Michel had harvested the same way since childhood. In fact, he used to help his mother and father, and even remembered one time helping his grandfather when he was very young. Alex, Sara and Jean-Michel worked together as a team, and looked and felt like a close family working in harmony on their very own little olive farm.

A large old bell chimed, the sound carrying across the hilly terrain for miles and miles. 'Lunch time,' announced Jean-Michel. The harvested olives were carried by basket and placed inside the store room of the second stone building.

Entering L'Hermitage, they found fresh bread laid out on the table, with cheese, pate, homemade pickles, fresh ripe juicy tomatoes and more. A carafe of red wine and another full of chilled water stood in the middle of the table, all already there, as if magically waiting for them. The host invited the couple to sit down. Once settled in the chair at the head of the table, Jean-Michel lowered his head and closed his eyes as if to pray. Reopening his eyes just a few seconds later he smiled and spoke. 'We'll go to the cave this afternoon, but for now let's eat, *bon appétit!*'

Alex and Sara told Jean-Michel everything that had happened. They had so many questions, but felt it was the right thing to be patient. They ate well and consumed a bit too much red wine for lunchtime, but then so had Jean-Michel.

It was around 2pm. Pamplemousse was in a deep sleep, busy chasing rabbits in his dreams, so Jean-Michel decided to leave him behind. As they set off for the building that guarded the caves, Alex noticed a light darting across the hillside, but couldn't trace the source. And none of them spotted the red sports car carefully parked and well hidden behind rocks on the far side of the valley.

'They're on the move again,' said Alina Wicky as she peered

through the powerful, top of the range binoculars. The sunlight reflected off her large solid gold Lebanese bangle and, occasionally producing a sporadic light on the far side of the hill, it was the only thing that indicated her position. She was well camouflaged otherwise, even in combats she had an undeniable womanly shape, just like the starlets of Hollywood's heyday. Fritz was taken away into a fantasy of sexual desire for a split second looking at her, but he would not act on it, not with her anyway, and certainly not right now.

'Let's be sure this time. We can't afford to make a mistake,' said her husband, looming ominously behind her, nudging her back, as if to intimate that any mistake 'they' made was only ever her fault. Alina winced a little, as her husband's nudge was right above her recently bruised kidney... just another of Fritz's 'gentle' reminders.

They had been watching for a while, and now looked on as Jean-Michel unlocked the grill to the stone dwelling, folded it back and opened the wooden door, and the three of them entered. Unfortunately Jean-Michel was not only a little worse for wear with the red wine from lunch, but was getting a little forgetful too, as he forgot to secure the door behind them.

Fritz and Alina spotted their opportunity, and the red sports car with the Swiss number plate was on its way towards L'Hermitage. The couple parked a little way from the building, on a back road leading up to Jean-Michel's fermette. They made their way up to the entrance of Élan and listened carefully. Not a sound came from within. 'Wait here and keep a look out,' Fritz instructed his wife, as he stealthily gripped the door handle. The door creaked open and he peered inside. Old sacks, a well, a few tools, some old oil lamps, a couple of old barrels, but apart from that the room was pretty much empty. He walked over to inspect one of the barrels. It was three-quarters full of olive oil. Then he noticed the wooden lid of the well was slightly ajar. He approached and pulled on the small dark metal handle protruding from the well lid, moving it to one side. Looking down the hole, and lighting his view with the small pocket torch, he could only just see the water. His eyes flicked here to there as he tried to figure out where they had gone. He shone the torch once more and looked down the well. This time he dropped a stone.

As the stone hit the water, the noise suggested it was quite shallow. Then, leaning over, Fritz spotted the foot holes on the sides of the well, and realised it was a way in, an entrance. With his small torch held firmly between gritted teeth, Fritz Wicky hurriedly replaced the old wooden lid to the well, and turned to leave the dwelling. He made his way back to where Alina sat, secretly nestled in the rocks of the hillside. 'There's a secret entrance. I think this could be it,' he said excitedly.

Do you want me to make contact now?' Alina looked at him approvingly.

'No, let's wait a while to be absolutely sure. We can't risk getting this wrong,' replied Fritz taking a swig from his silver hip flask, before nervously biting his nails and looking to the ground deep in thought.

'Are you sure?' asked Alina. In response his face froze as he instantaneously became enraged, lifting his hand above his head as if to strike her.

Deep inside the cave, Jean-Michel, Alex and Sara were completely oblivious to what had occurred on the mountainside above them. Jean-Michel decided to leave and return to his olive harvesting, reminding the tentative pair to go with their 'gut', and if really unsure to ask for help.

Alex remembered what he had intuitively said in St. Guilhem, about breathing and relaxing into knowledge rather than pushing himself to find the answer. They sat quietly, listening and waiting. As the silence built, the air seemed to become charged with an electric anticipation, as if something or someone was coming. The feel of the cave surroundings altered as they became enveloped by an invisible blanket of pure energy. All thoughts vanished, and the entire cave came alive in a way they hadn't noticed before.

Alex sank to his knees, as did Sara, for out of nowhere, right in front of them, appeared a man dressed in simple clothes, the same man who had spoken to Jean-Michel many times over the years. 'It is time for you to go to work in the world,' he said. 'You are the guardians of a great truth, the key to which is the shell. Do what you are here to do. This is your life's mission.'

'But where is the shell?' asked Alex, a little uncomfortable to be in conversation with a non-physical being of some sort.

'Follow the water, for there is its home,' replied the old man.

'Follow the water...?' repeated Alex out loud, but the old man dematerialised as quickly as he'd appeared.

'Follow the water... what does he mean, do you think we need to go and follow the water out of the cave?' asked Sara.

'Yes and no. We just need to be still,' said Alex.

As their minds became quiet, Sara became aware of a dripping sound.

'Listen... water...'

'Yes and its coming from that huge stalactite,' noted Alex.

Drip, drop, drip, drop... water trickled down the stalactite, falling some thirty metres into a pool of purest water, the very same pool where Jean-Michel had healed Pamplemousse, and from where he had gathered his healing waters.

Approaching the pool, Alex felt sure he knew. 'It's in the pool. The shell is in the water.' They walked together around the sides of the pool. They looked everywhere but couldn't locate the shell.

Occasionally, glittering crystal particles radiated fluorescent beams of light which caught their attention, but still the shell was nowhere to be seen. Alex, wearing shorts, tee shirt and sandals, and filled with an inexplicable surety, took it upon himself to climb into the cool water to take a better look around, but still nothing. The pool of water deep inside Clamouse felt cold, as it covered his body up to the waist.

Still wearing leather sandals, he could feel the wobbling form of something beneath his feet, and imagined it to be a dislodged rock of sorts. Alex stuck his head under the cold water. There, just to one side of where he stood, he could see something shimmering. He came up for air, and looked from above the water in exactly the same spot, but nothing.

'I think I might have seen something,' said Alex, 'I'm going to take another look.'

Taking a deep breath, his body now bent over in half, Alex submerged his head in the water once more. There it was again. He could just about make out the near transparent shimmering gold reflection. Only when he was underwater and in the same 'dimension' as the shell could he actually see it. That was why all those years ago Adameil could not see the shell in the water, because he wasn't immersed in water himself.

Alex leaned down and picked up the golden shell. From above Sara was unclear about what was going on, because Alex's hands appeared completely empty. But then, as his hands came out of the water, the gleaming golden beauty of the shell was exposed to the air. The walls of the cave were illuminated as the golden light shimmered in the semi-darkness. In an excited silence, Alex and Sara both spent time touching the shell. Was this a dream? All Jean-Michel's stories and all the experiences now seemed to make sense, and yet they could hardly speak to each other. It was a real case of shock and awe. The legend of the shell was true, and they were the new guardians. Alex put the shell back in the pool, knowing it to be the safest place for the time being. As to what to do from here, they weren't really sure other than they had to let Jean-Michel know.

Adrenalin pumping, they left the cave, entered the short tunnel, came up the well, into and out of the stone building, making sure to close the door and grill behind them. The door and grill were firmly shut, but remained unsecured as, lost in the drama of their incredible discovery; they forgot to click the heavy duty padlock into its locked position.

A loud snoring bellowed from L'Hermitage as they approached. 'He's probably having a siesta,' said Sara. Though desperate to share their news, they decided not to disturb the old man.

It was early evening by the time they returned to their holiday cottage, showered, and changed into fresh, presentable attire in time for the dinner invite at the De Morreze's. Arriving at the tall spiked iron gates of the De Morreze's main residence, which was more of a grand manor than a regular house, they walked up the old carriageway. Palm trees, dry-stone walls and antique garden ornaments complemented the unique classical setting as they approached the dominating over-sized double door.

Before they could pull the antique iron chain to sound the doorbell, Marianne appeared dressed to the nines, and covered in jewellery as if she was on a VIP night out in Paris. 'Come in my dears,' she smiled, beckoning them inside through the immense double doors. 'Jacques... Jacques... our guests are here,' she announced, raising her voice to a level so that her husband could hear the news. Turning back to them she lowered her voice again. 'Come on into the salon and we'll have a little drink first. Please make yourselves comfortable... I won't be a minute... just need to check on the kitchen,' and, with that, Marianne disappeared out of sight.

Alex and Sara looked around the well-lit room. Old oil paintings in ornate golden gilt frames covered the walls, a white marble gold figure of Louis XVI clock with the makers name 'Schmit a Paris' sat on the gigantic mantel above an enormous fireplace, which Alex guessed was about ten feet wide. Chandeliers, candelabra and the most intricate tiled floor either of them had ever seen completed the decors of the *petit-chateau*.

A door opened. 'This is my husband, Jacques,' said Marianne, now accompanied by a man holding a silver tray containing several glasses of what looked like champagne. The smiling grey-haired man with kind eyes, and still wearing his slippers approached them.

'Very pleased to meet you both...' he said offering them each a glass of bubbly, 'And before you ask, it isn't champagne, but *Blanquette de Limoux*, considered to be the first sparkling white wine ever produced in France, created by Benedictine monks in the early sixteenth century at the Abbey of Saint-Hilaire in the nearby Aude. You must visit it if you...' he suggested, but was unable to say more as he was cut off mid-sentence by the sound of the old clanging doorbell.

'I'm coming!' called out Marianne as she left the room, returning with her two other guests.

'Yes, if you get the chance, it's an interesting place... very worthwhile,' said Jacques pleased to complete his sentence, before being cut off once more by the new arrivals.

'This is Fritz and Alina Wicky from Switzerland, who are looking to buy a holiday home and are renting another one of our properties while they do,' announced Marianne. The couples smiled politely at each other, though Sara found Mr Wicky's ogling look was far too familiar for her liking. And she had an uneasy feeling they had met before... but that would have been impossible, so she endeavoured to just go with the flow for now at least.

Dinner was a five course gastronomic delight consisting of *Petite Quiche au Fromage et Jambon, Poulet au romarin et Choufleur au gratin, Salad Niçoise, Plat de fromages* and ending with the famous *Limousin dessert Clafoutis aux cerises*.

The conversation eventually turned to the subject of their preoccupations. Alex couldn't help it, he wanted to tell them everything. He briefly mentioned a strange experience at the bridge and in the village of St. Guilhem, and their recent visit to

Clamouse.

'I love mysteries and exploration, and the caves here at Clamouse are amazing,' said Alex. Sara, worried he was going to say things he shouldn't, tried to kick him under the table, but his shins were just out of reach. Alex continued, 'There's even a secr...' his words were cut short as he heard a loud voice barking in his head telling him to 'Shut up'. The voice didn't seem to come from anyone's mouth, but he had clearly heard it.

'Oh, there are plenty of caves here. Isn't that right, dear?' said Marianne looking over to her husband, who by now was slightly slumped to one side of his chair, head on shoulder, dozing at the table. Marianne rolled her eyes and continued, 'Yes, the caves here at Clamouse are amazing. There's even a pool reputed to hold an ancient secret power.' She rolled off the words nonchalantly as if she had told the mythical story a thousand times before.

'Oh really?' said Alina, catching her husband's eyes as she leant forward, placing the point of her elbow on the table with her hand folded neatly under her chin as she became increasingly interested.

'That's ridiculous,' spurted out Sara in an attempt to cover over the truth. Alina winced as she looked away from Sara, a little too dismissively for Sara's liking.

'Now my dear, don't be so quick to dismiss the unknown. Alex's grandmother Lucette would beg to differ...' said Marianne looking over at Alex for confirmation, who Sara could see was in a dilemma because he had no idea what she was talking about. To save Alex further embarrassment of openly asking for an explanation, Sara quickly turned the conversation away from Lucette.

'So other than property hunting, how do you spend your time?' she said looking over at the Wickys.

'Well, we both love birdwatching on the hillsides,' said Alina.

'Yes, actually we're specialists,' added Fritz smugly.

'How interesting, and what sort of birds have you spotted to date?' asked Marianne.

There was a pregnant pause. 'Birds of prey mostly,' said Alina

'Have you seen the Andorran bull-nosed eagle?' asked Sara.

'Oh, my favourite,' came a swift reply from Fritz Wicky.

'Oh mine too, such a beautiful bird' said Sara.

'Yes, quite,' interjected Alina, before turning to Jacques with a rather seductive smile and changing the topic '... but Jacques, do tell me of your hobbies.' A rather half sober Jacques swayed in circles as he lingered a little too long on his guests smiling lips, before regaling the entire group with some of his more colourful undertakings, causing much laughter and frivolity for some time.

It was getting late and Sara signalled Alex to make a move, which he did grudgingly. They said goodbye to the Wicky's and thanked Marianne, while Jacques showed them to the door.

'Thanks Jacques, it was lovely,' Sara commented, making the man very happy by giving him a peck on the cheek.

'Yes, it was a lovely evening, thank you,' repeated Alex.

He yawned and waved goodbye to them both and closed the door as he and Sara began their walk back down the beautifully lit park at the front of the house. To the far side of the gravelled drive was the small red sports car Alex had spotted several times over the past few days. The red convertible Morgan plus was a stunning looking car, so Alex wandered over to have a look.

'This is the one, the same one I've been seeing everywhere,' Alex said a little surprised.

'Lush, isn't it, but a bit lavish for birdwatching don't you think?' On the dashboard Sara spotted what looked like a wedding invitation with a scallop shell printed on it. 'Nusk Calb Eht Fonoitar Belec', marked with the following day's date. She studied the bizarre language and was just about to lift up the card and take a closer look when the front door opened once more, startling her. Sara motioned Alex to leave. They briskly passed the display of garden statues, ornaments and palm trees which now seemed to take on a completely different light under the luminosity of the clear starlit sky. Not wishing to look back, they could hear laughter coming from the front door of the property, then a car engine roaring into life.

'Sara, I heard a voice telling me to say no more.' blurted Alex.

'I know you did. It was me,' replied Sara 'I tried to get your attention but you were getting so carried away with your story that you couldn't hear me.' Sara stopped talking as the Wicky's rolled by in their sports car waving goodnight, making their way down the old drive and out of the park. 'So I spoke to you in my mind, I needed to warn you something wasn't right.'

'Okay, so now you're saying we're telepathic?' Alex quizzed.

'Well, it's like you said, if you don't limit the thought of what you can do and what can happen, then anything can and will happen. Anyhow that couple...'

'The De Morrezes?' Alex interrupted his wife.

'No, the Wickys, they're lying through their bloody teeth,' said Sara, her eyes enlarged, visibly miffed.

'Lying about what?' asked Alex, who, following countless glasses of wine, hadn't noticed anything out of the ordinary.

'Well not only did they have an unhealthy interest in the caves, but they also made out they were some sort of specialist twitchers.'

'And...?' asked Alex hoping for a swift explanation.

'The Andorran bull-nosed eagle doesn't even exist.'

'How do you know?'

'Because I made it up!' replied Sara pointing her finger heavenwards, as if to emphasise she had caught them red-handed.

Alex looked at Sara, nodding his head as if to acknowledge her investigative prowess. 'Somehow, Miss Marple, nothing surprises me anymore.'

Having eaten such a wonderful meal, they were absolutely

stuffed and decided to get some fresh air by taking a walk down one of the tracks overlooking the valley. Hand in hand in the moonlight, they strolled past rows of vines and numerous small antiquated agricultural buildings in various states of disrepair, enjoying the cool refreshing night air and the beautiful lights emanating up and out into the night sky from the houses down in the valley below.

After half an hour, Alex turned to Sara to suggest going back, but the old romantic in her wanted to continue a little farther. It was now past midnight. The moon shone brightly, lighting up the panorama of the hillside and the houses below. They continued a while longer, and came across some lights at the far end of the track. Coming closer to the source, they could see the faint, vague outline of an old ruined building. As they reached the end of the track, there was just enough time to see that it was an old fort or tower, before they were dazzled by the glare of several powerful halogen security lights coming from the left of the old chateau. A pack of four Doberman guard dogs sprang out to the edge of a nearby metal fence and barked angrily, startling Alex and Sara.

Alex and Sara squatted uncomfortably for a while in the unwelcoming prickly underbrush, their hearts racing. Awkwardly balanced, and unnerved by the lights and the hounds, they decided enough was enough, time to go. Alex led the way as they weaved in and out of the bushes, running along the side of the track so as to avoid the unwanted attention of the little road. Although a little scared, Sara was intrigued by the old building, and suggested they return the following day in good light, when they would be able to see what was what. 'I don't know why I'm saying this... but yes... why not...' agreed Alex.

Alex and Sara woke late the next morning. Nonetheless, Alex stuck religiously to his new morning Tai Chi routine in the warmth of the sun on the outside terrace, then made fresh coffee and took a cup up to Sara who was still getting dressed. They spent a few minutes discussing the night before, and both agreed that they felt as if they were taking part in somebody's dream. It was as if they had little time to think, and 'things' were just happening of their own accord. Sara was adamant about returning to the old ruined tower they'd discovered to uncover exactly what it was, as the place had really gripped her imagination. So before long they were pulling on their hiking shoes, walking down to the drive and onto the track towards the old part-ruined chateau.

As they neared the buildings, they heard vehicles approaching from ahead, and reacted quickly, taking refuge once more low down in the scented bushes of the scrubland. Sara's heart was pumping fast, but she was comforted by Alex as his hand squeezed hers tightly. As the cars passed by, they could see it was a small convoy of half a dozen or so vehicles heading away from the ruined tower. One was an official looking dark coloured saloon with a little flag flying from the bonnet, on which there was a golden scallop. Alex's heart skipped a beat as he felt a bolt of energy pass right through him. It was a strange feeling which made little sense, but then, nothing much did anymore. Alex shook his head as if to cleanse himself.

'Did you see that?' he said, as Sara nodded confirming that she had. Some of the vehicles had tinted windows, and all of them travelled at speed along the dry agricultural track, kicking up great clouds of sandy dust, making it difficult for Alex and Sara to see inside the vehicles at all, which only fuelled their imagination of the mysterious looking convoy.

Once the small motorcade was gone they got back to their feet, dusted themselves down and carefully made their way through the scrubland down to the old chateau. At the end of the lane, looming to their right was the once proud now tired old half-ruined stone chateau. Alex guessed it was circa twelfth century. The ancient castle or chateau was in part covered with a thick veil of green ivy, enveloping about half of the walls of the ruined building with a considerable natural bushy cloak as if to protect her from newcomers.

Sandy walls gave way to a large turret where several *meutriere* windows were sited, narrow slits from which arrows were once fired in almost complete security. To its left hand there was a large modern plain looking house with some sort of lengthy extension all of which appeared to be connected to the old part-ruined chateau. There was no one about. The dogs were outside barking aggressively again, but thankfully penned in by an imposing metal, barricade-like fence, which wrapped around the modern house. To the right of the group of buildings, the old chateau ruins appeared deserted, so Alex and Sara decided to investigate further. They were desperate to know more about the place, especially after spotting the scallop shell insignia on the car.

Like a man on a mission, Alex was in the zone, and pointed out to Sara that owing to the line of the buildings, if they approached from the far right, once they were close enough to the old arched doorway of the chateau, they would be well hidden from view. They simply couldn't be seen from the house and other buildings to the left. Still aware of the dogs barking, the two took a wide route around the edge of the underbrush so as to be as well camouflaged as possible. The rather worn but still sturdy arched wooden doors to the right hand side of the building were partly opened, but difficult to budge, so they squeezed inside. Here they discovered an overgrown grass courtyard and a far less impressive remainder of the building to its rear. However, being a couple of feet high the old walls allowed for stunning hilltop views over the varicoloured Hérault valley.

To the left of the overgrown inner courtyard, a small wooden door clung precariously to its tenacious medieval hinges, behind which they could see a large very secure looking two piece door, to the right of which was a stone staircase, a little worse for wear

from continuous exposure to the elements, and looking rather
bowed having been gently worn away from the parade of
thousands of footsteps over many hundreds of years.

With a wink from Alex, and a reassuring nod from Sara, the
intrepid couple crossed the grassy courtyard, slipped through
the smaller door and climbed the staircase. An unlocked old oak
door greeted them at the top, which lead to a variety of rooms.
There were several antechambers within the rooms, full of
scattered old wooden crates and boxes. They carefully made
their way through all the unrestored rooms until they arrived at
a closed door.

Adrenalin rushing, Alex grabbed the worn metal handle and
turned, opening it just a fraction to discover a fully restored
stone passageway leading ahead, past a door on the left, to a few
steps which lead onto a small ornate stone terrace. The door to
the left was securely locked. So they continued to the terrace
where they found themselves overlooking a beautifully restored
former banquet hall. There were various coats of arms and tapestries hanging from the walls. And to the couple's amazement,
they all shared a common theme – the scallop shell. Something
wasn't right. Why was this image everywhere? Alex and Sara
couldn't imagine it was just coincidental. 'That's the same
insignia I saw on the invitation in the Wicky's car. Put that
together with the shell emblem we saw on the car just now… and
it's getting beyond weird. Something's definitely going on here,'
Sara finally remarked in a hushed tone, pointing at a large
banner hanging centrally in the hall.

Down below, a door opened and shut, startling the couple,
who dived for cover, even though they were already well hidden
high up on the stone balcony. 'I don't like the look or feel of this.
Let's get out of here… now!' whispered Alex with some urgency.

Back at L'Hermitage, Jean-Michel, busy in his olive grove,
spotted the worried looks on Alex and Sara's faces as they

approached him, 'Hello my friends, something wrong?'

'We need to talk,' said Alex.

Okay, just give me a few minutes to finish here, and I will be with you,' obliged Jean-Michel without hesitation, and he quickly went about packing up his tools and making himself ready. Alex and Sara helped him put the tools away in the store, La Cabane. Jean-Michel nodded his appreciation and before long they were all done. 'So what is it, what's the problem?' he asked, concerned.

'We've discovered the shell, we know where it is' said Alex, barely able to contain himself.

'That means...'

'Yes, we know. We are the new guardians,' interrupted Sara in a rather matter-of-fact fashion.

'So it begins. And now the quickening.' Jean-Michel looked upwards and nodded his head, remembering what had been foretold.

'But there's something really strange going on down at the old chateau over there,' said Alex, pointing in the general direction of the ruins a couple of miles away

'Ahhh, you mean the Chateau des Cathares,' Jean-Michel added.

'Yeah...what do you know about it?' asked Alex both out of curiosity and concern.

'Well, apparently the building was abandoned in the thirteenth century and came under the ownership of the Church. It was sold in the 1940s to a wealthy aristocratic family from Paris, who built a large house to one side of the property which they apparently use as a *maison secondaire*.'

'But, Jean-Michel, we've been inside and seen...' Sara butted in, again unable to vocalise the end of her sentence.

'Seen? Seen what exactly?' Jean-Michel had now focussed his gaze totally on Sara; it was almost tangible, as if his eyes were actually gripping her shoulders and pulling her in.

'There are scallop shells all over the place, on coats of arms and tapestries. They've all got the same markings' she replied.

Are you sure?' asked Jean-Michel. Sara and Alex nodded a very definitive 'yes'. '*Merde*... DVK,' said Jean-Michel. Clearly now he had become rather agitated.

'That would also explain the vehicles coming and going' deduced Alex, looking at the pensive, uneasy Jean-Michel, while at the same time beginning to realise the seriousness of the situation which he and Sara had gotten themselves into. Jean-Michel explained to them that what they had uncovered was most likely a European cell of the DVK, and taking into account the size of the meeting and the number of vehicles, an important one.

'These are the people working to establish a one world government. They're the ones using covert methods of population control. They are close, literally, which means that they're on the trail of the shell now, which must mean...' he hesitated with his train of thought, not wishing to alarm the young couple further. 'Yes, it all makes sense...' said Jean-Michel, as in his mind he tied together the break-ins and the bugging devices.

'What can we do?' asked Sara anxiously.

'Perhaps tonight, when its dark, we could get back into the Cathar Chateau and see what is really going on?' suggested Alex.

'That's a good idea, but dangerous. Perhaps Sara should stay away,' replied Jean-Michel.

'You've got to be kidding, I'm going all the way on this...' voiced a determined Sara. So they agreed that they would all go to the chateau late that evening. They would all wear dark clothes as plain as possible; at least that was the plan.

Later that afternoon, Jean-Michel continued his work on the olive trees, totally unaware he was being watched closely by the Wickys. Having done enough Jean-Michel took his afternoon nap, however he had forgotten one thing – to check the grill and door to Élan, which had been left unlocked by Alex and Sara on their last visit. From their spy roost on the hillside, the Wickys spotted their opportunity. They entered the stone dwelling, and climbed down the well...

When Alex and Sara returned to Jean-Michel's they found him snoring loudly. So they decided to let him be and check on the shell alone. They found the grill and building open, but, guessing that Jean-Michel had forgotten to lock up again, they entered without hesitation. 'Oh look, the well cover hasn't been put back either,' noticed Sara, completely oblivious to the fact that deep in the caves under the mountainside, the Wickys had been exploring. They had found the stone seating area, the pool, the altar and the scallop shell engraving in the walls. They'd even discovered the engraved Latin words, but hadn't found the shell. Now hearing Alex's and Sara's footsteps approaching, they scrambled to hide.

At that moment Fritz lost his footing on the wet cave floor, banging his head on the narrow opening as his ankle gave way with a loud 'crunch'. 'Arrrrrrrrrrggggggggghhhh!' he yelled out in agony. The combined noise of the bone, muscle and sinew meant that his ankle was undoubtedly broken. The ankle swelled rapidly, and the fibula was almost poking through the skin of his leg. He reached for his hip flask.

Alex and Sara, who were making their way into the upper chambers of Clamouse, heard the shouts of distress. In a rush they spotted the couple and immediately went to help. 'How did you get down here?' Sara asked Alina.

'Look, it's broken.' Alina avoided the question, diverting attention to Fritz's shattered foot. It was clear he was in trouble.

Alex, moved by overwhelming compassion, reacted instinctively. 'Let's carry him down to the pool.' Lifting Fritz's belt and shoulders, and without touching his damaged ankle, they managed to move him down to the nearby pool, where Alex unlaced his walking boot, and Sara ever so gently removed his sock.

Alina watched on suspiciously, one hand on the small pistol hidden in the secret pocket of her top.

Alex intuitively soaked the sock with a little water from the pool, and gently squeezed the cotton stocking, allowing the cool liquid to slowly drip onto the damaged ankle. Within seconds, the silence was broken by the squelching sound of moving bone, muscle and liquid, as the swelling went right down, and the ankle was completely healed, good as new. It seemed as though the waters had healed Fritz Wicky, as they had healed Pamplemousse all those years ago.

'How in the hell did you do that?' asked a relieved yet bewildered Fritz.

It wasn't us, it was the water. You see, the...' Alex's explanation was cut short when he felt a sharp dig to his rib cage from Sara.

'It's healing water' said Sara.

'Thank you, thank you so much...' Alina said looking deep into their eyes and then hugging Alex, grateful for his help and the warmth she felt from his embrace. The Wickys went on to explain how they had come across the open stone dwelling by chance and looked inside, finding a well. Desperately needing a drink, and having no way to retrieve the well water, they had climbed down the well, which revealed the entrance tunnel. Being naturally inquisitive, they had decided to explore from there. Sara was sure they were lying but Alex seemed somewhat 'out of it' and seemingly oblivious to everything.

They all made their way out of the caves and up the well into the little building. Sara watched them suspiciously like a hawk all the way to the door. Alex made sure that the door was closed and that the grill was locked by clicking together the padlock. As the door of the dwelling slammed tight, Alex could see the three quarters full drinks bottle attached to Alina's waist. 'This cave must remain a secret, we need your promise,' said Alex.

'We owe you so much. Thank you, thank you…' replied Alina.

'Yes, I promise no one will hear of this,' added Fritz with a rather disingenuous smile, at least that's what Sara thought.

The Wickys then made off across the hillside muttering to one another, heading in the direction of their parked car. Alex and Sara returned to L'Hermitage where Jean-Michel was a little surprised to see them. They explained what had happened, and Jean-Michel looked gravely concerned. 'For them to have found the tunnel, means they're after more. They know now. We must be prepared to act as and how we need to in order to protect the shell.'

Alex confirmed he had clicked the padlock together and the grills were now secure, but thinking that the Wickys opportune intrusion was all down to his own forgetfulness, an embarrassed Jean-Michel took his keys and this time made sure the door and grills to Élan were securely fastened. He slammed the door of L'Hermitage solidly behind him. They could take no risks and make no mistakes. At that moment, Alex heard his mother's voice reciting the first line and a half of Rudyard Kipling's poem 'If'; 'If you can keep your head, when all about you are losing theirs…'

Eleven

The Return

Alex and Sara were having aperitifs on the terrace, with just two things dominating their thoughts; the late night escapade at the ruined chateau and the exposure of the tunnel to the Wickys. For the night ahead, they had some small wind-up torches and dark clothing. Alex, having turned from 'doubting Thomas' to a strange hybrid of a special ops soldier and 'Hercule Poirot' had keenly accepted his new role, and even decided to 'darken up' using some greyish sticky clay he'd uncovered in the garden.

'You look like a commando,' Sara remarked with a nervous smile. Waiting for the rendezvous and the cover of night to come, they sat there trying to pass the time by playing cards, all kitted out and feeling rather surreal.

'What time do you make it?' Alex asked with a confident and deliberate tug on his ponytail for good measure.

'Eleven ten,' Sara replied tentatively.

'Okay, let's make a move,' suggested Alex putting his handful of cards on the table and standing up, chest puffed out in a show of bravado. Leaving the TV and the lights on around the cottage to mimic someone actually being 'home', they pulled the shutters to and set off up the hill, where they were to meet at the old water tower as Jean-Michel had suggested.

'Shhh…what's that?' Alex bobbed down putting his right arm out to indicate to Sara to do the same. They heard the crackle of debris as the ground seemed to be humming. A wild boar flashed at immense speed across the hillside just two metres in front of them. 'Shiiittt,' came the muffled cry from a startled Alex, adrenalin pumping and heart beating fast. A few seconds later, as if on cue, a tawny owl hooted its haunting melody like a forewarning. A light flashed once, twice then stopped, followed by the same again.

It was Jean-Michel, who had also camouflaged his face. 'Are you both okay?' he whispered.

'Just about,' said Sara.

'Good, let's go.' Jean-Michel nodded, and with that they set off towards the ruined castle, crouching down low and walking through the scrub about twenty metres to the right of the track. As they arrived at a large oak tree they could see that the whole area clear as day, thanks to the halogen security lights.

'It's like *Escape From Colditz*,' whispered Alex in Sara's ear. At night, it really did have the eerie appearance of a prisoner of war camp. They sat quietly and patiently. To their left they could see cars parked behind the hedge and fencing. Then they heard a door open. Two men came out, immediately lit cigarettes, as if gagging for a smoke. The light intensity increased and four vicious-looking, dark-haired dogs barked repeatedly. until one of the two men commanded them to back down.

From their shelter behind the tree, Alex explained again to Jean-Michel how they'd entered the old chateau. The men from the house finished their cigarettes and went back inside, and the heavy metal door closed behind them. Once the security lights dimmed, Alex, Sara and Jean-Michel made their way around the natural perimeter of the estate, taking them farther away from the electric gates and the car park, but closer to the ruined entrance of the chateau. They had to be quiet because the guard dogs were jumpy, barking at the slightest noise be it a hooting owl or a snapping twig, and as sure as hell would go completely mad at the sight of three strangers approaching.

Following Jean-Michel's lead, and keeping themselves close to ground, they reached the far side of the ruin, manoeuvring a line of temporary metal-works barriers and onto the chateau grounds. They slipped through the huge arched wooden doors unnoticed. 'Over there on the left,' whispered Alex, recalling the route, pointing it out tentatively, just enough to be sure Jean-Michel could see.

They slipped through the smaller gateway and, on approaching the large doors, they heard music and laughter. The noise of a large sliding door bolt alerted them, as the wrought iron handle on the ancient wooden door turned and the metal latch lifted. Quickly they made for cover. The crumbling stone staircase to the right would have to do. They clambered up as a man and woman came out of the doorway. Pulling the immense door shut behind him, the man leaned closer to the woman, their gaze of desire magnified. They kissed, and lost in the moment didn't see the three motionless intruders, all darkly dressed, with their backs glued to the old stone staircase.

Jean-Michel touched Sara on the shoulder and pointed upwards. The couple by the doorway were now oblivious to anything beyond themselves. So Alex, Sara and Jean-Michel continued up the staircase till they reached the landing and the collection of rooms. Alex led the way, through the interconnecting rooms until they reached the small stone balcony where the noise exploded as they found themselves overlooking the fully packed banquet hall. Jean-Michel saw the scallop shell banners and tapestries and realised the gravity of the situation. He waved Alex and Sara towards him with his left hand, while at the same time signalling them to keep low with his right. They shuffled towards the ornate arched 'Fleur de Lys' shaped opening which Jean-Michel was hiding behind. As the three peered down from above, they could see a large table of diners, with a lavish banquet underway. The table was filled with a vast array of food and drink. Sara noticed the whole hog roast and wasn't impressed. All present were well dressed and appeared to be a mix of nationalities. At the far end of the hall hung a large pair of purple velvet curtains, looking a bit like a home theatre.

'That coat of arms there is the Papal coat of arms of Pope Benedict XVI,' Jean-Michel revealed, 'the scallop shell on the coat of arms is said to relate to St Augustine, as well as being a symbol of baptism and pilgrimage. For them it is a symbol of recognition. Of course the scallop really signifies the Divine heart within us all, and the embodiment of love.' Sara and Alex nodded.

'Benedict XVI was the first Pope since the Middle Ages to resign the seat of St. Peter, in a move that shocked the Catholic Church and made headlines around the world. Rumour has it his resignation was prompted by a scandal involving secret Vatican documents.' Jean-Michel put a finger to his nose and tapped it three times.

'Like I said, nothing surprises me anymore,' Alex remarked.

Just then, a high-pitched metallic screech hit the room. 'Five minutes, ladies and gentlemen,' a voice boomed out from the speakers, which were strategically positioned around the walls of the large room. Jean-Michel, Alex and Sara all looked at each other in wonder, and were transfixed as one of the servers pressed a button causing the pair of large curtains to be drawn back.

The crowd in the banquet hall hushed as the screen lit up to reveal what appeared to be the shadowy figures of a group of businessmen sitting in a dimly lit basement. The setting looked like a cross between a war time operations room and a secret corporate AGM. There, on screen, sitting in the middle, was the 'European Obama', Jared Kingston. Sara grabbed Alex's arm, barely able to contain herself. Seeing strange men and women display such vile trains of thought and desire, but seeing this familiar face, this 'man of the people' in the mix too, was something else.

'Alex, bloody hell, isn't that...' Alex gave her a look and she fell silent again.

The murmur of anticipation died down as the dark haired spokesman at the head of the table onscreen addressed the crowd with the surgical clarity common of a well-educated German linguist. 'Good evening, brothers and sisters. Welcome. We are here to update the global situation. We are rapidly expanding our plans to move forwards. So let us begin. As you all know, the recent deployment of G9 global mobile technology has given us the opportunity to implant electromagnetic chips in all mobile phones and media devices.'

Alex got out his phone looked at it nonchalantly and began videoing through a small opening on the ornate stone balcony as the man continued...

'This causes people in general to become increasingly fatigued, and their ability to think clearly is scrambled, giving us greater freedom to act. The 'manimals' no longer question what is right or wrong, as their minds desensitise. Very soon the encoded chips will be triggered to increase that sense of malaise, and infiltrate their bodies in the form of growths and cancers. I like to think of this as techno-euthanasia. We supply the 'know-how' and they do it themselves!'

The man on screen smirked. The crowd in the room joined together in muted laughter. Sara was appalled, and touched Alex, who turned towards her. 'Well, well, well,' she said nudging him again. Alex let out a muffled puff of mild annoyance as he followed the direction of her pointing finger. There, sat in the middle of the long table was the grey-bearded figure of Fritz Wicky, flirting outrageously with a young, buxom blonde, half his age. Opposite, a frustrated Alina Wicky tried to ignore her husband's lawless libido. Alex frowned as the speaker continued...

'This is all part of the process of the manifestation of the Cremation of Care. A new "enterovirus" is being released this winter to help alleviate the present population problem. As usual, the main target is reduction in numbers of those who do not carry the desired traits. And you know what this all means, there will be more for us because quite simply, there will be fewer manimals.'

Once more the arrogant, self-congratulatory group around

the banquet table joined each other in audible appreciation, which sickened the onlookers behind the stone balcony. 'Well you can book that $250,000 space trip now,' they overheard one man say.

'The European passport regulation is in the throes of becoming law, and this will necessitate implants. That will allow us an opportunity to introduce whatever we like, to whomever we like, whenever we like. Ladies and gentlemen, the possibilities are immense. The application of drugs and alcohol is being stepped up, increased untraceable biochemicals will be systematically upgraded. The weapons industry is in depression, and we have a couple of campaigns planned this winter which will no doubt lead to a boom in sales. Remember war is great business.

'And to this end it is worth noting that we have made great inroads in cyber-propaganda. Using modern technology to sow the seeds of doubt and spread global fear has worked better than we expected. Manipulation of the masses has never been easier. Our efforts with cyberterrorism are so convincing and so readily accepted – we know how to push the right buttons, literally. The great advantage here is anonymity. No one really knows who did what.' Alex, Sara and Jean-Michel looked at each other in disbelief as the guests in the hall of the Chateau murmured and nodded approvingly. At the grand table, a smartly dressed man in his forties looked at his female partner, a lady who had clearly been under the plastic surgeons knife on more than one occasion, overdressed and dripping with gold and diamonds, as together they delighted in the thought of the huge profits they would soon be making. It was a shocking scene, particularly for Alex and Sara, who until very recently had believed that such goings-on within secret societies were simply bedtime stories from the damaged minds of conspiracy theorists. But no, it was true, and it was stomach turning to witness talk of such Machiavellian actions actually being implemented in the world.

The man continued, 'We are presently looking at ways to deal with the boom in "new age" spirituality. As people increasingly move away from religions and belief systems, we have implemented a worldwide programme of "residential centres" for people to attend. These centres propose and idealise freedom, truth and transparency, but will in fact facilitate the neutralisation of seeking. In these times, people are emotionally and mentally encouraged to go to such places, and we will help them, for they will be allowed to "seek", to a degree, but only to a degree. This will keep those searching for deeper meaning and freedom quite separate from knowing and realising more.'

By now the gloating crowd were so psyched up and fuelled by the speaker's words that they began to scream and cackle, openly displaying their support of the ongoing nefarious global plot. A smartly dressed man with dark hair and a slim beard was so wrapped up in what was going on, in one moment of celebratory ecstasy he slammed his steak knife down on the wooden table with such force that it stayed there, bouncing side to side.

'As you know, we have heavily benefitted from our role in global leveraged buyout's over the last fifteen years. It's easy money, no questions asked. The recent global financial crisis has led us to the present situation, wherein many of our supporters and contributors from banking, markets and global businesses are under pressure. So using the crisis as cover, we have introduced varied and confusing financial charge structures where possible and convenient. The manimals are so locked into their own tiny minds and worlds they don't even question things anymore! It's a great way to work, introducing laws which apparently benefit the whole, but which in fact only benefit us. This is why at this time the trade commission is putting in place new laws which legalise the treatment of all livestock designated for slaughter to be given courses of antibiotics and growth hormones. And here's where it gets really clever.

'From next month, all European marketed food will need to

be irradiated by law, as a positive measure to ensure the purity of the supply, but in fact will mean that in time increasing numbers of manimals will be prone to preventable diseases due to malnutrition, and many will be eradicated. And then there were none!

'The present cycle of earthquake escalation will continue in the designated areas, and the pole-shift technology application will mean increasing natural catastrophes, again in the nominated hotspots. In world politics, eliminations are on-going. And we have big news for later on this year. The 45th president of the United States will be our candidate. She is delighted to continue her family's role in our organisation.' A lengthy applause and shrieks of support echoed around the hall.

'God bless America!' shrieked the voice of a middle-aged woman, glass raised to toast the prospect. The whole room exploded in whooping and hollering, verging on a wild hysteria.

'It's beyond belief,' whispered Alex, looking anxiously at Sara, who by now had her eyes closed in prayer-like contemplation.

Now the man on the screen held both hands in the air, calming the raucous crowd, before continuing. 'The geo-engineering programme is escalating, with blanket media explanations being that the action taken is to combat global warming. The on-going spraying of the atmosphere with aluminium particles will escalate the electromagnetic disharmony in designated areas, and contribute to the toxification of soil and degradation of surface water. Our electro-magnetic campaign is still in its infancy, but all the initial signs are excellent. All in all, we are winning. But we need more.'

'My God, if people knew all this, there would be worldwide revolution,' whispered Alex.

And still the onscreen presenter continued to feed his baying audience, who were calling for more, and banging glasses, bottles, cutlery, whatever they could find on the large oak table. The din was becoming almost unbearable as the noise pierced the eardrums of the three high up on the stone balcony. 'And now, a poignant treat. For those of you who haven't heard the Hanussen tapes, we have a surprise in store. We have original footage...'

On the large screen in the hall, an old cine-film began to play... 'And what can you tell us about the future?' asked a voice. There, in the room, and in cloudy eyed trance state, was Eric Hanussen. It was one of Himmler's private tapes.

'You will find and lose the power of the shell, but it will be yours. The year of the sheep, between the passing of the Draconids and the Orionids, a unique window of opportunity will open. On one single night you will have the chance to retrieve the shell and manifest eternal ownership through a human offering. He who returns the shell to the body of life will receive the secret of eternity, and hold the universe in his hands. A ceremony must be convened using that which the shell has touched, and that which has touched the shell. For the highest spiritual working one must offer a life within a life, thereby superseding the natural cycle of birth and harnessing the most powerful metaphysical force imaginable. This energy, combined with the knowledge of the shell, will render the shell's power your own. The gifting must take place within the sign of the Black Sun so that the energy cannot escape.'

'What was all that about?' asked a perplexed Sara, but Jean-Michel had seen and heard enough. He signalled to leave. They crept out of the balcony, down the stone staircase and with the roaring cheers from the hall masking their every footstep they exited the Chateau. Following a few half-hearted barks from the dogs, and keeping down low, they reached the cover of the old oak, and were safely away. As they crept away under the cover of the scrublands, a robotic noise could be heard. None of them had noticed the CCTV cameras discretely mounted on the buildings and in the trees, and in a room in the new house to the side of the old castle, a man picked up his radio, 'Intruders spotted on section C, awaiting protocol request'. The answer to search and retrieve came immediately.

Back at L'Hermitage, Alex, Sara and Jean-Michel sat around the old table. Shell-shocked by what they had just witnessed. Jean-Michel stroked his greyish stubble while Sara looked on in silence.

'Un-bloody believable.' Alex finally spoke out, head in his hands, his elbows supporting the weight of what his brain had just taken in on the table.

'Yes, but it must all be true,' Sara responded, almost heart-broken.

'We need to be sure that the shell is safe,' insisted Jean-Michel.

'Let's check in the morning.' Sara was desperately weary.

'No, we must check now,' Alex almost barked this out like an order, oblivious to his wife's deteriorating state.

So Alex and Jean-Michel left Sara at L'Hermitage where she promptly fell fast asleep in front of the warm log fire Jean-Michel had lit. It was not long before dreams engulfed her... She never noticed the shadowy figures of two men appearing at the window.

'Wake up' said the man. It took Sara a while to realise she wasn't dreaming. There in front of her was a man pointing a semi-automatic two tone pistol right between her eyes. 'Get up,' he ordered. As she did what she was told, she noticed a second man stood by the doorway of L'Hermitage.

The tall, shaven-headed man with tattoos on his hands and a nasty looking facial scar below his left eye spoke to her in a soft eastern European accent, 'Where are your friends?'

He looked about the room, as if she might have squirrelled them away somewhere. Sara was too nervous to speak. 'I said, where are your friends?' her interrogator repeated, louder still.

'I... I don't know, I'm not sure,' replied Sara trying her very best to act the innocent. But this fell on deaf ears. The man slapped her hard in the face, and pulled her blond hair downwards with so much force that the momentum caused her to fall to the floor, hitting her head. A small amount of blood started to trickle from her nose. Not satisfied with that, the man picked her up off the floor and hit her again. Once more, she fell down, and this time started to sob in pain and fear. The shaven-headed torturer yanked her up and spun her around like a ragdoll, so that he was behind her as she stood helplessly, the warm blood trickling from her aching nose as she trembled uncontrollably in shock. He took his gun and placed it against her head. Sara could feel the cold metal pushing hard into her temple and in that moment, she was sure she would die.

'Come with us,' ordered the man with an abrupt army-like directive. With that, the second man, who was rather more Mediterranean looking, and who until now had been standing there silently, like a burly mafia bodyguard, drew back his large, muscular leg and kicked the door open, as Sara was dragged out of the house. Too weary, shocked and broken to put up a fight, she could do nothing but comply as she was bundled into the waiting 4X4 vehicle. Within a few minutes Sara recognised the route; it was on the track heading back down to the Cathar Chateau, lit up with moving red lights, giving the building an eerie, fire-like glow.

The vehicle went through the electronic gates and came to an abrupt halt. Sara was pulled out of the truck and taken to the side of the house, which they entered via a reinforced metal door secured by a coded digital lock. Dragged down an old winding stone staircase by her abductors, she found herself in the cellars. To the rear was a hatch in the floor. One of the men lifted the grill, beneath which was a small opening to an even deeper cell. She was dropped inside the dungeon-like room, falling down from a height and hitting the stone and dirt floor with a heavy thud. The metal grill covering the hatch was slammed shut.

Her head spinning and body aching, she felt utterly and desperately alone in the world, hidden away in the depths of the old Cathar Chateau, with no escape. She was imprisoned in the *oubliette* (a dungeon with the only route in and out being the hatch in the high ceiling). As she listened to the footsteps of the two departing men, all the lights went out, and all Sara could see in the small dark room was a tiny unglazed opening at a height of about ten feet. With her hands now tied, and an out of reach barred window not even big enough for a child to pass through, she sat on the uncomfortable damp floor. The French dream vacation had become a living nightmare. Sara sat with her back tight up against the damp algae covered wall and sobbed.

Out of the silence of the night there came a rumble and a shaking, followed by bright glaring lights. As the din reached a crescendo, in the car park of the Pont du Diable, a large twin rotor helicopter was landing. As the rotors of the helicopter slowed, the doors flipped open and one by one out leapt two dozen soldiers, heavily equipped and dressed in dark combat gear. No sooner had the aircraft delivered its human cargo, it lifted up and disappeared into the night sky. The soldiers vanished into the surrounding darkness.

Oblivious to the imminent threat to Sara's life, and tucked away within the depths of Clamouse, in the Cathédrale du Temps, Jean-Michel and Alex reached La Source Vitale. Alex put his arms under the water, desperately groping for the shell. For a moment, he panicked, thinking it had gone, but regaining his composure, he submerged his head and caught sight of the glimmering outline. 'It's still here Jean-Michel,' said a hugely relieved Alex.

'Thank God,' replied Jean-Michel, releasing a rare, audible breath of built-up tension.

Alex brought it to the surface, and, as he did, the shell radiated a golden shimmer around the cave. In the shadows, the heads of several onlookers could be seen. Quickly Alex and Jean-Michel moved away from the pool and past the stone altar. Out of the silence, the metallic noise of a gun being cocked echoed around the cave. Alex and Jean-Michel turned around to see the barrels of several M4 carbines pointing directly at them.

'We'll take that,' said the mercenary, indicating to Alex to hand over the shell. Like Sebastian Cavalles, all those hundreds of years ago, he instinctively clutched it tightly to his chest.

'Hand it over, or the old guy gets it,' came the precise English-toned voice of the mercenary. The well-built darkly clad soldier of fortune standing in front of Alex appeared to be the leader of the group. Alex wondered who he was and where he was from. After all, he was British too, they had that in common. However, any idea of a combination of being decent and English immediately fell away from Alex's mind as the hired gun pointed the barrel of his automatic pistol with attached silencer directly at Jean-Michel.

'Don't hand it over Alex, whatever they do,' said Jean-Michel looking directly in the eyes of a now fearful Alex, who slickly transferred the shell behind his back.

'Last chance,' warned the thickly moustached English leader, as he moved his available outstretched hand forwards to receive the shell.

Alex glanced at the pool then back at Jean-Michel who gave a subtle nod. Then, without a word, and with all the force he could muster he launched the shell high into the darkness of the cave, hoping to reach the invisible camouflage of the pool's water. Three metallic muffled shots came from the pistol. Jean-Michel fell, collapsing on the cold hard floor of the cave. Alex rushed to Jean-Michel and held his friend's head in his arms.

'I'm sorry... I... I...' whispered Jean-Michel as blood poured profusely from the triad of bullet holes in his chest.

The mercenary leader turned screaming to his men 'Find it, and find it now!'

The shell, although well projected by Alex, was deflected from its planned path by a stalactite and bounced awkwardly around the cave, eventually coming to rest in the darkness, but short of Alex's target of the secure invisible haven of the pool. In the depths of Clamouse, a small glow appeared as the two halves of the shell opened a minute fraction.

Jean-Michel closed his eyes. Alex looked at the mercenary who had shot him with hate and a desire to kill. The other soldiers now frantically searching for the shell, while the commander kept shouting as he loomed over Alex and the near lifeless body of Jean-Michel. Alex could see Jean-Michel was fading fast; his breathing was shallow and very weak. Then a last breath came from him and he was gone. Alex held him close as tears came to his eyes. Gently lowering his friends head to the floor, Alex slid to one side and stood up, all the while under the watchful guard of the mercenary commander.

'Slowly, very slowly...' said the commander. The leader moved towards the unarmed Alex, his automatic pistol now pointing at Alex's head.

'You don't scare me,' said Alex in an angry, fearless tone.

'Well I should... you...' but before he could finish his sentence, Alex moved his leg round in near silence and at such a speed that it swept Jean-Michel's killer off his feet. The commander fell to the floor piercing his temple on a slender white stalagmite which killed him outright and without a sound. The pistol flew across the floor of the cave, lost in the shadows. Alex ran. The soldiers, spread out in the shadows and engrossed in their search for the shell, failed to see the fleeing Alex or their commander, who now lay dead on the floor of Clamouse.

'I have it, sir!' shouted one of the soldiers with great excitement. But he got no response and by now Alex was well on his way out of the cave, and climbing up the well and into Élan. He paused momentarily. He was intent on finding Sara, but flashbacks of the death of Jean-Michel occupied his mind like a recurring nightmare.

'Got to keep focussed,' said Alex aloud, attempting to keep calm in the chaos of his shock and despair. He managed to keep going, to exit the well, up into the outbuilding and out onto the heathlands.

By now the soldiers had discovered the two bodies of Jean-Michel and their commander, and realised that Alex had escaped. 'Not to worry. What can one man do against us?' said one of them and they all broke out in laughter. 'We have what we came for. Confirm collection and return to base,' said the second in command. The CSO (communication systems operator) contacted HQ with the long awaited, welcome news, 'We have the unit. Repeat, we have the unit.'

Jean-Michel found himself in a long, dark tunnel. At the far end was a light so bright he couldn't look directly at it, and yet somehow the strange luminescence drew him in. As he approached the golden orb of light spanning the dark tunnel, the pain and trauma of what had just taken place seemed to dissolve, as his mind became peaceful and silent. He had no desire to think. There was no need. In the distance he thought he could see somebody waiting to greet him. The figure appeared to be standing in the light, and although it was difficult to make out who it was, Jean-Michel sensed a masculine presence. The light seemed to emanate from the figure and rays of gold shone all around him. Jean-Michel felt increasingly joyful, safe, protected and loved.

Without moving his lips, the figure spoke to Jean-Michel, 'It is not time. You are not ready. There is still work for you to do. You must go back, to help the two become one. That is your destiny.'

Jean-Michel felt saddened, because by now he was so happy and peaceful where he was that going back seemed so far away from that moment, and somewhat pointless. Jean-Michel had never felt so at home, so full of joy and so peaceful, yet he found himself incapable of arguing with the resounding truth.

The voice repeated, 'It isn't your time. You still have a purpose to fulfil. When that purpose is realised, and you are ready, then you can return, but not before. That time may be much longer than you realise.'

Jean-Michel was warmed by the light, and filled with an overwhelming sense of being completely whole. Then the light began to fade. He could smell something, a pungent slightly disturbing odour which he could almost taste with his lips and then his mouth. His eyes rolled, and opened to find his faithful friend Pamplemousse licking his face in an attempt to revive his beloved master.

Jean-Michel came to, in a dreamlike state of consciousness and 'snapped' back fully into his body. Stretching out his hands, he found the strength to begin crawling, leaving a trail of blood as he slowly but surely crossed the floor of Clamouse. On the verge of passing out, and with the words of the spirit world he had heard just moments ago resounding in his heart, he found an inner strength which can only be described as coming from his soul. He continued slithering and sliding like a dying wounded reptile, scraping the skin of his arms and legs raw in places as he rubbed against several crystal clusters on the floor of the cave. And then there he was on the edge of the sacred pool. With his last ounce of will and life, he flopped into the water. The blood flowed into the pool, turning the crystalline waters a strange luminescent pink. In his head he heard the words, *'Ela patzan min bischa'*. He didn't know what the words meant, but they came to him just in that moment. It was ancient Hebrew and meant *'Let us be freed from that which keeps us from our true purpose'*.

Jean-Michel lay suspended in the water, seemingly lifeless. The faintest trace of a thought flashed through his consciousness. Perhaps the vision telling him to return was just in his mind, and it really was the end after all. He accepted his fate, whatever the outcome. An explosion of light filled his mind's eye, as, one by one, the metal bullet heads rose out of the bruised fleshy wounds, and spiralled down to the bottom of the pool, dancing their way to rest. The three entry holes in his chest began to close up, and the darkly bruised, swollen impact areas started to heal over.

Pamplemousse barked his encouragement. Jean-Michel's eyes opened once more, and he found himself semi-submerged and face down in the tepid waters of the ancient pool. Gasping for air, he turned his body, and in one glorious movement arose out of the water roaring back into life like the mythical Greek God, Triton.

Meanwhile, Alex had made his way back to the cottage, only to discover the door wide open, a chair lying on the floor and specks of blood splattered across the wooden floor. 'Bastards,' said Alex, the adrenalin pumping through his veins. He knew Sara had been taken. She became his focus. The only thing on his mind was to find and liberate her. *Sara...where are you?* he enquired telepathically.

Sara responded, *Alex... Alex, I'm in the dungeon beneath the old Cathar ruins. Help me, get me out of here.*

Be strong. I'll find a way, he promised.

Running at full pelt for about fifteen minutes, he eventually reached the ruined Chateau, which he found was buzzing with lights and movement. He took the now familiar route down the side of the metal fence, and through the ruined overgrown courtyard towards the same back steps that he, Sara and Jean-Michel had climbed just a few hours earlier. Before he could get to the stone stairway, the old metal door handle creaked as it was twisted from the inside passageway. Alex dived for cover.

A statuesque, red-headed woman appeared from behind the large metal studded door with a cigarette in her hand. She placed the cigarette in her mouth and produced a classy looking art deco lighter. Alex's attention was broken as he felt something crawling up his trouser leg as he lay flat on the overgrown grass of the ruined courtyard. A snake was making its way up his groin. Alex shook his leg, repeatedly. The snake was thrown sideways in the air, landing with the noise of a wet cloth as it struck the old stone walls, before sliding off into the undergrowth.

The woman fruitlessly glanced over in the direction of the wall, then walked about tugging on her pink Sabrinie cocktail cigarette. The door opened again. 'Come on, they're back and they've got it, it's happening,' the man announced rather excitedly. The two of them went back inside and the heavy door clunked shut.

Alex took his chance. He ran towards the door and made his way up the stone staircase, all the way along to the balcony. The banquet hall below was relatively quiet, with just a few people moving in and out, seemingly preparing for yet another feast. He decided to wait it out. As he sat crouched in silence, the few minutes seemed like hours to the impatient and worried Alex.

He remembered what he had learnt in the last few days, that to really know something he must quieten his mind to the point of clarity. He shut his eyes and thought of Sara. Nothing. Then he remembered to relax into the present moment and to be aware. As soon as he did he could see her sobbing in a dark, cell-like room. As the image became clearer, Alex felt he could almost reach out and touch her. He could make out the room, and the small area of light coming through what was a barred cellar type window. He could see that Sara was bruised and beaten, which angered him further and made him even more determined to reach her.

'There's no way out, the exit is only accessible only from a hatch in the high ceiling,' Sara's voice resounded in his head.

'What about that window?' he suggested, finding the whole telepathic gift getting better and better.

'Well I could squeeze through if I was five stone and twenty feet tall,' said Sara with a hint of sarcasm, which Alex took as a sign that she was in good spirits.

'Hold on, I'm coming,' said Alex, spurred on by the way she looked and his desire to get her out anyhow he could.

He moved from his balcony hiding place and entered the old large rooms looking, searching, for inspiration. There were various old wooden tea chests scattered around the place, which Alex rifled through in turn, hoping to find something useful. Desperately seeking inspiration, and not knowing exactly what he was looking for, he stubbornly continued searching all the same. He noticed the old light switches and his eyes followed up the walls and to the old wooden chandelier which held at least twenty old light bulbs. At one point he nearly fell into a hole where some of the old boards gave way because they were riddled with woodworm. A sprinkle of wood-filled dust fell unnoticed down onto the tiled floor beneath.

Laying down, he looked through the hole in the wide ancient floorboards and could make out an antechamber, positioned behind the large wooden courtyard entrance doors, which contained a small hallway with large curtains leading to the banquet hall. He got up from his knees and covered the hole with one of the boxes for safety. Next, he flicked the switch but no light. He tried it again. He returned to the boxes and uncovered several items, including a rusty axe head. Taking the axe head, he smashed it down just above the light switch and cut straight through the cable. Ripping the cable from the wall, he pulled so hard that the old cable clips pinged off the wooden partitions in sequence. The cable was loose now, but remained connected to the timber chandelier. He pulled and pulled until the cable sprang free from the old connection at the top of the chandelier. This gave Alex about ten metres of cable which he wound round his palm and elbow, coiling it like an adept artisan. Grabbing an assorted batch of huge old nails and bits of metal, he made his way back down the stone stairs and out into the courtyard, where he found a safe spot on the far side of a ruined wall.

Sitting with his back against the wall, he could feel where Sara was. It was as if he had the use of a natural built-in navigation system. He could sense her energy and feel her presence. From where he sat, he would need to get to the far side of the immense building, remaining low and well hidden.

Sliding through the grass, and keeping close to the walls so he was a less obvious target, Alex began his dangerous expedition.

Alex could hear the commotion inside the chateau. Something was going on. Keeping a calm head, he made his way around the far side. There, low down and partially covered by the overgrown grass, he could see the small opening to the *oubliette*. It was covered by old metal bars, which were rusty but still looked solid after several hundred years of life. Alex crept to the opening and peered inside.

Hunched against the dark damp wall of her isolated stone prison was Sara. She looked up almost immediately. 'Alex,' she said, finding it hard not to raise her voice with excitement and relief. Alex put his index finger over his mouth to quieten her. Then taking the large old nails, the axe head and an old, handle-less wood chisel, he quietly went to work. Removing the partially worn granite was an arduous process, enhanced by the fact that he needed to remove the stone as quietly as possible so as not to attract the unwanted attention of the guards. After twenty minutes of stop and start stone removal, Alex finally managed to free up one of the bars. There were three bars in all, and so he continued on to the second. The hubbub in the chateau was building, and music and voices could be heard as preparations grew, which all helped to further disguise the noise of Alex's handiwork.

Alex was now busy trying to loosen the second bar, and struggling. *How well things were made in the old days*, he thought. Just then a shaft of light appeared in front of Sara as the lid of the *oubliette* lifted and a rope ladder dropped down. Alex hit the grassy terrain in an attempt to hide. He listened attentively like an animal fully attuned to his surroundings as the goings-on unfolded. 'Climb!' the guard barked at Sara. She didn't want Alex getting caught, so she clambered to her feet and with difficulty climbed the long rope ladder. She winced in pain as she struggled to ascend. Then, in one swift movement, the rope ladder and Sara were gone as the guards pulled her up and out of the *oubliette*. Alex popped his head up just in time to see Sara's legs disappear.

'Where are we going?' asked Sara in a loud voice hoping to get the guards to provide a clue that Alex could overhear.

'You are going to dinner, you're the guest of honour, and it's time for you to shower,' replied one of the guards suggestively. 'Don't worry, I'll make sure you're really clean and fresh...' he smirked as the stone lid to the cell slammed shut. Alex closed his eyes and gritted his teeth, desperately wanting to forget what he'd just overheard.

Jean-Michel was now inside the store of La Cabane. Lifting up the old oak flooring in one corner, he knelt down and pulled out the dark dusty canvas sacking. There they were; the old munitions he had kept from his time in the French Foreign Legion. This included a 9mm semi-automatic pistol, a trench knife, grenades and smoke bombs. He had kept them hidden, never thinking that he would actually need to use them, but now it seemed the day had truly come. Cleaning the pistol down and checking it was still operational he filled his pockets with various munitions and a number of shells, and with a long deep breath readied himself for what was to come.

Twelve

The Offering

Sara was in real danger. Alex had to get inside the chateau, and attempt a rescue. Panic started to take over. 'Be calm,' said a voice, 'Be calm.' Shutting his eyes to the distractions Alex took a moment to pull himself together. The panic subsided and the clarity he needed presented itself. Keeping close to the wall, and camouflaged by the overgrown grass, he crept and slithered like an army sniper making his way around to the old courtyard. It was all clear. Alex prepared himself to make a dash for the outer stone staircase, when he felt something touch his leg, and this time it wasn't a snake. The hand tugged on his trousers. Alex slowly turned his head expecting to see a guard...

'What the hell? How did you...? You're... I saw you die...' said Alex as he looked at Jean-Michel in utter disbelief.

'Not now, we've got work to do,' replied a very much alive and determined Jean-Michel. 'This way.' He beckoned Alex to follow. Alex noticed the pistol and grenades strapped to the green canvas belt secured around the old man's waist – how ironic, Alex thought, having begun to regard Jean-Michel as the epitome of all things spiritual and peace-loving. In the undergrowth they discussed the situation.

'She's inside, they've got her... getting her ready for something,' fired Alex, his voice now bubbling with tension. Then, as if it was the first time the thought had occurred to him, he looked at Jean-Michel and asked, 'And the shell?' Jean-Michel shook his head. 'I guessed as much,' replied Alex.

Just then a large dark vehicle arrived at the front of the property. The two dived for cover, ensuring they could not be seen. Jean-Michel heard the mechanical whirr as he pointed upwards towards a large tree nearby. The CCTV camera was patrolling the area. In silence Jean-Michel looked at Alex, pointed again at the camera and then at his watch, signalling that they should figure out the time delay of the movement of the camera. They watched patiently as the camera scouted the area in front of them. 'Thirty-three seconds per shot,' whispered Alex.

Jean-Michel signalled again with his hands. They watched and realised that the CCTV camera was filming three areas, so rather than create attention by rendering the camera inactive they agreed to follow on behind each shot, and move rapidly at intervals of just under half a minute. They waited while the camera returned to the first point. As the whirring sound commenced, they sprinted forwards taking cover behind part of the ruined courtyard walls. A few seconds later, the whirring could be heard once more, as they concealed themselves in the long grass around the courtyard. A few seconds more and on Alex's finger count, they made for the stone staircase.

Alex sprinted as fast as he could, with Jean-Michel following on behind. He fell on the staircase, but managed to pick himself up and get to the top to re-join Alex. They stealthily crossed the old rooms where Alex had stripped the cable and found the old tools, and onto the balcony where they hid, overlooking the banquet room. Feeling somewhat safe and in familiar territory, they looked on as the room below filled with masked people.

Drinks were flowing, spirits were high, and voices were raised and rowdy. This time though, there were no dining tables, but huge cushions providing places for people to lie down. Masked topless waiters and waitresses coming from a swing door kitchen area served copious amounts of wine, and the whole scene had the air of a modern day Roman orgy.

Alex and Jean-Michel looked on in disbelief as a large gong was sounded and the crowd fell silent. There, in the ancient paving stones, embedded in the floor, the two onlookers could make out the crooked twelve legged wheel shape of an occult symbol called the Black Sun, on the farthest side of the room, below the large screen. The crowd hushed as the charismatic Zarco De Vlinder moved towards the top point of the paved circle in the floor and stood there motionless, eyes looking straight ahead, waiting for the room to quieten. Within seconds an eerie silence became extended further still as De Vlinder took the time to make momentary eye contact with everyone present.

Then the mesmerising figure spoke in a moderate tone, 'Tonight is the night,' his clear voice easily reaching the back of the room and the balcony, 'the night we have waited so long for. This moment will mark the seal of our superiority, and lead to the embodiment of our divine birth right. For tonight, ladies and gentlemen, the Black Sun rises!' He looked around the room as the crowd murmured with excitement. Silence quickly returned to the hall as the audience awaited more.

De Vlinder continued his speech, getting louder and more passionate with every passing sentence. 'In years to come, you will be able to say "I was there" to witness the golden dawn, the rebirth of our species. We are the strong, solid and determined new race. This organisation of great honour and strength is entering a time of regeneration, a rebirth, a window of awakening. Celebrate now because this time belongs to us!' De Vlinder nodded his head in a conceited manner as if what he was saying was undoubtedly true. 'And, following this unique moment in world history, you will stand as the enlightened ones. This is an illumination we will never relinquish. The power is ours. The world is ours!' The blond, blue-eyed De Vlinder thrust his arm forcefully into the air in a victorious gesture as the golden exterior of the shell gleamed and flickered in the candle light. Triggered by the passion and power of De Vlinder's words, the crowd erupted in rapturous applause and cheers, gloating over the symbolic capture of the relic.

Alex looked over at Jean-Michel, whose eyes were transfixed on the floor, as if he was in the throes of accepting defeat, and was coming to terms with the sad inexorable consequences.

'Do not question anything you see or hear tonight, and do not ask why, simply follow, and all will be revealed. Trust in the law. There is only one law, and tonight it is ours.' De Vlinder paused as the room echoed with applause once again. 'We will now prepare for the Great Exchange, the gathering of the light...' Again the onlookers murmured in excitement and expectation at this powerful man's words. 'Go now and prepare yourselves, for at midnight we seal the offering.' De Vlinder smiled, the smile of a person who knew he was about to get away with murder.

Alex felt sick in the pit of his stomach, as if he had been poisoned. He sensed the room was full of dark energy. De Vlinder walked towards an ornamental fireplace, touched his hand on the lion head carving on the left hand side of the mantelpiece, and left the hall via the opening which appeared. The two onlookers sat quite still for a while watching as people left to prepare for the ceremony. Alex looked anxiously at Jean-Michel. 'My God, they're going to kill Sara,' said Alex through gritted teeth.

'Not if we can help it,' assured Jean-Michel who seemed to have found yet another lease of life. 'I have an idea.'

'So do I,' replied Alex and the two began a whispered conversation. Within a few minutes, they made their way back into the upstairs rooms. Alex waved Jean-Michel over to him. When they stood together Alex pointed towards the floor, and, pushing the wooden box aside, he exposed the area of damaged boarding he had covered over. Jean-Michel nodded. Alex looked down through the floorboards to see a couple return through the courtyard door and enter the banquet hall. Alex remained still, hoping they wouldn't look up. They didn't.

Using what useful implements they could gather, they set about levering up the floorboards as best they could. With all the preparations taking place, and with everyone preoccupied, this was their chance. Alex removed the electric cable from around his waist and tied it to an exposed solid wooden purlin, checking it was secure. He nodded at Jean-Michel who reciprocated the movement, and, with Jean-Michel holding the tension, he slid down the cable like a fireman on an emergency call out. Once Alex hit the floor, Jean-Michel let go of the cable. Just then the banquet hall door opened.

Alex flipped the electrical cable over the huge curtain pole, where it became safely hidden. A loud voice boomed across the hall, 'Frederic, you'll have to wait, we've got too much to do.' The door shut and it was clear once again. Alex flipped the cable free of the curtain pole and Jean-Michel descended. Once he was on the floor, he quickly made it over to Alex, who flipped the cable once more back over the curtain rail. It hung there, like an old cable, which, after all, was exactly what it was.

As planned, Alex and Jean-Michel waited for the banquet hall door to open. It seemed like hours to Alex, who was so impatient to proceed. Jean-Michel was doing his best to keep a tight lid on his friend. Then, as if by magic, the door opened, and a waiter carrying a packet of cigarettes and a lighter, but little else, came out.

He removed his mask and headed for the courtyard exit. Just as he reached out his hand to open the immense studded door, Jean-Michel struck. With a precise and powerful 'shuto' (karate strike) to the side of the unsuspecting waiter's neck, the young man passed out immediately, falling seemingly lifeless to the floor.

Dragging him behind the curtains to the side of the hall, Jean-Michel looked at Alex who had already begun to undress. Using Alex's t-shirt, Jean Michel gagged the unconscious waiter, removed his mask and shiny black leather shorts, and pulled him to one side. To the rear of the curtains along one side of the hall was a store cupboard and toilet, where Jean-Michel tied up and hid the unconscious gagged waiter, jamming the base of the door shut with two large old nails. Alex, now virtually naked, slipped the shorts on, which were close enough to be a reasonable fit, and pulled the mask over his head, he had never been more grateful for his well-honed physique than right at this moment, for it could save Sara's life.

Opening the banquet hall door just a fraction, Alex could see people scurrying here and there, some in and out of the kitchens and some through the large swing doors to the top right hand side of the hall. He had no choice; he just had to go for it. Standing directly behind him, Jean-Michel nodded indicating it was the moment, and, clearing his mind once more, Alex entered and began to cross the immense room. 'Take this to four immediately,' instructed a rather official-looking man, as he passed Alex a tray which contained a bottle of 2002 Dom Perignon vintage champagne and a number of smoked salmon and cream cheese *amuse-bouches.*

For a second, Alex stood there, frozen to the spot, like a helpless child. 'Come on, now!' barked the man, pointing towards the door on the top right. Alex walked away, tray in hand and followed the instruction. At the door he nearly dropped everything as a bare-breasted busty waitress came back through with an empty tray, nearly knocking each other over. 'The right, remember the right,' snapped the waitress, as Alex looked away in embarrassment and continued on his way. Through the doors he could make out that it was designed rather like a hotel, which once Alex had found the signs to the rooms, made it easier for him to pass unnoticed.

Looking for a way to ditch his tray, Alex tried a door marked private, but to no avail as it was locked tight. A large, burly guard spotted Alex and moved towards him 'What room, boy?' he asked stroking his scarred and battered hand down Alex's slightly damp chest.

'Four,' Alex replied fighting his natural urge to punch the pervert in the face.

'Just there,' the guard pointed to the room. Fortunately for Alex it was the next door across the hallway. 'Perhaps I'll come and find you later?' said the guard cocking his head to one side and raising his unkempt eyebrows, as Alex smiled nervously. The guard continued to look at Alex both suspiciously and longingly. He had no way out but to follow through the role play.

Knocking at the door of room four, he heard a mumbled response and waited. The guard waited too, eyeing his prey. The door opened to reveal a huge private suite, and standing there in the doorway was Alina Wicky. Her eyes were red and swollen and Alex was sure he could make out facial bruising, pretty well camouflaged under layers of makeup.

She looked away quickly. 'Put it in the sitting room.' Alex moved inside and stood motionless. 'Over there.' She gestured to a seating area where the white sofas were gazed upon by impressive works of art. Alex placed the tray on the ebony table. He could hear a shower running and a man's voice singing in the background. As he moved towards the table, he lost his concentration, the ice bucket toppled over and the entire contents of the tray fell across the floor.

'I'm sorry, Madam,' said Alex bending down to retrieve what he could.

Alina Wicky approached and looked Alex up and down. He was a sight to behold, all tense and lean; she could almost feel the adrenalin pumping through the protruding veins of his toned forearms. She flicked her eyebrows with appreciation and smiled seductively. Then it clicked. 'I know you… You're…' for once she was lost for words. Alex stood motionless. In that moment he felt sure the game was up. Alina looked deep in his eyes and slowly put her finger to his mouth. 'Shhh…' she moved towards the large ornate wooden partition and closed the section between the hall and the lounge. Alex was unsure as to what was going to happen next, but sensed he had little option than to go with the flow of the moment. Alina approached, putting her hand on Alex's shoulder, 'I want to help you. You saved my husband… I owe you that.'

'I need to find her,' said Alex not bothering to explain and it seemed no explanation was needed.

Alina nodded. 'She's being prepared for De Vlinder in the ceremonial suite.'

'Who's De Vlinder?'

'The main man, the boss, the one who's in charge of it all,' Alina replied.

'And where's the suite?' Alex was nervous but had little option than to cling to the hope that he could trust this woman.

'Downstairs, it's part of De Vlinder's private chambers. But it's guarded and difficult to get into, unless...'

'Unless what?' asked Alex. 'You know how to, right?'

'Yes... Look that greedy bastard has really used me, he's used us all. He's such a shit! It's time he had his comeuppance. Come on, follow me, I'll show you, that's as much as I can do, then you're on your own.' Alina stroked Alex's arm, she was unquestionably attracted to him, but it was now not just because of his body and looks, but her realisation that the young man standing half naked in front of her was genuinely prepared to risk his own life for the sake of the woman he loved. In her entire life, she had never experienced the type of selfless courage that Alex was showing through his desire to save his beloved Sara, and she found that action powerfully intoxicating.

Opening the sliding partition, Alina found Fritz coming out of the shower, 'For Christ's sake woman, where the hell is my new razor?'

Nervously stepping forward and pulling the sliding door to behind her, a shaking Alina quickly made her way to the bedside table, and opened the drawer.

'Here we are,' she said ushering her husband back into the bathroom area. He looked at her long and hard.

'I'll talk to you about this later,' he said threateningly as he pushed past her, heading back to the bathroom. Within seconds the whirr of the electric razor was accompanied by a man's voice singing and humming a strained version of Richard Wagner's 'Ride of the Valkyrie'.

Sliding open the white louvered lounge area partition, she waved Alex to move her way, and they quickly exited the bedroom together. Making their way downstairs, Alex was relieved that there were people beginning to circulate. The predatory guard was now standing at the far end of the corridor facing away from him, busily talking to another young masked waiter, with his muscular arm extended blocking any escape for his next intended victim.

Moving into the now frantic banquet hall which was fast filling up for the evening, Alina said, 'Offer me a drink,' and Alex grabbed a tray of glasses filled with wine from the side table. Following her over to the ornate fireplace Alex braced himself for his next move. Alina looked over at the guard longingly and smiled suggestively. She grabbed a second glass from the tray Alex was holding and honed in on her prey. Turning the guard slightly by stroking his shoulder and pulling him playfully, she offered him a glass, which he refused. Alina looked at Alex, leaned across and gently touched the carved wooden face on the top left of the fireplace. Alina was now standing closer to the guard, biting her lower lip suggestively and whispering in his ear. The next thing Alex knew, Alina had disappeared off around the corner with the guard following in hot pursuit. He chose the ideal moment to put down the tray as he pulled on the lions head and, hey presto, the door opened.

Alex slid inside unnoticed as the door closed quickly and silently behind him. The long, dimly lit passageway was difficult to make out. Alex could hear voices up ahead. A small group of armed guards were playing cards in a kitchen area set back from the hallway. He heard footsteps approaching and made for the nearest doorway. The footsteps were coming closer and Alex's heart was beating loud and fast. He felt a hand over his mouth and was pulled backwards through the now opened doorway with tremendous force. He struggled, but quickly realised that he was being constrained by a powerful force, a force none other than Jean-Michel.

Pulling him backward, they reversed into the store room, Jean-Michel closing the door behind them. The room was full of clothes and masks, 'You were supposed to get Sara, and I was supposed to get the shell.'

'Well, looks like they're both here somewhere in these rooms,' replied Alex rubbing his shoulders with both arms.

'Here, put this on.' Jean-Michel passed Alex a blue one-piece work suit which he slipped on over the leather shorts.

'And there are guards up ahead,' continued Alex.

'Yes, four men... I know,' replied Jean-Michel. 'I can deal with that, but can you free Sara?'

Alex recalled how he'd sensed Sara's energy, and how they were able to converse telepathically. He sat quietly while Jean-Michel looked on faithfully. In his mind's eye, Alex could see the guards sitting on chairs around a large table in the smoke-filled kitchen area, littered with banknotes, half-empty drinks, and smouldering cigarettes in makeshift ashtrays. A bundle of sub-machine guns were hanging from the back of the door. Moving his vision down the passage, he noted the existence of several more empty rooms followed by a pair of large pleated velvet curtains blocking the way forward. Alex seemed to pass straight through the palatial looking barrier with his third eye view. Behind the tall overpowering hanging fabric he looked on as a wide corridor split to a left and a right with doors at the far end of each passage. In the storeroom, Alex was in a trance-like state, his eyes aloft and fixated. Like a floating incorporeal spirit with unlimited visual access, he could see Sara in the right hand room, all dressed in a white material, gagged and sitting on a chair. At the other end he could make out De Vlinder's private suite, with a hand holding a shell but no sign of De Vlinder himself. *Sara...* *Sara!* he called out in his mind. This time however, there was only silence.

'I know where she is, and De Vlinder's room is at the far left end of the corridor. I think I can see the shell,' said an animated Alex, now more determined and sure of himself than ever before.

In complete silence, Jean-Michel placed his index finger over his sealed lips to quieten the excited Alex, who was speaking too loudly for comfort. Holding the same index finger aloft as if he had formulated a good plan, he beckoned Alex closer by waving all the fingers of his hand back and forth. He whispered in Alex's ear with the calm assuredness that comes from insight and experience.

A few seconds later, the former legionnaire prepared himself and took a deep breath, grabbed a towel from the shelf of the storeroom and wrapped it around the pistol. 'It's now or never Alex'. He opened the door of the storeroom sufficiently to see the way ahead was clear, before fully opening the door to quietly approach the kitchen, like a wise old lion carefully stalking his prey. Alex pulled the door back to keep himself well hidden in the store cupboard, peeking out from low down like he was a child in a game of hide and seek. The guard's voices could still be heard and it sounded like they were playing poker. Jean-Michel drew a deep breath and slithered down the wall of the empty corridor. It was time for action. One, two, three... bang! The door slammed shut just a second before Jean-Michel could pounce.

With the door to the kitchen now closed, Jean-Michel immediately took advantage of the impromptu window of opportunity to make his next move. In an instant, he carefully and almost silently slid past the closed door and, once safely on the far side, motioned Alex to move towards him, which he did. Together, they continued in silence at a slow walking pace past several more doors, most of which were shut tight. Alex noticed that one of the doors was partially open, but the room seemed empty. It was clearly a bedroom. Carried by the momentum of adrenalin, the two continued on down to the junction at the end of the hallway, and through the heavy purple coloured velvet curtains. In an exchange that spoke more than any words could, they looked at each other reassuringly one last time, as if to wish one another good luck. They nodded at each other. Jean-Michel went left and Alex took the right. Alex's heart was beating faster than ever, but he put his head down and moved forward.

Jean-Michel gently squeezed and turned the handle till the door now in front of him was just so slightly ajar. He peered into the room through the small gap. Just as Alex had said, the shell was sat in a stone sculpted hand on one side of the room with no De Vlinder in sight. He flicked the light switch. With the stealth of a man many years his junior, Jean-Michel made his way over to the shell. On closer inspection he could see that the heavy metallic object clasped in the hand of the stone sculpture was only a replica, albeit a very good one. He couldn't help but notice the beautiful inscription on the solid golden plaque attached to the lower body of the effigy.

Translating as best he could, he read it out loud to himself, 'Ultima Cumaei venit iam carminis ætas (now the final era of the oracle's song); Magnus ab integro sæclorum nascitur (the great order of the ages is reborn); iam redit et Virgo, redeunt Saturnia (order returns); iam nova progenies cælo demittitur alto (a new lineage is sent from heaven)'. It sent a chill down his spine.

At the foot of the inscription were four interconnected circles underscored by the heavily embossed letters DVK. Shaking his head and expelling the air from his nose in a muted snort of contempt, he turned and continued to scour the room. He caught sight of the nearby smoked-glass table and a large ornately hand-carved desk, which was firmly locked, thwarting his germinal plan of a rummaging search. Running his hands and fingers under and around and lip of the mirror like walnut veneer, he felt a protrusion underneath the escritoire, and carefully kneeling down discovered two buttons, one red the other green.

He withdrew his shaky hand, mopped his brow and

continued to investigate the interlinked chambers for any clues leading to the whereabouts of the real shell. The white polar bear rug dominating the floor looked fierce and intimidating, as if it was about to leap off the floor and attack him. As he searched, the rooms increasingly reminded him of an elegant bunker. It was huge, but bizarrely there were few windows, and the three that were there were small and nigh on purposeless.

At the far end of the corridor, Alex also entered a room. Fully trusting what he had seen with his fast developing 'second sight', he had gone straight in. In the far corner of the room, there was Sara, just as he had envisioned, strapped fast to a substantial metal chair. She was dressed in white, with a sagging white cloth hood covering her head. Alex shivered. It was hauntingly reminiscent of the old Ku Klux Klan outfit. Distinct burgundy coloured, rune-like markings intermittently covered the loose fitting robe. A few strands of Sara's hair protruded like soft golden grass just below her chin on both sides. Alex took a deep breath, ripping off the hood in anger.

'Sara?' Holding her head in his hands and lifting it gently towards him, he stroked her lifeless face, but there was no response. She was warm to the touch, alive but unconscious. He tried to shake her awake, but without success. 'What have they done to you?' he remarked, noticing the vicious looking bruises to her face, gritting his teeth once more as he felt the anger within filling his entire being, but no time to vent it now.

Out of the corner of his eye he saw a small table, with a little bottle of transparent liquid and a half-full syringe on it, which Alex presumed had been used on Sara. He pulled up the baggy sleeves of Sara's ivory cotton garment to reveal a small smudge of blood where the needle had penetrated the delicate soft lilywhite flesh of her inner arm. He knelt down to see if he could free her from the chair, and discovered she was firmly secured with large, unforgiving cable ties, the kind used to bind electrical wires, pulled so tightly, they were cutting off the blood supply. Nothing to cut with, he thought.

Alex held her head tightly to his chest and shut his eyes briefly. Upon opening them, his attention was drawn to a selection of masks and cloaks suspended in a purpose built recess in the wall. There was also a dark leather macabre looking gurney, complete with arm, leg and torso restraints, ominously standing guard in the room. 'They will pay for this, I swear they will pay,' Alex muttered, as a muffled noise caused him to turn around.

'Too late for that,' the figure emerging from the back of the room spoke menacingly, 'you'll both pay now.' De Vlinder, automatic pistol in hand, stood firm at the partition to an adjoining suite.

'You'll never get away with it... you can't do this,' said Alex attempting to buy time and clarity.

De Vlinder smiled, amused, 'You... boy, you think you can spoil my moment of glory? You're nothing. This moment is the manifestation of our higher destiny, our long prophesied fate... and this...' he waved his pistol in Sara's general direction and then towards the leather gurney, '...is her fate. Two souls, for the price of one are to be offered so that omniscient power may be eternally granted to a select few. Your wife and your unborn child have been chosen and you should be grateful. It's a real honour. Your wife, my friend, is the key to unlocking the greatest power imaginable.'

Alex was dumbstruck, the words 'unborn child' rang in his ears' and De Vlinder must have instantly seen this news came as a shock to his hapless opponent. With a grin of pure delight De Vlinder came up close to Alex staring into his eyes relishing the fear and shock and agony that was reflected in them, like some sort of ghoulish emotional vampire, 'What? You didn't know? *Ja*, priceless isn't it... It's quite amazing what a few well-placed kicks and blows will extract from a person or even just the threat of them, why do you think we made such a mess of her face instead eh? And to think I will be the first and the last to see that little life inside her before I end it all for them both.'

Alex, a single tear escaping down his left cheek had never felt more hopeless in his life, but somehow managed to speak, as much to assure himself that this was indeed really happening and not a horrific nightmare, as a last ditch attempt to stall for time, 'But how did you know about us?'

De Vlinder's index finger flicked intimidatingly between the trigger and the trigger guard as he smirked and raised his eyebrows. 'We have been watching you far longer than you think. You see we have ways of obtaining information you cannot possibly imagine. We know all about you... all of you.' De Vlinder was positively revelling in his ill-gotten power over Alex, his eyes glistened and his smile expressed the genuine pleasure only real sadists reserve for their victims – a real love for the fear they can inflict with just a word, a look or a gesture.

'But why, why take her life... and the life of a total innocent?' Alex was now genuinely asking from his heart, rather than as a ploy to delay the horror about to unfold.

'*Ja, ja*...why? Ha why, ours is not to reason why, ours is but to do and die,' De Vlinder almost sang the words in his harsh Afrikaans accent, as he continued with his relentless verbal bombardment. 'Look boy, your *lekker bokkie* is just the means to an end, a temporary and disposable tool for establishing something far greater than you can possibly imagine.' His open arrogance and exuberant self-gratification sickened Alex to the pit of his stomach.

'I don't think you know what you're doing, can't you see this is absolute madness, you're just following an insane belief with a demented idea, it's perverted and sick,' said Alex looking De Vlinder straight in the eye, holding De Vlinder's attention, while his hand collected the syringe on the side table next to Sara. Without hesitation Alex stepped toward his captor.

De Vlinder, equally quick, raised his empty gloved hand, 'Don't you tune me. That's enough boy, no closer. You've been warned.' The index finger of his raised gloved hand now pointed only inches away from Alex's face. 'Watch my lips boy, I only give one warning.' De Vlinder lowered his hand slightly and indicated to an armchair. 'Now be a real good *rooinek* and sit down over there.'

Alex shuffled towards the chair beside Sara, just managing to hide the syringe in a back pocket of the cleaning uniform.

'I tell you what, as a special treat you can have the additional honour of watching the ceremony,' De Vlinder offered, mockingly, as Alex watched him move his free hand to the pocket of his suit. 'This is the reason, this is the power, this is our destiny... my bloody destiny,' said De Vlinder darkly, as he produced the golden shell. A beam of light appeared momentarily, an occurrence which inflated De Vlinder's ego further still, as he believed it was a sign the shell was speaking directly to him. 'Look don't you see... it's already begun. This fateful moment in history will ensure that we will have exactly what we want in the world we desire. And it's all because of you that we were able to finally recover it. So thank you boy,' De Vlinder winked, sliding the shell back into his pocket.

Just then a gong sounded three times from the banquet hall.

'It's time. They will come for her shortly. So now boy you can be part of this world changing event... and do some bloody work.' De Vlinder pulled a large hunting knife from his canvas web belt with his empty hand and, pushing Alex to the floor, walked behind Sara and cut the large plastic ties holding her arms secure behind the chair. Now he was less the poet and more the executioner, as he waved his pistol between Sara's head and Alex's face yet again to make his resolute demands crystal clear. 'Put the mask back over her bloody head and lift her on to the couch.'

As Alex replaced the mask and carefully lifted Sara, she let out a slight murmur, as if regaining consciousness. Her blue eyes opened, looking straight at Alex through the small slits in the material. Alex shook his head slightly then blinked, holding his eyes shut for longer than normal, attempting to convey that she should continue to appear to be unconscious. Sara looked on confused, and was just about to speak when Alex shouted out in his mind 'Shut your eyes now. Play dead!' Sara quickly understood and obliged.

De Vlinder missed the subtle exchange as he was too busy locating and then tossing a bundle of large plastic cable ties at Alex, hitting him on his face, before they fell spiralling down to the floor. 'Pick them up. Now tie her securely. Hands and feet.' Alex looked up and grimaced at De Vlinder. 'Or it's over... *Jisis* man don't think I won't *bliksem* you,' threatened De Vlinder, pointing the pistol at Alex's temple. In that moment Alex looked at De Vlinder and fought with the idea of trying to tackle him. De Vlinder wouldn't expect that, thought Alex, and he was running out of time.

'What the fok are you looking at?' said De Vlinder growing ever more impatient. He waved the pistol from side to side ordering Alex to get on with the task at hand. That was enough. Alex leapt at De Vlinder, managing to knock the gun across the floor. A struggle ensued as Alex fought not just for his own life, but for the life of his beloved Sara and their unborn child. The two men rolled around the floor, crashing into furniture as each tried to get the upper hand in the battle. Alex had both hands around De Vlinder's neck and tried to squeeze the life out of him. De Vlinder's hand found the pistol and hit Alex powerfully across the back of his head, dazing him just long enough that De Vlinder could get to his feet. Now standing directly over him, the mercenary aimed the pistol at his forehead. A warm rain of blood trickled through Alex's hair and began dripping onto the floor. On the verge of passing out, Alex was done, and he shut his eyes ready to accept his fate.

In the outer corridor the small group of priests and priest-esses were getting impatient. The intercom spurted into life. 'They're ready, Sir...' a priest announced aloud, hoping De Vlinder could hear him and was ready to make his entrance. The guards were on standby in the kitchen. A door opened and closed. The curtains moved a little. Another door opened and closed. Then in a fluid sweeping movement, the velvet curtains finally opened to reveal a figure dressed in ceremonial costume and mask. Next to him was the cloaked and masked, blond haired 'offering' securely strapped to the bed on wheels. The master of ceremonies opened his arms in a welcoming gesture. 'Take her,' he ordered beckoning the guards, who obeyed, wheeling the couch towards the entrance. The gong sounded a second time.

'But De Vlinder... the shell?' enquired the high priest.

'*Ja?*' replied the man.

'It must be in place, otherwise...' the bewildered high priest continued, nervous to be questioning his master.

'You know what to do,' came the curt response.

The priest was confused, and this did not go unnoticed by his boss who was growing impatient. 'Do not question. I have been told by the shell you must do it ... you!' and with that he handed the shell to the shocked priest. The high priest looked at De Vlinder quizzically before being overcome by a rapidly expanding sense of self-importance and the inflation of his own ego.

The small party moved into the banquet hall, where the guards moved the couch into position as instructed by the priests and the high priests congregated in a line. The room was full of guests all wearing robes and masks. The gong sounded a third time. 'Bring forth the ceremonial wine,' announced the priest as the scantily clad masked waiters and waitresses passed goblets to all and sundry and exited the room quickly through the kitchen service doors.

Looking through the small gap in the door, Jean-Michel could just about see what was going on. The couch was in position within the symbol of the Black Sun on the floor, surrounded by a large circle of red roses. The shell was consecrated, lifted high and placed on a small cushion. The room was dimly lit with candles and naked flame torches.

'In the name of Baphomet. With this shell, and with this blood, we unite what is rightfully ours, that we may share the limitless riches of this sacrifice.' The entire room raised their goblets high into the air. One priest moved forward with an orange-handled dagger placed upon a small black cushion. The high priest took the large dagger in both hands and kissed it. Words were spoken by the high priest and repeated by all present. The wine was drunk, as another priest presented the shell. 'He who returns the shell to the body of life will receive the secret of eternity, and hold the universe in his hands,' said the priest echoing the recorded words of Hanussen.

Taking the dagger, the high priest plunged it deep into the chest cavity of the offering, the razor sharp blade slicing effortlessly through the material and human flesh simultaneously. Dragging the large sharp blade downwards from the chest cavity and then back to the middle, efficiently carving its way below the rib cage first to the left hand side and then to the right. A cross of blood appeared as the high priest took the shell, raised it above his head for all to see, and with the word 'Mamon' plunged the shell deep into the chest cavity of the victim. 'Now we have eternal life!'

Just then the eyes of the body opened, blue and piercing, but it was a man's voice that gurgled, 'Foools... Foo...' as a final breath spluttered from the blood drenched torso. The high priest ripped the mask from the victim, confirming to his horror that it was De Vlinder, drugged, haemorrhaging and now lying dead before him. 'Fuck!' But his obscenity was smothered by the noise and smoke of grenades exploding in the banquet hall. As shots rang out absolute mayhem ensued.

'Go, go, go!' roared Jean-Michel firing more shots into the air as he, Alex and Sara now rushed through the smoke filled room making for the side door to the courtyard. In all the chaos, guards were panicking and shooting their own people, a massacre was unfolding.

By the time Jean-Michel, Alex and Sara reached the side doors they were already wide open thanks to those few who had made their way out to the safety of the courtyard. The waiter who had been accosted by Jean-Michel and Alex, still wearing his t-shirt gag finally freed himself from the little room, but, noticing the smoke and chaos, quickly returned inside, slamming the door tight.

Alex, Jean-Michel and Sara, who were now dressed in the same attire as many of the guests, rushed out to the safety of the long grass, but aided by the dark cover of the night, they decided to keep going. They ran past the courtyard, scrambling through the metal fence and out into the safe camouflage of the scrubland. Looking back they could still hear panic and screams in the distance behind them. People were stampeding over each other. Others were by now clambering into cars, desperate to escape.

Then a new noise, getting louder and louder, approached them from the opposite direction. Blue lights flashing and sirens blaring, a number of police cars marked *gendarmerie* appeared, travelling at high speed on the track to the house, blocking the escape of most of the cars parked outside the castle and adjoining house. They noticed headlights fast approaching from behind them and just managed to dive to safety as a large 4X4 vehicle sped past them across the stony hillside. 'You're idea of the phone call was brilliant timing,' said Alex looking at Sara as they lay on the dusty ground.

'There's one that got away,' said Sara.

'There'll be more... it's not over' said Jean-Michel.

'Well they will definitely struggle to explain what's been going on here... guns, bizarre costumes and at least one dead body,' said Sara. Alex held her tightly.

The shell, securely contained in Alex's zipped up pocket glowed its divine light. 'It's the shell, it's glowing,' said Sara.

'Let's get out of here.' Jean-Michel stood up waved his two friends on.

Thirteen

Rendezvous

By some incredible twist of fate they had managed to escape the chaos and mayhem of the chateau. Tired, but pumped with adrenalin, they reached the relative calm and safety of L'Hermitage where they were greeted by the frantic barks of a much relieved Pamplemousse coming from inside the house. Jean-Michel retrieved a small bunch of keys wrapped in a plastic bag from under a large granite stone. He approached the front door finding an envelope wedged tightly between the door and frame marked 'JM', which he quickly tucked into a pocket.

Once inside Jean-Michel was ambushed by his old canine friend. On finishing with his master, Pamplemousse darted headlong at Sara, licking her bruised face and neck in wild celebration, making her giggle out loud. Alex smiled. Jean-Michel slipped the lock on the front door, and with the shutters already closed tight, L'Hermitage was now relatively secure. Alex ran the kitchen sink tap, gently placing the shell in a large saucepan and watched it disappear in the cool water, lying invisible once more on the base of the pan.

'I'm getting changed,' said Jean-Michel as he disappeared upstairs, followed by Pamplemousse, only to soon return with towels and spare clothing, which he placed on the chair by the fireside so that the couple had something fresh to wear. 'Help yourselves to showers and whatever you need,' he said thoughtfully, bending down to light the already laid fire.

Sara chose some clothes and went off to shower, returning a few minutes later looking like a hillbilly with a red checked 'lumberjack' shirt and worn denim overalls. Alex laughed a little, which felt good.

With all that had taken place over the last few hours the three of them were shattered but struggling to relax. Alex returned from the shower to find Jean-Michel treating Sara's battered face with a small bottle of oil from a little homemade wooden stand he kept in the house. The little rack was full of bottles with different essential oils and remedies Jean-Michel had made from the various herbs and plants he had gathered from the Languedoc hills. He passed the cotton wool to Alex, who continued to treat Sara's face as he explained how he had learnt the art of herbalism over the years, which was his attempt at shifting their attention and hopefully calming the nerves a little.

But it made little difference to Alex, who interrupted Jean-Michel in mid flow. 'So it's all true; the shell, the history, the DVK, the future of the world. Everything you said is completely true.' He paused and looked straight at Jean-Michel awaiting the inevitable reply as the shocking reality began to hit home.

With a silent subdued nod, Jean-Michel confirmed that it was. Putting away his ointments and swabs he spoke to them like a father protecting his young. 'We need to let things settle a little, my friends. You two had better stay here tonight.' Sara and Alex both agreed that was a good idea, they felt safe and secure around Jean-Michel, and completely trusted him with their lives now. 'How you both managed to keep clear heads, think on your feet and pull off that amazing stunt, swapping De Vlinder's body for yours, Sara I will never quite get my head around, other than I know it completely validates your custodianship of the shell.'

'Jean-Michel, it was nothing that you would not have done for a woman... and child... that you loved,' revealed Alex, recalling in his head the scene of stabbing De Vlinder with the syringe and rescuing his love, just as the words and vision of his mother had guided him to do in the split second he thought his life was over. 'Congratulations!' Jean-Michel smiled and nodded on realising the joyful news of Sara's pregnancy, then breathed a heavy sigh as the smile on his face turned to a sad, almost forlorn downward gaze.

Sara looked at her husband lovingly and took his hand in hers. And in that moment they both shared a vision of a baby cradled in their arms and knew instinctively there was still hope.

Wine flowed and the recent traumatic episode at the Chateau and blurred recollections of miracles began to calm in the minds of the three. With the effects of a powerful combination of relief, tiredness and alcohol now hitting home, they finally started to unwind and relax. It was around 6am, not long before dawn, when Jean-Michel produced spare bedding from an old chest of drawers, bid them goodnight and wearily clambered up the wooden staircase to the sanctuary of his small mezzanine bedroom. He was followed as usual, by the pitter-patter of four hairy legs as Pamplemousse toddled up right behind him.

Feeling safe and secure on the solid floor of the house, cuddling in front of a warm healing fire, the young couple held each other tightly and kissed. 'You know it's still unbeli...' Alex stopped mid-sentence as the soft purr of Sara's gentle snoring overshadowed his words. She had succumbed to a blend of alcohol and exhaustion, which Alex deduced was now combined with the residual traces of De Vlinder's sedative.

Alex lay there slowly drifting off as his thoughts struggled to make sense of everything. What had taken place was all very real, yet beyond the confines of his conditioned mind, and therefore incredibly hard for him to accept. It had happened, but still it made no sense. Like a mind-blowing drug induced 'trip' of a dream, a weary Alex found fact and fiction dissolving into a confused unsolvable blur.

Alex awoke to the intermittent flash of a glowing light coming from the back of the house. At first he believed it was coming from a torch beam outside, and panicked, thinking, *'oh shit someone's trying to get the shell.'* He leapt up from the homemade bed where Sara still lay dead to the world. Alex rubbed his blurry eyes, trying to focus. The glow came and went, and came and went, like a slow alternating flash from the beacon of a lighthouse. And yet the light seemed to make Alex feel paradoxically peaceful. Every five seconds or so, whenever the golden glow appeared, it lit up the end half the house like a Christmas tree.

Heart pumping nineteen to the dozen, Alex stepped forward towards the luminous energy and pulled back the kitchen curtain. He didn't need to go any further. From where he was standing, he could see that the halcyonic, pulsing light was coming from the metallic saucepan beside the sink. Approaching, with one hand now covering his eyes for protection, he cautiously peered into the water.

Sure enough, there was the shell opening and closing, appearing almost alive when open, as if trying to speak. As the shell opened it became visible, even under water, and as it shut it completely vanished again. Carefully he took the shell in his hands, lifting it out of its watery haven. As soon as he did, the figure of a man appeared at the back of the small kitchen.

At first Alex was shocked, but quickly calmed when he realised it to be the very same spirit who had spoken to him and Sara in Clamouse. Alex looked into his vibrant lifelike eyes, as the man began to speak once more. 'Alex, you're task here is not finished. When the two become one and the shell is in its rightful home, then, and only then, will all be accomplished...' With that the apparition departed, and as it did, the shell stopped glowing, giving the little house over to the opaque dark of night once more.

The next thing Alex was aware of was the warmth of sunlight on his face. It must have all been a dream he thought, as he came to from a deep sleep. But all it took was a glance across the bedding to the bruised face of his wife and the realisation that he was clutching the golden shell in his hand to understand it was far from a dream.

Alex rubbed his eyes with the palms of both hands, and squinted in reaction to a bright beam of light in the room. The shutters of the living room were partially open, and the room was beginning to fill with the healing warmth of daylight. Alex could hear Jean-Michel talking to Pamplemousse outside, telling him what had happened, 'But I will never leave you my friend…I will always be with you.' The dog whimpered a response as if to say 'I hope so'. Alex thought it best to leave Sara asleep, and made his way outdoors to join Jean-Michel and Pamplemousse.

'Plenty of coffee in the cafetière. Just made it, help yourself,' said a jovial Jean-Michel. Alex smiled wrinkling his brow wondering how and why Jean-Michel could be so happy after all they'd been through. 'When you're ready, we're taking a little trip.'

'But wh…' began Alex, both a little startled and confused.

'No questions Alex, just follow,' said Jean-Michel assuredly, as an infectious grin spread across his sun tanned face. With impeccable timing, Pamplemousse barked and wagged his tail furiously in agreement, which caused them both to chuckle.

So Alex woke Sara, and they drank coffee together, as Alex explained the unexpected idea of Jean-Michel's little jaunt. Jean-Michel made sure that Pamplemousse had sufficient food and water before explaining that they were all going out for a while. He stroked and calmed his friend, and put him at ease before getting him to lie down in his small wicker basket. As they prepared to leave, Alex made absolutely sure to secure the shell, which he placed most deliberately in the large inner pocket of his borrowed jacket, zipped tight for safe measure.

Locking L'Hermitage Jean-Michel voiced the fact that they had a fair way to travel, and suggested picking up the rental car still parked outside the couple's holiday cottage. They trusted the grey-haired old man implicitly, and knew they no longer needed to question his plans or his motives. Setting off slowly across the countryside, the stillness in the air was almost deafening. There was no evidence of what had occurred the previous night, and it struck them as substantially odd that nothing looked out of place in the aftermath.

Arriving at their cottage, Alex retrieved the key which he'd stashed in the hanging basket and entered with Sara, who was keen to change into the habitual comfort of her own clothes. Returning with the car keys to the waiting Jean-Michel, Alex clicked the central locking tab on the rectangular key. 'Where are we going?' asked Sara, who imagined it must be the local police station.

'Just wait and see…' replied Jean-Michel with a twinkle in his eyes as they all climbed into the rental car.

Along the track they drove, following the old man's directions by crossing the Pont du Diable away from the village. They continued on, travelling down past Beziers then Narbonne, heading inland towards Carcassonne. At Carcassonne Jean-Michel navigated Alex down a smaller cross country route heading south through several small hamlets.

In the centre of one charming but seemingly deserted village, Jean-Michel sprang into life, blurting out further instructions, 'Pull over and park here and wait. You're perfectly safe; I'll only be a few minutes.' He patted Alex firmly on his shoulder as he climbed out of the car and disappeared inside a pretty house, in the street called 'Maison L'Orchidée'.

'What's he up to?' asked Sara.

Inside the bed and breakfast, after speaking with the friendly proprietor, Jean-Michel was stood in front of a door with a sign on saying 'Asie'. He breathed heavily and shrugged his shoulders nervously before knocking. No reply. He knocked again. The key rattled in the lock, as the door opened and there stood Lucette. 'So wonderful to see you,' Lucette greeted her old love, looking deep into Jean-Michel's eyes. No denying the spark between them, which hadn't altered in all those years. 'So you got my note then?' Jean-Michel nodded, tears in his eyes, reciprocating her tender smile with a huge grin. Lucette placed her hands on his forearms and leaned in to kiss him on both cheeks. 'I guessed you were all busy. I went to the holiday cottage last night, then to L'Hermitage and still no sign... so I came back here.'

Jean-Michel looked at her quizzically. She took hold of his arm and without further hesitation began to walk to the car. 'Come on let's go and talk with Alex and Sara, there's lots to discuss isn't there?' said the wise woman with a youthful glint in her eye.

Alex was quite astounded to see who was with Jean-Michel, he got out of the car smiling, though baffled. 'Lucy... what are you doing here?' Lucette smiled, and, letting go of her old flame, she approached Alex and gave him a huge hug.

She stood back as if admiring a child she hadn't seen in years who was now all grown up, 'Come now, can't be that much of a shock, I did say I would like to visit, remember'. Alex smiled.

By now Sara was out of the car too and Lucette hugged her affectionately. A knowing smile between the two women seemed to be all that was needed, as Lucette gently stroked Sara's cheek all too aware of the bruises, but knowing she was safe now. Lucette suggested they find a nice quiet place for lunch where they could talk. She directed them out of the village and after about ten minutes they arrived at Preixan. There they followed Lucette into 'Le Relais de Preixan' and sat on the sunny terrace protected from the sun by rolls of bamboo roofing and green parasols. It was there, in privacy that Lucette explained about the vivid dreams she'd been having.

She knew far more than any of them expected. That was one of the reasons why she had suggested Alex and Sara visit Jean-Michel in the first place. She had seen into the future, through her dreams. She knew about the shell, its history and even some detail of the recent goings on at the ruined Chateau.

'So why did you wait to come until now?' asked Alex.

'Because there was so much work to do which had to be done by the three of you alone... it was not part of my journey,' she said, tenderly reaching her arm out to lay her hand reassuringly on his.

They continued eating and talking for hours, sharing their stories. When it got to Alex's description of Jean-Michel getting shot he was stopped dead in his tracks by a cutting look from Jean-Michel as if to say 'not now'.

Having shared so much good food, wine and extraordinary experiences, Lucette was definite about the meal being her 'treat' and left a decent tip as was always her way. They all returned to the rental and set off once more, now driving through the deserted vineyards. 'I knew that my role in this was to help you complete the next phase,' announced Lucette proudly after a comfortable silence.

'The next phase?' quizzed Sara.

'To help solve the problem of the shell, Sara,' Lucette smiled.

'Problem?' Now it was Alex's turn to play 'twenty questions'.

'Listen *mon cher*, you don't think you can walk about with a ticking time bomb in your pocket forever do you?' Lucette raised her eyebrows at Alex, as if he should have known better. And with that a golden glow radiated from the shell, he was still holding, filling the car with light.

'It's been doing that a lot recently,' Alex commented.

'That's because the window that Hanussen talked of applies to us too,' piped up Jean-Michel, who had been quiet for some time, clearly deep in thought. 'Remember what he said, *You will find and lose the power of the shell, but in time it can be yours once more. That very same year, the year of the sheep, between the passing of the Draconids and the Orionids, a unique window of opportunity will open...* Well the Draconids meteor shower passed ten days ago. And, if he was right, we now have less than thirty-six hours until the Orionid meteor stream begins,' explained Jean-Michel.

'So you're saying we've only got a day and a half to completely solve the enigma of the shell?' queried an anxious Alex, pulling rather forcefully on his pony tail. Jean-Michel nodded. 'And what if we don't?' Alex's wide eyed glare made it clear he was far more than just a little worried.

'Then the world as we know it will plunge into the abyss... and a living hell on Earth will begin. Chaos is coming.' said Jean-Michel as an eerie silence filled the car and the shell once again let out another burst of light, as if to confirm all he had said was perfectly true.

'But there's still time to act. Listen, the only way to solve it, is together. This isn't a Hollywood film, this is here and now and very real, and it's down to us. It's not about a hero saving the day, it's about all of us, together, sharing what we know and feel to uncover an authentic and lasting solution,' said Sara quite calmly, and almost philosophically.

'Exactly my dear,' Lucette affirmed in a supportive and positive manner, patting Sara on the knee as she spoke.

They continued driving, till they got back to the B&B where everyone helped Lucette with her numerous bags. Sara smiled as she looked about the bedroom decorated with pink Chinese looking fans and bright lanterns. 'A bit glary...' whispered Sara to Alex. Alex simply smiled.

'Can you both take these down to the car' said Lucette 'and we'll finish off ...'

'No problem... we'll meet you down there,' replied Alex.

'We'll only be a few minutes,' said Lucette looking at Jean-Michel lovingly.

Alex carried her largest suitcase down from the bedroom and Sara balanced a stack of presents which made visibility difficult. In that moment it struck Sara that Lucette was always generous and kind, and how that spirit of giving was the reason for Lucette's almost perpetual happiness. Carefully placing the luggage and gifts in the car boot, they decided to return to reception and get a couple of cold drinks. They sat in a small lounge area waiting for Jean-Michel and Lucette to finish packing.

In the bedroom, the couple held hands and looked at each other lovingly as Jean-Michel moved slowly forward, kissing Lucette tenderly. 'I have always loved you,' said Lucette looking fulfilled.

'And I...I have never loved anyone else,' replied Jean-Michel as they kissed once more and held each other in their arms swaying to and fro in perfect harmony.

Downstairs, Alex and Sara watched as shocking news was announced on the television in the salon.

'...*a giant earthquake has hit the west coast of the United States of America causing unparalleled chaos and loss of life. First reports indicate that the 9.6 magnitude super-quake is the strongest and most devastating quake mankind has ever recorded. For many miles around buildings have been flattened, and both the Golden Gate and Oakland Bay Bridges have been seriously damaged. Latest reports say witnesses looked on in disbelief as the Golden Gate Bridge shook and twisted like a broken toy before crashing down into the ocean. The super-quake also caused a deadly tsunami attaining estimated wave heights exceeding eighty metres. The tsunami hit the west coast mounting the natural protective barriers of the Presidio cliffs, surging up across the tablelands eastward into northern San Francisco facing San Francisco Bay. Latest reports suggest major problems with huge backflows in the surrounding river systems. The devastation has prompted the authorities to prepare all citizens living within a thirty mile radius of the San Francisco Bay Area to evacuate and to get to high land as quickly as possible. Water supply is bound to become infected and people are advised not to use tap water. The authorities are asking people to keep calm, pull together and help one another in this devastating crisis. The epicentre is believed to have been in the Gulf of the Farallones mid-way between San Francisco and the Farallon Islands. As to the cause, accusations are rife with many blaming authorities for using the area as a nuclear waste dump. It is estimated that at least 50,000 steel drum containers have been dumped in the area...*'

'My God, Jean-Michel was right, it's catastrophic,' Sara said, unable to hide her reaction to the inconceivable news.

'Well I can't say I'm shocked,' said Alex, rather too clinically for Sara's liking, who glared at him, registering her disapproval. Attempting to explain his seemingly callous comment he continued, 'Mankind has raped and pillaged the Earth for greedy and selfish reasons for so long, for far too long. You can't simply suck the life out of your habitat and expect it to retain a lasting healthy balance.

'Banncchhh' the sound of something hitting the floor behind them caused the nervous Alex and Sara to look round, only to find Jean-Michel and Lucette standing in the room, suitcases by their sides.

'It's time' said Lucette with tears in her beautiful hazel eyes.

'In more ways than one, there's little time left,' commented Jean-Michel. Somewhat subdued, they made their way to the car parked outside.

'I have a strong feeling we need to visit the abbey before we leave. It might give us some peace, or maybe we could all pray for guidance?' said Lucette thoughtfully.

'Why not?' replied Alex, half hoping that he would be able to empty his mind and see clearly what steps to take from here, if any.

It wasn't long before they were mounting the stone stairs to the abbey's entrance, finding themselves in a simple shop-like area with a middle-aged woman sat behind a desk selling entry tickets. They paid their admission fees to the affable bespectacled lady and entered the Abbey of St Hilaire. They toured the beautiful buildings, stopping at brief intervals to digest the information posted around the site including passages on Charlemagne and the crusades against the Cathars. Sara loved the small central flower shaped fountain, Alex, the old chessboard engraved on a solid block of stone. The stunning fourteenth century cloisters consisted of fifty-four pointed arches separated by double columns, each decoratively carved.

As they explored the dark and dingy cellar of the West Gallery, they recalled the De Morreze's dinner party and the story of how the monks had created Blanquette de Limoux, the first sparkling wine in 1531. 'Hey, doesn't that look like you?' Alex asked Sara.

'No. But that one looks like you,' said Sara as they stood in front of the painted spandrel of the north gallery.

'Yes, it's two angels, sent to protect the world from calamity!' said Jean-Michel from behind them.

Leaving Jean-Michel and Lucette sitting quietly overlooking the courtyard, the young couple continued their tour around the cloisters. Sara twigged, 'It was here... here in this place that Charlemagne's men reburied Mariam Magdalana.'

Alex's eyes lit up, 'Yes, the twelfth pillar, the sarcophagus...'

Farther around the cloisters lay the simple stone sarcophagus embedded in the floor. 'Look, here it is,' said Sara excitedly.

'And here, opposite...' said Alex moving towards the pillars of the cloisters, 'is... yes, look!' The emblem of the pillar had been hacked off just as Jean-Michel had told them.

'To think the body of Magdalana was here,' Sara said in awe and wonder.

'Everything he said... everything!' remarked Alex, wincing as he recalled how he had originally misjudged Jean-Michel's incredible tale. They turned and looked across at Jean-Michel who nodded in humble acknowledgement.

Lucette and Jean-Michel gathered themselves and calmly entered the Abbey Church, the burial place of Saint Sernin, which was marked by an impressive white marble sarcophagus. It was almost the opposite of the simple unmarked sarcophagus in the cloisters, but somehow and in some ways far less in meaning. Jean-Michel and Lucette sat in the wooden pews, heads bowed, their hands locked in a loving embrace.

After a while, Alex and Sara entered the Abbey Church and the four sat silently together in a form of group prayer. Not a word was said, there was nothing to say. The shell, now safe in Alex's pocket glowed several times in the stillness.

Time was running out. Alex broke the silence as he was drawn to get up and walk over to the impressive ivory coloured sarcophagus of Saint Sernin. He felt there was something to discover there, something beckoning him, calling him closer. It was like a voice but inaudible, like a signpost but invisible and yet it was definitely there, he could feel it deeply and unquestionably. He was joined by Sara as they studied the white marble sculpture depicting the martyrdom of the saint.

Aloud, Sara read the information hanging on the wall, 'In 250 AD Saturninus, the first Bishop of Toulouse met with a violent death for refusing to worship pagan gods. Roped to a sacrificial bull by a mob gathered on the steps of the Capitoline Temple in Toulouse, St. Sernin was dragged down the main street to his death. The saint's body was buried by the local Christian community in secret...' she paused taking it all in, then continued, 'The Abbey of St. Sernin in Toulouse attracted many pilgrims from the start, but its importance increased enormously after the Emperor Charlemagne donated a quantity of holy relics to it, as a result of which it became an important stop for pilgrims on their way to Santiago de Compostela, and a pilgrimage location in its own right. Visitors poured in with the rise of the pilgrimage to Santiago de Compostela in the early eleventh century.' She turned to her husband, 'Sounds like a familiar story doesn't it Ali?'

Alex didn't respond. He was standing gazing at the stone water font carved out in the wall to the side of the white marble sarcophagus. In contrast, it was a simple stone basin, but it intrigued Alex for a couple of reasons. The first reason was, it was exactly opposite Miriam's stone sarcophagus on the far side of the wall, and secondly it was in the shape of a shell, a scallop shell. 'Is it here, is it here where the shell is meant to be. That would make sense, this is Magdalana's final resting place,' Alex wanted to be right, but an uneasy feeling in the pit of his stomach indicated he wasn't.

'Yes and no,' said Jean-Michel, 'this is a burial site of Magdalana, but as you are aware, it's not the original site.'

'And what about the *two into one*?' Alex was chomping at the bit.

'Do you think we need to get to Rennes-le-Chateau then?' asked Sara.

'What do we all feel?' asked Lucette encouraging them all to hold hands in a small circle, in an intuited sacred silence. After a few minutes, they opened their eyes simultaneously and nodded in complete agreement. They quickly made their way out of the abbey, through the cloisters, stopping momentarily to honour and acknowledge the empty stone sarcophagus as they passed it on their way to the exit.

With the aid of Jean-Michel's explicit directions they travelled south through Limoux and within forty minutes arrived on the outskirts of Rennes-le-Chateau. They continued travelling south for a few minutes as directed, until Jean-Michel signalled to Alex, who pulled over bringing the car to an abrupt halt on an agricultural track just to the side of the narrow and winding country road. The land was brimming with light and colour, and an inexplicable serenity permeated the air. It reminded Sara of the Holy Land, but with greenery.

'This way,' Jean-Michel waved them on. In silent expectation the group crossed the dry landscape, crossing a quaint archaic stone bridge leading over a babbling brook, underneath which the pure crystalline water washed over a multitude of brightly coloured pebbles. 'That's why they call this the Stream of Colours,' said Jean-Michel, gesturing his open hand towards the beck. Everything appeared so animated, vibrant and alive. A small pyramid shaped pile of sandy coloured stones sat to one side of the track.

The hilltop village of Rennes-le-Chateau was now visible, as was the striking red sand hill in the distance. The sound of chirping crickets and chattering birds filled the air as they descended the semi-parched scraggy hillside overhanging the crystal clear stream below. They carefully crossed a narrow ledge of white reflective stone before Jean-Michel came to an abrupt halt and pointed ahead to a small but almost perfectly formed opening on the rocky hillside surrounded by trees. 'The locals call this the Grotte du Fournet but it is known as the burial place of Mary or Magdalana's Cave. This place has been violated many, many times by hordes of treasure hunters at Rennes-le-Château. But they weren't looking for what we're looking for, and they didn't know what we know,' explained an upbeat Jean-Michel. 'Anyone got a light?' he asked, but as Alex stepped up to volunteer with his mobile complete with flashlight app, the shell in his pocket briefly opened. It was a sign. They were in the right place.

It was an amazing feeling. It was here that Miriam Magdalana's body was buried and eventually discovered by Charlemagne's men. It was here the shell was recovered more than twelve hundred years ago. One by one they ducked their heads and entered the cave, hoping for a sign or at least some form of acknowledgement or encouragement. The malachite residue rising from the floor gave the cavern a strange green hue, while several low nooks and crannies led off intriguingly at various angles from the main chamber.

Alex volunteered crawling down the holes to ensure a thorough search. Lucette had a better idea, 'I suggest we do the same here as we did in the Abbey'. They were all in agreement. They had a combined sense they could only solve the dilemma of the shell if their collective intention was pure and unadulterated by desire, greed and ego. So they stood in a small circle, hand in hand, sensing what they could and what they should do. Time was running out and they were still none the wiser. Something was obstructing them.

'There's nothing here,' Alex said out of the blue.

'No you're right Alex,' confirmed Jean Michel quite defini-
tively.

'Well it feels great just being here,' said Sara.

'Mmm... So peaceful and so beautiful,' agreed Lucette.

So they exited the grotto and sat outside on the sun-baked
white stone for a while taking in the beautiful scenery. Sara and
Lucette discussed the what's, where's and why's of the situation.
Jean-Michel looked out across the valley and listened in silence.
Alex impatiently expelled the air from his chest, loudly
commanding everyone's attention. 'Look, how can you talk like
it's just another day, or sit there doing nothing. We're running out
of time, this is just hopeless,' he said and kicked out at a nearby
rock which sent it tumbling down the steep slope until it disappeared from view. The disappointment he felt was met by a stony
silence, for they all understood his frustration and anger.

The silence was broken by a shocked and inquisitive Lucette.
'Mon Dieu, just look at that!' Behind the pretty backdrop of
Rennes-le-Chateau a Cimmerian mass of cloud was rapidly
approaching from the north as a gargantuan storm moved ever
closer.

'Time to move, let's go,' said Jean-Michel. Sara grabbed Alex's
hand as they made their way back to the car. It can't have been
more than a second or two after they clambered into the vehicle
that the skies opened and the rain started bucketing down, the
persistent noise of the water striking the roof reminiscent of an
unnerving and violent burst of gunfire. So the weary deflated
group travelled back silently through the turbulent winds and
rain. On the way, occasional glances and looks were shared but
not much more.

Arriving at L'Hermitage, they were met by the ever consistent
celebration of Pamplemousse. As they removed some of their wet
clothes, a vaguely hopeful rather than optimistic Alex lifted the
shell from his inner pocket, but was greeted by a stony silence.

He placed the shell on the mantelpiece. Jean-Michel winced as he knelt down to light the fire.

It was now early evening. They sat having a simple warm dinner around the old wooden table, with candles and cosy fire lighting up the room. Outside, the storm continued its relentless aggressive bombardment, which didn't help. It was evident Alex and Sara were both deflated, so shortly after the meal concluded, a positive Lucette suggested they join hands and share the energy of their intention, which was to somehow return the shell to its rightful home wherever that was.

Alex took the shell from above the fire and placed it in the middle of the table. One by one they put their hands on top of it. A long silence followed – still nothing. The lights flickered. Fifteen or twenty minutes passed before Lucette spoke, but when she did Alex was shocked, for the voice, though not Lucette's, was very familiar to him. 'It wasn't your fault; you share no guilt for my death, my darling boy. I know what you promised me, but it was my time to go. Thank you for the songs Alex, I do love you so very much,' the words flowed easily and lovingly from Lucette's mouth, but Alex could only see and hear his mother...

Tears welling up, he rubbed his eyes, and, assuming he was the only one to have heard what was said, he just lowered his head and asked quietly, 'How did you know that? No one knows about my last conversation or what I promised in hospital, or that I wrote her songs.' Lucette lifted his chin gently, looked into his misty eyes, smiling lovingly. Alex, who had never truly healed from the loss of his mother let his head drop again and wept. Sara put her arm around him as he sobbed, 'I promised to save her... but I couldn't.'

In the middle of the table, the shell glowed, opening suffi-ciently to bathe the entire room in a radiant golden bath of light. The four seemed unable to think or to reason logically as a heavenly peace permeated the room. 'The shell must return home, two into one,' said a voice as if from nowhere. They could all hear the words, but no one could be seen speaking them. Was the shell itself now talking? The mysterious male voice continued, 'This is the great adventure awaited so long, the awakening to a world of beauty and freedom of thought...liberation for all.'

Raising his head, eyes wet with tears and with a mixture of desperation, sadness and frustration in his voice Alex called out, 'But what do we have to do!'

'Two into one, two into one,' echoed the voice. The shell closed, the golden light was gone and the voice dissolved into the ether.

'Two into one' and 'the shell must return' floated around Alex's head, completely dominating his consciousness that night. He tried to empty his head and be really present, but there was too much swirling around in his mind. They finally managed to get some sleep, but Sara was worried about Alex who, accompanied by the battering noise of the rain, kept waking her up throughout the night with his feverish mutterings.

A bang on the door awoke them the following morning. Alex unlocked it to find two Gendarmes on the other side. Jean-Michel swiftly appeared, partly dressed, and approached the doorway as Alex backed off. Pamplemousse yapped. Pulling the door to behind him, Jean-Michel stepped outside with the two officers.

The rain had finally stopped but the sky was dark and stormy. A concerned Alex could hear the officers asking questions, but couldn't quite make out the exact words. At his feet, a nosey Pamplemousse whined and scratched at the door. The questioning went on for some time before Jean-Michel bid them farewell and the officers went on their way down across the windy hillside.

Jean-Michel came back inside, his hair astray, like the Wild Man of Borneo, and explained the reason for the visit. 'They were just making enquiries about the other night. I told them we know nothing and heard nothing; they appear to have believed me. It's best we keep out of that mess.'

No one could actually eat much breakfast, but they all downed coffee until it was coming out of their ears. Jean-Michel turned on his old valve radio which reported updates of the super-quake in the US. Shaking his head, he turned it off realising that it was another disheartening distraction which would serve no purpose at that point. 'It must be linked to the cave, the pool, the altar, the engraving in the wall. I reckon we've just got to take the shell there,' said Alex tying the bright pan-African coloured hairband around his long fibre-like tresses, and pulling resolutely in an attempt to convince himself and the others to take action.

'Yes, the words of Sebastian Cavalles's father *Now take it son, take the box, get to the cave, go into the Cathédrale du Temps, and you'll know what to do when you get there*, perhaps that's the place,' Jean-Michel said animatedly. Pamplemousse barked.

'Of course, coming home to Clamouse,' echoed Sara.

'It's got to be worth a try,' Lucette said encouragingly.

'Remember, we only have until tonight to find the resting place,' Jean-Michel reminded them, deliberately attempting to motivate the group by looking each of them in the eyes, which inspired and heartened them and simultaneously reminded them of the time which was fast ebbing away.

They left immediately, with Pamplemousse leading the way. Once outside, the sinister threatening hue of the normally idyllic Languedoc sky unnerved them all. Occasional squalls struck the now desolate looking hillside causing them all great difficulty in keeping their balance as they laboriously made their way towards the cave entrance. This was followed by the unwelcome arrival of rain, rapidly and chaotically cascading around them, striking their hands and faces in a bitter relentless onslaught.

Upon reaching the sanctum of the thick walled solid stone building, Jean-Michel placed Pamplemousse carefully in one of the hessian sacks, fastened it securely to his solid back, and down the well and into the caves they all went. Along the route, they walked slowly owing to the unusual amount of water present in the caves. Arriving at the Cathédrale du Temps with the pool and stone altar, they stopped.

Alex tried everything he could think of. First he put the shell back in the water and repeated aloud the Latin words carved in the cave wall – nothing. Next they tried placing the shell into the scallop engraving in the wall, but it simply dropped out. For a further half hour they explored every option plausible, but still no success. Tired and worn out, Alex and Sara sat on the floor as the shell partially opened once more, giving off a beautiful light. For a few seconds they were hopeful that some miraculous solution was going to occur, but the shell simply shut tight once more.

Outside the skies were ominously dark, and it was raining again, so fast and so heavily that the streams and rivers were swelling and rising. The penetrating rain was now flooding in from all directions, causing the water level in Clamouse to rise rapidly. 'Go...' said Jean-Michel, 'now, and I mean right now!'

The way back up to the tunnel was treacherous. Water poured through every crack and seam of the cave. Jean-Michel held Lucette's arm and Alex supported Sara. Out of the blue Sara lost her footing, and as Alex struggled to hold her, he fell backwards, accidentally freeing the shell from his deep pocket. It tumbled into the gushing water. 'Jesus H...,' shouted Alex as he secured Sara on a protruding rock and flopped down into the gushing stream which was now more than a metre deep.

Jean-Michel, Lucette and Pamplemousse carried on ahead, oblivious of the unfolding nightmare. Sara sat stranded on the rock face, watching on in trepidation as the waters continued to rise by the second. Alex had disappeared under the surface, and in his desperation to find the shell which had been carried by the powerful current of the flood, he had cracked his head on the side wall of the cave and was now lying unconscious in a small cavern set off from the main cave, which was rapidly being filled by the surging torrent.

In the darkness, Alex was captivated by the exquisite shimmer of an unusual light. He had a vague sense that he should be helping Sara, but was becoming overwhelmed by the power of the light emanating from the end of the tunnel. He was drawn like a moth to a flame; the beckoning glow seemed an inevitable destination. It was as if the celestial light was not just a home or even another home, but *the* home. The closer he got to it, the more beautiful it felt and the less interest in worldly things he had. In fact all his worries seemed to fall away, and even the fact in physical terms that he was drowning seemed a vague dream, and in a sense entirely untrue.

Alex approached the blinding light, raising his hands to shield his eyes as he stepped forward into the powerful luminescence. What he found was most unexpected. He seemed to be falling, spiralling downwards in a wormhole, catching glimpses and sights of his own life, and that of those who came before him. At one point, the face of his beloved mother smiled at him, but floated away in a whirling mass of sounds and memories. Then in an instant it all ended as he was 'snapped' into the body of a cloaked man holding an oil lamp.

The spacious candlelit room was constructed with large blocks of stone, resembling a fortified medieval manor or castle. He was standing in a crowd of similarly dressed folk gathered around what appeared to be a dying man. The man was being given the 'last rites' but to Alex's surprise, not by a male priest but by a woman. She wore a purple gown with an ornamental thread tied around her waist, holding the garment in place. *'Benedicite, Benedicite, Domine Deus, Pater bonorum spirituum, adjuva nos in ommibus quae facere voluerimus.* (Bless us, bless us, O Lord God, the Father of the spirits of good men, and help us in all that we wish to do)', she recited lifting a leather bound book and touching it on the dying man's forehead. 'Do you forgive and pardon your wrongdoers, love your enemies, pray for those who accuse you, turn your cheek to those who aggress you and neither judge nor condemn anyone.'

The dying man faintly whispered, 'I have this will and determination. God give me strength.'

The priestess continued, 'In the beginning was the Word, and the Word was with God, and the Word was God. All things were made by him; and without him was not anything made that was made. In him was life; and the life was the light of men. And the light shineth in darkness; and the darkness comprehended it not. There was a man sent from God, whose name was John. The same came to bear witness of the Light, that all men through him might believe the true Light, which lighteth every man that cometh into the world.'

She bent over the dying man asking if he had any last request. Now barely alive, and struggling to breathe, the man harnessed the final remnants of energy he could to speak 'These are not my words, but the words of Spirit. Humankind must remember... remember the way of the soul. Who you are, the Christ within us all, must not be overlooked or forgotten, for therein lies the destiny of mankind and the kingdom of heaven. So this may come to pass, the divine key – this gift, is left here to remind you. Please God, may it rest with me in Gellone.'

A silence filled the underground stone room. The priestess took the shell from the between the man's clasped hand and turned away towards the far wall. The woman returned to the dead man's side, gently kissing both his cheeks. Then, just as the crowd turned to kiss each other, Alex's dream like attention was broken by a feeling; a feeling that was quickly joined by a voice, and yet it wasn't a voice. It was a light, a golden light inevitably calling him.

Within seconds he found himself being spun violently and as his eyes opened he could just make out the shimmering light. He summoned what strength of mind and body he had and stretched his arm towards the light, struggling to succeed. As his hand touched the light, he grasped his fingers around the light and pushed upward, which was his natural inclination. As he did, his head appeared above the water line, and as his hand rose out of the water, he could see... he had the shell.

'Alex! Alex!' screamed a distraught Sara, now stranded, surrounded by the unforgiving ferocious water. Forcing his way back against the power of the deluge, he fought with all his might, drawn from the depths of his being to answer the distress call. There on the large rock, now greatly swamped in the on rushing tide was Sara. Grabbing her, shell in the other hand, he pulled her into the killer current. Alex and Sara were almost submerged. There seemed no way out.

'Whatever you do, don't let go, and take a big breath,' said Alex. 'I love you, with all my heart,' said Sara.

'Me t...' but before he could finish they disappeared into the powerful swirling current. Water flowed outside Clamouse, pouring down the hillside and across the road leading to the village. At a crossroad in the cavern, the flow seemed to change and was now pulling and pushing the two human bodies faster and faster.

In the little stone guard house, Jean-Michel and Lucette watched as the water level in the tunnel continued to rise. Jean-Michel had tried to return, but the oncoming force of the water was so great, the pressure had forced him back. They sat peering over the circular rim of the well, hoping, praying. As the water continued to rise, the panic stricken whines of Pamplemousse reflected how Jean-Michel and Lucette felt, as they were beginning to think the worst. The last lamps were extinguished as the flood of water rose up the well and began overflowing into the building.

Lucette and Jean-Michel looked at each other. Lucette held

her hands in prayer, as Jean-Michel held his strong arm around her. Water poured out under the stone barn door. Outside, the apocalyptic storm was still raging, as the chilling sight and sound of thunder and lightning dominated the entire landscape.

Then out of the depths of the well, a hand reached out. Jean-Michel and Lucette grabbed the trembling limb and pulled. It was Sara. Lucette held her tight as Jean-Michel looked downwards. Nothing. Sara was in shock and wailing. The dark waters of the cave had taken Alex. Jean-Michel dived head first into the well, and disappeared. The electric lights tripped, as the water poured in from between the canal roof tiles which could no longer cope with the sheer volume of water and into the switch. Everything was dark, void of all hope. Jean-Michel appeared at the surface of the well and shook his head.

Alex's body had been dragged and pulled by the surging waters towards the old entrance that Jean-Michel had sealed with lime and sand when he restored the stone buildings, the same exit Pamplemousse had discovered, and the same entrance that Sebastian Cavalles had entered all those years ago. Alex was pushed with such force against the lime sealed exit that a small flow of water escaped. Alex kicked with all his might, again and again, even striking the man-made wall with the shell, before the stones finally gave way and he was carried out of the tunnel onto the hillside by the sheer force of the current.

Meanwhile Jean-Michel, Lucette and Sara had no option but to leave with Sara clinging onto Lucette for comfort. The gargantuan storm was still raging, and the sky lit up with strange colours and shapes as multiple forks of electricity bolted out from the dark mass of cloud above. In the flashing lightning, out of the corner of his eye, Jean-Michel spotted a lifeless corpse amongst the fallen rubble.

Water still poured from the hole, causing him to slip and slide as he made his way towards the opening. 'It's Alex! He's not breathing, he's not breathing!' Lucette and Sara ran towards the two men. Sara clutched Alex tightly as Jean-Michel placed his hand over Alex's chest and closed his eyes. Alex lay motionless. Jean-Michel moved him on to his side and struck his back forcefully. Several times he tried to resuscitate him, but it was over.

Sara looked at Jean-Michel and shouted angrily, 'No...why? Why!' as Lucette held the grieving widow in her arms to console her as best she could. After all they'd been through, it had come to this. Lucette tried to ease Sara away from the body, but she shook and struggled to maintain her vice-like grip on Alex's hand, not wanting to give up on the man she loved.

Still clutched tightly in Alex's right hand, partly concealed by the mud and firmly wedged under his body, the shell opened a little and a golden light surrounded them. A spluttering sound cut right through the tension as liquid spewed up and out of Alex's mouth and his eyes flickered before fully opening. He coughed loudly clearing his lungs. 'Alex, oh Alex,' said Sara throwing herself upon him. Alex, exhausted beyond belief, looked deep in Sara's eyes. 'I thought you were...' Sara, tears streaming down her face, was unable to say anymore.

Fourteen

Belief

Alex awoke to voices muttering in the background. He felt warm, dry and comfortable – no stone chamber, no last rites, no rushing water… It must all have been a dream, so vivid and so real, but just a bizarre dream. Drawn to his left, he found solace in the warm glow of a smouldering fire, the dying embers and smoke breathing in unison, as if the fire itself were a living being. It was both relaxing and comforting, and because of his tiredness, nigh on hypnotic. Partially sitting up on his elbows, he looked over to where the noise was coming from at the back of the room and saw the shapes responsible for the muttering.

'…two into one… it just doesn't make any sense.'

'It has to, we're just not getting it.'

'The home of the shell…'

The shell, safe on the mantelpiece, glowed. Pamplemousse whined. Then Alex sat bolt upright, 'I know where we need to put the shell… where it belongs. I've seen the answer,' he announced excitedly. Pamplemousse barked enthusiastically as if to support him. 'Trust me… we need to go right now!' said Alex bursting with impatience.

Hurriedly dressing in the dry clothes Jean-Michel had already laid out for him, and grabbing the shell from above the fireplace, Alex snatched the keys from the kitchen table, and headed for the door. The others looked at one another in silence before following him, hoping for a miracle. With Pamplemousse in tow they jumped into the rental car still parked outside L'Hermitage and headed for St. Guilhem. Alex spurted out garbled bits of his story as he revealed details of what had actually happened to him in the depths of Clamouse. Sara tried to question him but Alex was having none of it. 'Listen, what I am saying is we need to get there, and get there now!' slamming his foot down on the accelerator, causing gravel to spray out from under the tyres, flying everywhere. Alex was in such a rush, he didn't even explain where 'there' was.

The roads into the village were almost deserted, thanks to the horrendous weather and rapidly fading daylight. 'Careful!' Lucette warned anxiously, hoping Alex would slow down and calm himself a little in the process. It didn't make any difference; Alex was driving like a man possessed.

Lightning bolts flashed across the darkening sky like tears of fire, causing an eerie, pulsating glow. Speeding as fast as they could down the winding country roads, past the treacherously sodden route at the Pont du Diable, Alex suddenly slammed on the brakes. They were almost opposite the main entrance to Clamouse, their passage was blocked. Water was gushing out across the road at various points in front of the car, and rocks and rubble lay strewn across the road, creating an impenetrable stone barrier. The force of the floods had created a rockslide completely blocking the route into St Guilhem.

The treacherous storm was intensifying, lightning now lit the sky for miles around, and just ahead a tree ached and strained, before it fell crashing down into the gorge. Several bushes and organic debris flew across the road at high speed, having been ripped from the ground with ease. It was hard to see ahead in the swirling chaos. The noise of the storm was getting louder and louder. 'Should we wait and sit this out?' asked Lucette, no longer worried about hiding her concern.

'We don't have time,' Alex snapped back.

Lucette looked at Alex, then at the others. 'But are you sure you know what you're doing?'

Alex slammed his fist down on the steering wheel. 'I am doing what I need to do,' he announced raising his voice to emphasise his conviction. Jean-Michel squeezed Lucette's hand.

Sara tried to calm the situation 'Alex is right, I know it's dangerous, but we don't have a choice.'

'Let's go,' said Jean-Michel calmly, almost as if he was unaware of the surrounding panic and chaos. With no other option open to them, they would have to make it on foot.

Alex clicked the driver's door handle, and began to climb out of the car, determined to get 'there' as quickly as possible. The force of the wind slammed the door hard against his legs, but he didn't react to the pain. He forced the door open, and stood up. A desperately worried Sara lent across and lowered the driver's side window, trying to catch him before it was too late. 'But Alex, where are we going?'

He turned calling, 'Just get to the abbey now!' Desperate to make his voice heard above the din of the storm. Alex was driven, pumped with adrenalin. He took off, first scrambling over the rocks blocking the route, then sprinted towards the village. He didn't look back. Pamplemousse barked as if pleading Alex to wait for them.

'Oh Jesus!' Sara shrieked as she struggled her way out of the car, desperately trying to catch up with him, while Jean-Michel, Lucette and Pamplemousse followed on behind as quickly as they could. Fighting the winds and rain, they struggled their way along the village road. In the distance the noise of a large explosion followed by a giant flash cut through the cacophony of the storm, shocking them all, except Alex who was in a world of his own.

Entering the village, which was now bathed in darkness, thanks to the power cut preventing any man-made light to shine, was like taking a step back in time, medieval time, the 'Dark Ages'. But the dense, quickly spreading cloak of obscurity was not solely due to the power cut, nor the sun disappearing over the horizon, for in the skies above the village blankets of menacing storm clouds suffocated the evening sky, shutting out any glimmer of light.

Unsurprisingly, the village square appeared deserted, apart

from the panicked voice of a cat scurrying for cover through the door of a creaking cat-flap. Alex crossed the square, past the immense solitary tree and closer to the abbey. Sara, still in tow, had given up calling his name and just tried with all her might to keep him in sight.

Soaked through and windswept, Alex arrived at the tower-like portal of the abbey clutching his abdomen, bending over and gasping for air, getting a few seconds much needed respite. Forcefully pushing the giant doors open, he stumbled inside, nearly collapsing as he entered the barely lit building. His eyes rapidly scouring the abbey, sweating profusely like an addict craving his fix. He was desperate to find what he was looking for, and clinging to the faint hope that the solution was there.

The intense concentration of his searching gaze was broken as Sara arrived running into the building, panting and out of breath. Alex, who was now half way down the right hand side of the building, turned and called to her, 'Look for a room, a separate chamber... that's what I saw, and we need to find it,' before rushing off to continue his search. Sara, filling with angst as the nightmarish feelings of her previous visit flooded back, moved as quickly as she could past the baptismal font on her left, clutching her stomach and mouth, barely looking at the grim reminder of the massacre.

On the far side of the abbey, Alex discovered an entrance which fed into a corridor leading to several further doors – he tried each of them, but they were all locked tight. He smashed his clenched fist hard against the hardwood barricade of the final door in frustration, and slumped to the cold tiled floor, his head bowed, dripping with sweat.

Sara was progressing quickly along the far side of the building, the little light she had at her disposal coming from votive candles placed before various statues of Jesus, the Virgin Mary and other Catholic saints. At the far end, she found the stone staircase she vaguely remembered from the last visit. It was pitch black.

'Over here Alex. This could be something,' she called out, at the same time grabbing two large unused candles from the candle rack and lighting them.

Alex was still slumped on the floor of the passage, exhaustion taking hold. Memories of his collapse a year ago were flashing through his mind, doubts and fear invaded his consciousness as he teetered on the edge of failure, gritting his teeth in frustration and despair. But Sara's echoing voice seemed to cut through the haze, breathing new life into him. Taking one more big breath, reaching out and gripping the door handle, he pulled himself up and made his way out of the corridor towards his wife standing on the far side of the abbey.

'Are you okay?' she asked looking at the approaching dishevelled figure. Alex nodded trying to keep it together, as Sara handed him a candle. Positioned at the top of the stairs, she stood lighting the stairway as best she could, holding the candle high above her head in one hand, and pointing down into the underground chamber with the other.

'This looks good,' said Alex as they descended the dark stairway into the catacombs. At the bottom of the staircase, Alex found himself virtually in the same spot he had been standing in his vision. But this time there was a padlocked iron grill protecting the ancient crypt. 'I don't believe it... this... this is... this is it,' shuddered Alex, 'Now we just need to get in...'

'I'll be back in a minute,' said Sara as she vanished up the stone stairwell. Alex stood transfixed, recalling what he had seen some hours before.

In the abbey, Sara had the foresight to collect several of the smaller votive candles, lighting up the route to the catacombs for Lucette and Jean-Michel. On the way back she grabbed a foot-tall statue of the Virgin Mary. When she returned Alex was still standing there in silence, vividly reliving what he had seen. 'Here, try this,' she said. Alex was unmoved. 'Alex, try this,' she repeated a little more forcefully handing him the solid statue.

He lifted it high above his head, and summoning what strength he had left, brought it crashing down onto the padlock. With a loud 'thwack' the head of the statue flew across the floor. The padlock was only slightly damaged and still fixed firmly in its place. 'It's no good, it's not strong enough,' said Alex impatiently, lowering the headless Virgin Mary, till she dangled upside down portraying a most forlorn and rather macabre sight.

But Sara was not about to give in and was off once again, in search of something more robust. 'Ah what the hell,' Alex made another attempt with the remaining body of the statue, and another, until all that was left was a brown base and two little peach coloured feet. Sara returned and slid the large metal crucifix between the bent and twisted clasp of the padlock, and together they pulled as hard as they could attempting to lever the damaged lock open.

Just at that moment a bark came out of the silence, and they both turned to find Pamplemousse standing at the top of the stone stairs yapping as if to ask what the hell was going in. Jean-Michel and Lucette appeared behind him and the three descended into the crypt. The crucifix bent, unable to compete with the old solid cast iron mechanism. Alex threw the crucifix across the stone floor outside the vaulted white stone funerary chapel.

'Stand back,' instructed Jean-Michel, urging Alex and Sara to give him some room. Taking a few seconds to quieten his mind and to focus his intention, Jean-Michel centred the energy within his body and with one concentrated quick kick to the metal door; it flew open as if it had never been locked in the first place. Even in the circumstances, they were all a little amazed. Lucette's eyebrows raised, and Pamplemousse panted and wagged his tail furiously. Finally they all entered the white limestone room. A sweet musty perfume filled the air, and it was remarkably dry considering it was underground. Alex walked over to the centre of the vaulted circular chapel, and briefly closed his eyes, trying to recapture everything he had seen in his vision.

'He lay here, the shell was taken from his hands,' Alex turned, painstakingly following the steps which the Liberae priestess had taken. 'We need more light,' said Sara, so Jean-Michel and Lucette moved closer holding the large candles. The direction Alex took led him to a small bay in the stone block wall and at the base of the carved niche was a scallop shaped stone recess with a slit above, looking like a vertical, elliptical letterbox or keyhole. Alex's jacket glowed. He fumbled for the zip, pulling out the shell from his inside pocket. It glowed again, opened slightly, then closed once more. Placing the shell on the base of the stone recess, it fitted perfectly and the shell glowed once more, but closed again, then nothing. Alex, shaking his head, looked bewildered 'It was here... I saw it with my own eyes ... I don't understand...'

Outside, the storm was creating havoc. Roof tiles, ripped from the local buildings flew through the air swirling on hurricane-like gusts of wind, were striking the abbey, thudding against the thick stone walls, disintegrating on impact. Electrical noises cascaded through the atmosphere as thunder cracked and lightning strikes lit up the dark abbey. A ferret-like figure gazed out from behind the immense Romanesque pillar on the far side of the abbey. Candle light reflected from the lenses of his spectacles, as the shadowy figure of Fritz Wicky crept closer. He had not given up, he was going to succeed. This was his chance. Sliding between the pews like a snake on the hunt, he stood to one side of the stone stairs, patiently listening, awaiting his window of opportunity.

Alex looked at his companions most apologetically. Sara, seeing he was on the verge of giving up, went to his side, clutching his hand. 'You can do it Alex.' but he still looked uncertain. Empty your mind, you'll know what to do,' she said looking right at him. Alex nodded, grateful for her optimism. He closed his eyes, taking several slow deep breaths, before opening his eyes again, shaking his head in frustration. He looked at Sara, who was unmoved, and nodding, encouraging him to try again.

It took a while until his mind became completely still. His senses seemed to expand and he could smell a familiar perfume in the air. Clear as a bell he heard the soft but firm tone of his mother's voice, 'Two into one, Alex, two into one.' Her smiling face appeared and in the background, Alex could see a man beckoning him closer, so he approached.

The man's voice was peaceful and calming as he looked into Alex's eyes and spoke, 'When you make the two into one, and when you make the inner as the outer, and the upper as the lower, and when you unite male and female as one... then you will enter.'

Sara reached forward to touch Alex, but Lucette, realising what she was intending, pulled her back. 'Don't break the energy of the trance,' she said looking at Sara, who nodded and backed off. Standing by his side, Marguerite, Alex's mother, placed her left hand in Alex's right hand, interlocking them, as if they were clasped in the prayer position. A golden aura appeared surrounding the two interwoven hands, which now resembled the shell. It was burning so brightly Alex squinted to protect his eyes. As he did, Marguerite took his left hand and positioned it against the outside of their two already clasped hands. Alex turned and looked on as his mother placed her right hand opposite Alex's on the far side. As she did, she looked at Alex, smiling as the light seemed to expand, filling him entirely.

Alex stood motionless, his eyes hazy. As he came back to earth, he opened them and picked up the shell. The shell responded, it opened wider than before and lit up the fluted grooves of the recess above where the shell had been laying. 'Sara,' he said calmly, calling his wife towards him. Taking the shell in his left hand, Alex gently placed Sara's hand over the shell. Now with her hand on one side and his on the other, Alex and Sara lifted the shell and together, as one, and fed it like a giant golden key into the deep fluted vertical recess. It was a perfect fit.

Immediately the entire room glimmered and gleamed as it was bathed in a golden explosion of energy. A blinding light shot straight up, out of the underground room, through the ceiling of the abbey, soaring upwards and burning into the heavens like an infinite, universal laser beam. The thunder and lightning retreated across the night sky, swiftly drifting away into the distance. A meteor shower began to rain spectacularly across the clearing night sky. High above the Abbey of Gellone in St Guilhem, a bright star appeared, radiating a golden, white glow across the sky, lighting up the entire landscape.

Fifteen

Time & Place

The intimidating snow-capped Alps of the Swiss Oberland stood out like a row of giant menacing teeth, patiently waiting to devour their prey. In the valley below, a myriad of log cabins dotted the lush green plateau some thirty kilometres south of Berne. As the evening fell, two large saloon cars with tinted windows were ushered through the security gate and crept silently onto the private airfield, heading towards an impressive bent winged Lear jet. The four circle insignia of the DVK adorned the white tailpiece of the lavish aircraft.

Coming to a halt beside the plane, the first car door opened to reveal the bespectacled, impish looks of the affluently suited Harris Thompson, the great grandson of the founder of the global pharmaceutical giant Petram & Thompson. He was followed (on the far side of the vehicle) by two cowboy boots and the silhouette of an oversized hat as a moustached James 'Duke' Foster III, the Texan oil magnate, bowed down to exit the car. Behind them, the doors of the second vehicle opened to reveal the dark haired, suave and handsome Swiss Central Bank chief, Timo Shultz. Saving the 'best' till last, the tall, dark figure of the English and European 'star' politician Jared Kingston, made his way to join the others.

Five short steps, and one by one the four men entered the customised plane, greeted by a most stunning, petite uniformed Asian hostess. Escorted down the black and white chequered veneered aisle, they took their seats in the heavily padded grey leather chairs of the futuristic spacecraft-like cabin.

Shrill mountain winds whistled and moaned as the pilot carefully manoeuvred into position, preparing for take-off. Being buffeted from side to side the aircraft whirred and hummed like a subdued giant hairdryer as it accelerated down the runway, the over-speed alarm siren briefly sounding as the plane stealthily climbed into the air, in a gentle ascent.

The welcoming aroma of freshly ground coffee filled the cabin as the small group of VIP passengers began talking, whilst their hostess prepared the drinks in the rear cabin. The jet was still ascending, now high above the Alps, heading east towards Munich. 'If this don't get solved, we're gonna have to take some real big steps, and there ain't no going back this time,' warned the deep Texan drawl of 'Duke' Foster from under a wide brimmed, beige Stetson.

'I hear what you are saying Duke, I do understand your concern, but listen when I tell you it's pointless talking about it, it's my responsibility and I will act accordingly,' came the curt reply from Kingston.

'You telling me you will do whatever it takes?' The Texan still wasn't quite ready to shut up as he stroked his moustache with thumb and index finger.

'Whatever it takes; that's my job, do remember who's in charge here, dear boy.' No hiding Kingston's condescension this time.

'Hell Kingston, framing these A-rabs is tougher than we thought. Shit... look what we did in 2001, and still we can't pin the tail on the Johnny Jihad, we need to stop pussy footing around and just frickin' do it our damn selves!' Foster placed the personalised *King of Denmark* cigar between his gritted teeth.

But before anyone could retort, the rear cabin door opened, and the hostess brought out a tray of drinks and passed a note to Kingston. He read the message, nodding his head. Having placed the refreshments onto the reflective extendable tables of each guest, the hostess returned to a small separate cabin at the rear of the plane, discreetly shutting the sound proofed door behind her.

Kingston put the note in his jacket. 'Now listen to me very carefully everyone...' The group fell silent, as the chairs swivelled in his direction. 'I've thought long and hard about this, and I see no other option than to implement the Megiddo Protocol. I've just received confirmation that we have a full shop, so it's our play. Now you all know what the benefits and consequences will be. I need your responses by midnight, before I take the necessary steps to implement the Megiddo Protocol. If we do reach compliance, and I fully expect your backing on this, then I suggest you get your families and associates to your specified DUMB (Deep Underground Military Bunker) by 4am Tuesday morning.'

'That is, unless like me, you're leaving the wife and taking the girlfriends!' piped up a smirking Schultz looking like a cat who'd got the cream. The cabin filled with laughter.

Not too far away, on a craggy mountainside, a lone, bearded vulture cracked his beak on the red hollow ribbed remains of a nearly devoured Valais Blacknose sheep. Unbeknown to the mighty scavenger, the carcass of the animal was riddled with 'Metarex', an extremely powerful, man-made analgesic. This painkiller originally designed for humans, had been withdrawn from the market following the coming to light of some rather unfavourable scientific evidence. It was proven beyond doubt, that the drug induced unacceptable side effects in humans, which included paramnesia, heart attack and renal failure. Following its withdrawal from the global market, the drug was subsequently rebranded and flogged off to the veterinary pharmaceutical sector, in a clandestine operation designed to minimise financial losses. This quickly led to its use on livestock and consequently infiltrating the human food chain.

The bird had consumed such quantities of the drug that its usually keen senses were seriously compromised. He was suddenly startled by the harsh sound of a quickly approaching Swiss army Cougar helicopter. So leaving the final scraps of his banquet, he flapped his giant wings as he repeatedly attempted to take flight to avoid the giant insect-like chopper's advances.

Several failed attempts led to one eventual success and the massive bird was finally airborne. Hurrying his broad wings to move faster, the unsteady bird flew higher and higher, away from the noise, effortlessly rising on the columns of moist air. The nauseous, confused bird continued to climb, as if suffering from a form of ornithological dementia. Thrown by the forces of an approaching storm, the bird was pulled towards the swirling grey mass of chaos.

'Some turbulence ahead gentleman, please buckle up. ETA in approximately thirty minutes,' the pilot's voice announced, confident and clear, from the Bose speakers outside the small soundproofed cockpit. He and his co-pilot could now see the approaching dark clouds and took the decision to reduce altitude rather than continue into the storm. The pilot reached over to lock his seat belt into place, when suddenly... bang! The left-hand side of the jet's windshield, disintegrated into thousands of pieces of glass and disabled several controls, including the alarms and radio. The cockpit was a mess of blood and feathers. The jet and bird had collided, and the pilot had been directly hit by the 17lb fleshy cannon ball smashing through the protective shield. Driven back by the force of the collision, the pilot's body was thrust to the back wall of the cockpit, before being pulled out into the atmosphere.

The co-pilot, blood streaming from a head wound, stunned and dazed by the noise, mist, and the force of the on-rushing freezing air, desperately tried to clear the glass and blood from his eyes. Within seconds he blacked out in his seat due to decompression. The remains of the vulture, snowballed by assorted debris, was caught wedged in the part-shattered side window of the cockpit, and the mass of feathers, flesh and bone was flapping around the depressurised cockpit, as the plane continued on its course.

In the main cabin, the group, who had heard the pilot's

message about turbulence, were joined by the hostess, yet all remained oblivious to what had actually happened, the sound-proofing and the autopilot system were working well. However Harris Thompson noticed the red spots splattering across the wing of the plane. 'What colour is aviation fuel?' he asked, as the bloody fluid made its way through the side window, splashing the wing.

The rest of the group were so engrossed in conversation, the question went unnoticed and unanswered. In the cockpit, the pressure of the mass of flesh pounding against the shattered glass of the side window finally caused it to give way. The sarcous bundle flew past Thompson, who saw the strange cluster get sucked directly into the starboard engine. A large 'boom' echoed around the jet, and orange smoke began to fill the central cabin. The plane shuddered violently. The hostess ensured everyone had their belts fastened and made for the cockpit, but was unable to open the door. The co-pilot's body slumped forward tripping the controls as the plane descended, spiralling out of control.

Shocked diners at the Ammersee Hotel in Germany looked on as the huge metal bird hit the water of the Bavarian lake before disintegrating into a thousand pieces. The hierarchy of the DVK were gone, and the Megiddo Protocol was dead in the water.

Sixteen

Beyond the Here & Now

B ack in the crypt beneath the abbey, voices and memories poured out of the shell, depicting bite size clips of its incredible history. Alex, Sara, Lucette and Jean-Michel were captivated as all that had happened to the shell revealed itself around them in a series of animated holograms. They saw and heard snippets of the entire journey all the way back to the huge explosion so long ago in Atlantis. Then, with an electromagnetic snap and crackle, the mass of energy circulating the subterranean chamber swirled back into the lower part of the fissure now holding the shell. From above the cleft in the white stone, another powerful bolt of energy shot out from the shell, circling the crypt in a swirling vortex before emerging into a large holographic three dimensional version of Metatron's cube, the Fruit of Life, the blueprint of the Universe.

In the middle of the multi-dimensional interwoven golden shape appeared a being of light emanating an energy that filled each of the four people present with a profound sense of love and wellbeing. Even Pamplemousse was transfixed.

Fritz Wicky stood watching at the entrance to the crypt as the energy exploded around them. He took out the gun, and applied the silencer. With the pistol now gripped tightly in his hand, he steadied himself, preparing to make his move. As the energy was released, he was unable to remain grounded in any sense of the word. His ego was flying, with dreams of power and success, looking like a man well and truly possessed by evil. His eyes enlarged, his mouth agape, Wicky was taken away to an illusory world of his very own making. There he stood, surveying the heavenly scene as every desire and whim was played out. He watched through his own eyes as he sat on a palatial bejewelled seat, his favourite drinks and foods laid out on the table, and several beautiful giggling girls sat on the floor before him, anything he desired was at his beck and call.

One of the girls caught his eye more than the others. He summoned her towards him, and asked her to remove the white veil covering her face. 'No my lord, you must do it,' said the girl, inviting his touch. Wicky leaned forward, and slowly removed the veil. As the disguise hit the floor, he let out a horrific cry. The face standing before him was not a beautiful girl, but that of a slimy, horrendous distorted demon, whose serpent-like tongue extended towards Wicky's face. As it touched his skin, slithering across his lips, he felt his skin burn as if acid was sinking through his mouth and piercing hot liquid was dissolving his teeth. He cried out and the torture stopped.

Opening his eyes, he found himself surrounded by grey and ash. The land was stripped bare, and smouldering as if an enormous fire had decimated the entire world. Bodies of animals and people lay strewn across the landscape as far as he could see; a kingdom littered with death. The stench of rotting flesh hung in the air like poisonous gas. He walked alone, trapped in a hellish world of his own making, with no possible escape.

Desperate, Wicky now ran up the steps to the abbey, distressed and distraught, he had no interest in the shell now, because he was tortured by the very real scenes repeating in his head. Crying out, with tears in his eyes and salivating like a mad dog, Wicky stumbled towards the exit, and reaching the ancient stone font, his hands rested momentarily on the huge basin.

As they did, horrific scenes from the past slaughter of the Liberae tore through his mind, and he fell to the floor, slumped between the font and the cornerstone of the building. He could not clear his head; a fire was raging inside his mind and there was no let up. With blood shot eyes and tears streaming down his face, Wicky looked down at the pistol he was holding in his trembling right hand, bringing it slowly but surely upwards, towards his temple. A metallic 'thwack', a puff of smoke and it was all over.

In the crypt, they looked on as images depicting the future of the world unfolded before their very eyes, a revelation that was both beautiful and shocking. The destiny of human life was inevitably to be aligned so that a sustainable balance would be restored to Mother Earth. Years of abuse and pillage from the ignorance, greed and desire of humans would not lead to the divine retribution of an angry 'God', but a consequential shift to redress the forces of the Earth, returning her to a natural equilibrium. A shift which would allow the planet to recover, heal and flourish once more. Major movement of the planet's land masses, a shifting of the waters, and a natural correction of the Earth were coming as part of its cyclical transfiguration. They could see that the Earth had already entered a tremendous cycle of growth and change, a time of incredible transformation. Images of metamorphosis in nature appeared before them, the tadpole, the dragonfly, and a snake shedding its old skin in order to be born again. A calm, assured voice spoke to them all, to Alex it sounded like his mother's tone, to Sara like two sweet children speaking in unison, to Lucette and Jean-Michel it was indescribable...

'Before the Golden Age of Humanity may begin, the Earth will shed its skin, thereby releasing the physical, mental and emotional negativity which is suffocating this world. The physical manifestation of this great shift will be precipitated by a tilting of the Earth's axis. This cycle is not a divine punishment, but an unavoidable holistic reaction resulting directly from Man's own deluded thinking. Humanity has forgotten the sacred nature of its habitat, taking has become the norm, and the art of giving back has been cast aside. The power of love has been replaced by the love of power. Joy has become synthetic, and is typically measured in belongings and appearances, and not in the realisation of our core being. And yet, you are spirit and all is not lost. For every single human being has an altruistic sense of what is right, for deep within you there

exists an innate wisdom of what is good, true and loving. That is the consciousness of the soul.

The Earth emerged from the Universe as an oasis, a true paradise. When humankind returns to the dimension of the soul, the Earth will become that utopia once more; and life will follow the authentic principles of self-knowledge, joy and love. The world will return to being a place where people intuitively heal themselves by facing their innermost fears. In this way, they will be experiencing what they need to, in order to grow. It will be an environment of awareness, a time when people will be able to discard thoughts of difference and separation, aligning their existence with the flow of the Universe. This world will become a place of peace where all accept the brotherhood and sisterhood of man, a place where people take responsibility for themselves, and are openly conscious of the oneness of life. They will see that the human being is beyond the confines of duality and non-duality. This will lead to a divine realisation, an equanimity of body, mind and spirit leading to the manifestation of wholeness of being.

The purpose of life in the multidimensional Universe is to share; to recognise, realise and actualise all that you are in the many plateaus of life. The nameless Source within all life draws people to reach out and discover who they are, what they are, and why they are here. The entire Solar System has entered the Initiation of the Golden Age... and the Earth is symbiotically stepping into a new higher vibration. Humans are emerging from a third dimensional perception of consciousness through the portal of the fourth dimension, and forward into the manifestation of a fifth dimensional consciousness (the embodiment of the soul).

In this unfolding, fresh water will become the most valuable commodity on Earth, far greater than oil or gold. Many of the ancient prophecies of the past have now begun; great floods, earthquakes, changes in land masses, volcanic eruptions, culminating in a complete pole shift. There will be chaos and confusion, but out of this catastrophe there will arise a new world (Terra Nova) and a new man – Homo Novus. Understand that the cataclysm presently underway is neither good nor bad; it is what is necessary and simply a stepping stone in the evolution of life on Earth. Many will leave this world, thereby fulfilling their soul contracts, but five times as many will leave because they cannot accept the changes which are about to take place.

Remember too, that death is but a chapter in the great book of life, and only relative to the physical plane, for those who pass over in the great shift will realise the infinite nature of their souls and their intricate relationship with Universal Intelligence. Humanity has long led itself into believing that it is the master of its own fate, that it is the controller of the physical world, that it alone decides the path it walks. But those of you aware of the Universal Intelligence in all things know that we are simply a part of a greater whole.

In the depths of your heart, you know that the cycle which has begun is a necessity. You are here as witnesses to that extraordinary path of evolution. The energy you see and feel here in this place has been waiting to find you, all of you. You are now able to embody this Divine life force. Bathe in its light, breathe its air, for it is your birth right, and the aspiration of all that is good in humankind. Do not worry about the past or the future, for they do not exist in this moment. Be present with the truth of who you are, for within the mind of the heart is the knowledge of what is to come and the part that you must play in it.

All humans are potentially beautiful beings with an incredible secret, a shared secret that is so powerful it can change the way you live and the world you live in. That secret has been waiting for you to remember the truth of who you are, so that you could recognise, realise and actualise your divine inheritance. To sense in surety that you are a multi-dimensional being of infinite potential. That Love is your truest language. And Heart is your noblest mind.

When you look back and realise everything that passed before was a blessing, and all that is to come is necessary for your learning and growth, then truly, you will have entered the consciousness of the Soul.

That time is upon us now. Today we are witnessing a new dawn for humanity. A time of hope and change. Let go of fear, for it has no place here. Breathe and embrace the sacred sense of life within. For there you *will find the peace and love that all seek. Be free. It is your birth right, your nature and your responsibility. When you are free, you cannot but help others to be free. That's how wonderfully kind and loving you are. So the secret of the shell is out. Souls are awakening to this world. And this world is awakening to Soul. It is time to speak and act from Love and Truth, then new life will come to one and all, and a new Earth will appear.'*

With that, the golden lights, voices, figures and all the vortex of energy in the room dissolved. Not back into the shell, but into the space surrounding them all, and into the very core of each present. The once golden shell, still locked in position in the stone cavity, turned from gold to stone and solidified in its position, looking like a sculpted part of the chamber that had been there a thousand years. The four of them stood there, unable to speak, bathing in the serene beauty of what they had just experienced. The silence was full, lacking nothing. In that moment, words were meaningless. The consciousness held within the shell for thousands of years had finally been released and found a new home.

Seventeen

Islands

The sun hung high in a radiant blue sky, the upper air partially coated with brilliant white wispy cirrus clouds looking like they were the result of deliberate strokes from a master artist's brush. Blue, green, yellow and orange light streamed through the high cloud, refracting the sun's light like a prism, which streamed onto the water, fracturing into a thousand flickering sparks dancing across the calm waves of the blue ocean.

A group of men and women pulled a large net full of fish onto a boat that sat peacefully in the placid sea. 'Looks like another big catch,' commented one man enthusiastically as they manoeuvred the large haul of exotic fish into position on the vessel. The colourful capture contained a variety of aquatic life, 'not like the early days, do you remember?'

'If our catch levels would have stayed at that level, well... we wouldn't be here now,' replied another of the fishermen. Murmurs of agreement filled the boat.

Cartwright discovered a small plastic doll which had become trapped and tangled in the frayed strings of the net. He held it in front of his face, staring at it long and hard. Everyone aboard noticed this melancholy find. An eerie silence came over the boat as the crew lowered their heads, clearly reminiscing times gone by which had deeply affected them all.

'Well who'd have thought that we'd all be fishermen,' piped up Fernandez, attempting to change the subject and cheer them all up.

'And fisherwomen!' corrected one of the women. Laughter broke out once more and they busily sorted the catch of fish into separate wooden containers. A few poisonous varieties were returned to the sea unharmed. Once they had tidied and put the homemade nets away, they held hands and gave thanks to the Universe for their bountiful catch, and set sail for home.

Home was a small group of large islands, now visible on the horizon. The hillsides were steeped in plentiful, luscious foliage, with abundant varieties of trees, including pineapple and coconut. At the ocean's edge, there was little sand, and more of a greyish stony silt, but still, overall it painted a stunning picture.

Flat plateaus on the island ridges had been dug and were being developed for growing vegetables and fruit. Ponds with vegetation were used for capturing and purifying fresh water, which then trickled down narrow channels dug into the hillside, taking the water to various irrigation and collection points. Other reed bed pond systems had been created to naturally resolve and recycle human waste. Additionally, by creating a number of 'solar-stills' seawater was being turned into distilled drinking water, so the islanders had a plentiful supply.

Scattered around the mountainsides sat a host of mud and earth built domed dwellings and homes, with turf-like roofs. Home-made pontoons and timber bridges strapped together with old ropes and twine connected the islands closest to each other. A few smaller rustic looking boats and coracle-like craft were gathered in wooden man-made protective harbours around the islands. A fast growing crowd of people stood staring up at the sky, chattering and pointing at a flock of birds cruising in layered 'v' formation across the islands. The only inhabitable areas for miles around were these isles protruding from the sea; so the horizon was dominated by a seemingly endless ocean of seawater.

Once back on dry land, the fisher folk began unloading their bountiful catch with the help of other residents. More or less everyone was dressed in light, multi-coloured clothes, made from a variety of recycled materials. Various collection points near the boat landing stage were set out as sorting areas for the flotsam and jetsam brought up by the water on a daily basis.

There was one area for wood, one for plastics, and another for rope and textiles which could be stripped before being woven by hand and made into clothes. Hardly any metal objects ever surfaced, and implements on the islands were hand carved, plates and bowls made from a poor quality clay which unfortunately, broke all too easily.

The climate was mild and warm, and the islands were abundant with food being so close to a rich natural fishery. Further along the beach area, a fire crackled into life, as the community came together to prepare the catch for dinner. Knives and cutting tools were also rare, and mostly used communally to prepare food. Some created knives from driftwood, twine and razor clam shells. The fish were gutted, prepared and slid on to the thick wire that had been fortuitously retrieved from the debris of a small yacht washed up on the shore. The fish sat in rows above the hot embers, and it didn't take long before they were ready to eat.

Back in his home, Cartwright removed the doll from his pocket, studying the plastic toy which was slightly disfigured and covered in green stains from the sea algae. 'Look what we found today,' he said to his wife.

Shanti turned around as the look on her face changed from interest to sadness, 'What shall we do with it?' Her question was pretty self-evident, not like they had any real use for it.

'I guess we'll put it in the chest with the other bits, because it's no use to anyone,' Cartwright replied.

'Only memories, my love,' added Shanti as an afterthought.

'Memories that we'd all prefer to forget,' said Cartwright. He moved into an adjoining room, and pulled out a wooden chest from underneath a rustic double bed. Taking the key from the chain around his neck, he opened the chest, placing the doll inside, and studied the contents.

His hands rummaged around inside the chest, before picking

up the objects one by one. An old mobile phone, a rusty can marked 'Corned Beef', a set of car keys and a broken digital clock with visible signs of leakage from the batteries. 'All completely useless,' muttered Cartwright to himself as he let out a long deep breath, replacing the items one by one into the old wooden chest, and closing the lid.

He returned to the room next door and put his arms around his wife. 'The girls okay?'

'Yeah, they're still at group exchange, they'll be back soon,' replied Shanti looking at the light in the sky to determine the time.

As the sun began to set on the mountainside, a white-haired man sat on a rock talking to a group of youngsters, 'And so thanks to people like Alex and Sara, we are here today, in a place of peace and beauty. We now live in a world where war is a distant memory of the past, for there is little doubt it is now geographical and scientifically impossible. Human consciousness has changed in alignment with the shifts that have taken place on Earth.'

'But what happened to cause so much destruction?' one child asked raising a hand.

The wizard-like white haired man looked upwards for inspiration to find the right words, 'After the shell was returned, huge advances in the electromagnetics industry coupled with the intention to rid the world of war once and for all led to the re-adaptation of TUW, or what was named Tesla's Unified Wall. The powerful electro-magnetic invention made all countries impregnable against attack by emitting a huge wave of energy. But that was not the end. There were celebrations world over, that humanity had somehow advanced to a new level.

'What the world had forgotten about was the rebalancing of the planet, which was inevitably bound to take place. From 2016, earth-changes escalated at unprecedented levels, beginning with the Golden Gate super-quake. Events unfolded at an astonishing rate. By the time the world began to really sit up and listen, it was too late.'

'But what caused these changes?' asked the same inquisitive youngster.

'Anyone know?' asked the kindly old man looking around at the group. They looked at each other, but no one replied. 'Well, the atom bomb tests from a few years prior proved to be major contributors to the acceleration in atmospheric changes. Military funded technologies escalated the damage by blasting the upper atmosphere with huge amounts of energy, literally moving the ionosphere of Earth, creating havoc with weather patterns. Then there was 'Low Intensity Conflict' – using electromagnetic weapons technology to debilitate people. That technology was initially designed to explode nuclear weapons in space, but the atmosphere of the planet was damaged irrevocably, and huge earthquakes, unheard of lightning strikes, storms and floods ravaged the face of the world in a few short years.

'Again humanity failed to take into considerations that the Earth is an intelligently balanced living organism, and when we alter that, we consequently alter ourselves. Earth is not here to be exploited but is a vital part of a harmonious and balanced system which gives life to all. Man played God in complete ignorance of the consequences.'

'I can't believe people were ever that stupid, why didn't they do something about it before it was too late, didn't they know what they were doing, didn't they sense as we do?' another pupil asked now baffled by what was being said, astounded by what sounded like something from the 'Dark Ages'.

Their elder took a slightly softer approach, 'People were never given the truth, and when they did discover the facts they were often projected as freaks by the media. Many were too far lost in the selfish materialistic ways of modern society to stand up and really take notice. They became increasingly isolated from each other and from the natural flow of life itself.'

The old man stood up and moved around his charges as he spoke, occasionally touching a shoulder a hand or top of a young head, 'You see it was always the great fear in the old human psyche that one day we would destroy ourselves and our planet by waging catastrophic war on each other. This never happened. And out of all of the chaos came something good, something new and beautiful. It brought about people like you.'

He stood still again in front of the children, looking at each one in turn to emphasise his optimistic point, before continuing, 'The earth-changes paved the way for the birthing of a holistic minded human being we call 'Homo Novus', a human with a holistic consciousness that now has the ability to lead the world into a bright, positive future. The holistic mind you all possess allows humankind to enjoy the benefits of a multi-frequency, multi-dimensional life. Benefits our forefathers would only have dreamt of. If you would have told them that following the changes on Earth life expectancy was going to treble, they would have laughed in your faces, and called you mad. But as we return to the true way of life, in harmony with all that is, extended life expectancy is a natural consequence. As is your ability to talk without words, or see without eyes, and listen without ears, these are all gifts of the soul coming to fruition.' The children were transfixed.

'Here, today thought flows without the controls and preju-dices of a designated authority. People no longer need a belief system but choose to follow and feel close to their inherent spiri-tuality. This way, the new way of humanity is peaceful. There is no poverty, famine, needless suffering or loss of life. There is no teacher here, only sharing between souls. We do not command, but suggest, we do not demand, but guide. And we do not enforce authority, for we all recognise the existence of a power beyond humankind.' He smiled, noticing that for some of these children it was the first time they had heard all this said aloud, you could tell them apart from the others as their small mouths hung open in astonishment.

He continued, 'Sharing and connection are the core values of us all. The true power of holism is revealing the quantum capacities of consciousness. We are now aware that all reality is built from a background of pure energy or proto-consciousness, and that Universal energy is the primary form of all creation.'

Now aware that this was quite enough for one day, and placing both hands on his thighs to lever himself up the great 'storyteller' said, 'That's about all for today,' smiling as the youngsters moaned a gentle disapproval that their story time had come to an end. 'I'll be here at the same time tomorrow... if you want to come,' said the old man as the group started to disperse.

As the youngsters made their way back from the gathering on the hillside to their homes, the old man sat looking out to sea. In the distance, he heard the bark of an approaching dog. 'Mousse, Mousse, come on boy,' said the old man as he stood up and took a deep breath. From around the rocks came Pamplemousse, running towards his friend and master. Jean-Michel stroked and cuddled his friend.

'Ready dear?' said a soft tender voice as Lucette arrived, and stood looking lovingly at them both. Jean-Michel put his hands to her face and kissed her tenderly. The couple held hands and began the short walk back down the hillside to their small simple home. Later that evening, lying on the simple handcrafted futon-like bed, Jean-Michel turned to Lucette, 'I wonder how they got on... if they made it.' Lucette smiled back knowingly as they snuggled up, with Pamplemousse curled up fast asleep at the end of the makeshift bed. Further along the shadowy beach, a large fleshy object was at the water's edge, being pushed too and fro by the constant movement of the tide. It was the body of teenage girl. A finger stretched out from the seemingly lifeless corpse, which was followed by the movement of a hand scraping the sand as the young woman gradually regained consciousness.

She wearily rose to her feet and staggered towards the light of a nearby hut. Mustering what little strength she had left, she slapped her hand against the wooden makeshift door. A muffled noise could be heard as Cartwright opened the door to see a young girl swaying before him, with barely enough strength to remain standing. She fell forwards into his arms, and Cartwright looked at the girl compassionately. He called for his wife. That's strange thought Cartwright, not so much surprised by the sudden arrival, but because he could have sworn that just before she collapsed, her eyes radiated the strangest red glow.

The following morning, a small boat was gently bobbing about on the ocean. As the sun continued to rise on a new day, a man's voice cried out from on deck, 'Land ahoy! Look…land!'

The woman scrambled her way from under the covers on the vessel and rushed to the side of the man stood looking ahead from the bow. The woman put her hand in the man's hand. The man put his arm around the woman as they stood looking out at the view. 'I'm going to wake John,' she announced, 'he'd love to see this, it's his dream.' As she turned to enter the shed-like cabin, a young boy appeared at the door, startling her. 'John, I was just coming to wake you' said the boy's mother.

'I know mother, I could see you in my sleep, and I knew you wanted me to see, so I woke up,' replied the boy.

As they approached the land in the distance, they could make out several small wooden built cabins. 'There are others,' said Alex.

'I wonder how many?' replied Sara.

'Enough,' said John with a golden beam of light emanating from his eyes.

'Enough to what?' asked Sara.

'To do it better this time,' said Alex, putting one arm around his son, and the other around Sara as all three gazed into the distance.

Acknowledgements

A big debt of gratitude to my family Wendy, Holly and Georges for putting up with me writing away like a bedlamite for many months and for allowing me the space and time to follow my dreams.

Many thanks to Kate Osborne, for all her spirit, patience and support, and for helping me fashion a book which honours the original intention – to share something of purpose and value, creating a soulful contribution to change and transformation.

Thanks to Grammy award winning writer and arranger Richard Theisen for his time and energy, and for his timely reminder: ".... a noble project.... and this world definitely needs it now."

Thanks to Jon Pogioli for contributing his passion, skill, enthusiasm and knowledge in the form of a great film-script.

My heartfelt thanks to the infinite Universe. From the very beginning there has been a powerful synchronistic flow of support allowing me to realise that love, life, passion and creation are inexplicably linked.

This story holds the whispers of my Soul – and in that sense it contains something for – and from – everyone...

About the Author

J.M. HARRISON is an Award Winning Author and Amazon #1 Best Seller who writes to support human consciousness. In 1987, Jonathan's love of contemporary music resulted in a short stint as the lead singer of *Frankie Goes To Hollywood* following the departure of Holly Johnson. At the close of his music career he was awarded a gold disc for his lead vocal on the Telstar compilation album 'Get on This 2'.

From '97 Jonathan underwent a series of experiences which radically altered his consciousness. Following a mystical death experience in 2007, he penned his first book *We Are All One: A Call to Spiritual Uprising*. It won the *Allbooks International Editor's Choice Award 2009 (USA)* and he was subsequently invited to teach alongside spiritual teachers Barbara Marx Hubbard, Esther Hicks, and Steve and Barbara Rother.

Jonathan's second book *Naked Being: Undressing Your Mind, Transforming Your Life* – was published by O Books in 2010. It was honoured as a Best Books Award Finalist 2010 (USA Book News) in the genre of Spirituality. Jonathan has been appeared in; Watkins Review, Kindred Spirit Magazine, Yoga Magazine, Paradigm Shift and many more. From 2010 he was the M.D. of *Gaunts House* in Dorset, one of the largest spiritual education and retreat centres in the United Kingdom, which blossomed until his departure in the spring of 2014. A third published book, YOU are THIS – Awakening to the Living Presence of your Soul is due for release through Mantra Books in early 2016.

He currently resides in rural Dorset, England with his family where he continues to write, supporting the current global expansion of human consciousness.

BY THE SAME AUTHOR

We Are All One – A Call to Spiritual Uprising
(2007) *paperback* (2015) *e-book (ALOL Publishing)*

Naked Being – Undressing your Mind, Transforming your Life
(2010) *paperback* (2015) *e-book (O-Books)*

YOU are THIS – Awakening to the Living Presence of your Soul
(2016) *paperback and e-book (Mantra Books)*

For further information and updates, visit the author's
website at:
www.AuthorJMHarrison.com

At Roundfire we publish great stories. We lean towards the spiritual and thought-provoking. But whether it's literary or popular, a gentle tale or a pulsating thriller, the connecting theme in all Roundfire fiction titles is that once you pick them up you won't want to put them down.

—

Following personal tragedies and spiralling financial problems, Londoners Alex and Sara are desperate to find ways to rediscover their zest for life. A free holiday provides the perfect opportunity for a second chance, but not long after arriving in France they discover that all is not what it seems...

A series of shocking revelations challenge their understanding of humanity, as they are propelled into a dangerous world governed by a ruthless occult society. Magical relics and extra-terrestrial objects promise to unlock incredible secrets, but what extremes will people go to in order to attain them? In a modern-day spiritual quest, Alex and Sara will be forced to take control of their destiny, facing their own demons along the way as time counts down, for them and the entire human race...

'*The Soul Whisperer* has the potential to be a huge bestseller. In the same spiritual-adventure mould as *The Da Vinci Code* and *The Celestine Prophecy*, J. M. Harrison's novel is a rich and riveting read full of hidden truths and unspoken possibilities.'
STEPHEN GAWTRY, Managing Editor, *Watkins Mind Body Spirit* magazine

'J. M. Harrison writes in a compelling style which draws you in to this riveting story that challenges your current beliefs.'
CLAIRE GILLMAN, Editor, *Kindred Spirit* magazine

J. M. HARRISON is an Award Winning Author and Amazon #1 Best Seller. A radical spiritual awakening in 2002 propelled him into a sequence of life changing events. He currently resides in Dorset, England with his family where he continues to write supporting the expansion of human consciousness.

www.roundfire-books.com

ROUNDFIRE
BOOKS

FICTION/THRILLERS
UK £9.99
US $16.95

US $16.95
ISBN 978-1-78535-246-1

Cover design by Design Deluxe

9 781785 352461